MY ONE AND ONLY

WESTON PARKER

BRIXBAXTER PUBLISHING

Copyright © 2017 by Weston & Ali Parker

All rights reserved. This book or any portion thereof may not be reproduced or used in any manner whatsoever without the express written permission of the publisher except for the use of brief quotations in a book review.

The novel is a work of fiction. Names, characters, places and plot are all either products of the author's imagination or used fictitiously. Any resemblance to actual events, locales, or persons – living or dead – is purely coincidental.

First Edition.

Editor: Mary Wolney
Designer: Kellie Dennis, Book Covers By Design

PROLOGUE
LEO

"Die, zombie fuckers!" My fourth round of Zombie Hunters was in full swing when I heard a tapping sound at my window that nearly sent me jumping out of my skin. As usual, I was home alone in my upstairs bedroom and making due with my time like every Saturday night of my life.

I froze in place and looked over my shoulder and then jumped to my feet as I saw Kya on the other side of the glass. As she mumbled something I couldn't quite understand, I rushed over to the window and lifted it.

"What the hell took you so long, Leonard?" Kya stepped into the room with her tall, spike-heeled boots leading the way.

"Why can't you use the front door? Your reputation would be severely damaged if you were to die falling off *my* roof." It would take a hell of a lot more than that actually because Kya was known for her carefree spirit.

She straightened her skintight jeans and smoothed down her jet-black hair that she'd added red streaks to only days ago. "I knocked on your door for twenty minutes, which you'd know if you weren't up here with your TV blaring."

I took in the sight of her slim hips, curvy ass, and tits that were way bigger than the time her bikini top had come off in my kiddie pool when we were only six. Back then, things were less complicated. We'd been best friends, and it wasn't until eighth grade when everything changed.

She filled out with curves as I grew as straight and tall as a weed and just as weak as one in a strong breeze. Her popularity soared as a talented singer with one of the hottest garage bands in town, and I became the butt of everyone's jokes with my horn-rimmed glasses and lack of muscle tone.

Luckily, my misery hadn't lasted too long, though. By the time I was a junior, I'd grown so tall and lanky that I was damned near invisible.

"What do you need?"

She rarely came over, and when she did, it was usually to borrow something or ask a favor.

"Do I have to need something to pop in and say hi?" She walked around my room looking at my science fair trophies and the banner I'd gotten for attending the school's mock trial.

"These days, yeah. I mean, it's been a while."

"Well, you don't exactly darken my doorstep these days either." She lifted her chin in a defiant way, and then her lips spread as if she couldn't help but grin. "Okay, so maybe I do want something. What are you doing tonight?"

"Hanging here while my parents are gone and playing Zombie Hunters."

"There's a big party over at Seth O'Haver's house. I was wondering if you'd give me a ride?"

"What's wrong with your car?"

"My parents took the keys. I got in trouble for letting Laney Peterson drive my car. She puked in it, and until I pay them back for the cleaning bill, I'm shit out of luck." She walked to the window and looked out to the rooftop where I usually sat to listen to her sing. "There are sunflower seed shells all over your roof, by the way."

"Ah, yeah. I dumped them out there." There was no way I would admit to sitting out there while her band practiced in her garage on the opposite side of the house. It was the only way I'd get close to the party that took place every other Friday of the month.

"Oh. So, will you?" She smiled sweetly as if to convince me.

"Sure, I'll give you a ride." I would have given my left nut to take her anywhere she wanted to go, but I was still at a loss for why she needed me. She had tons of friends, and any one of them could have gone out of their way to give her a lift.

"Perfect." She flashed me a big smile with her red-painted lips and then walked to my bedroom door as I stood there like an idiot. "Are you coming?"

"Oh, right." I didn't bother changing clothes. I had on a plain white T-shirt that I usually wore under my button-downs and a pair of jeans that were so baggy and loose, they looked like I could fit another one of me in them. I put on my sneakers when we got downstairs and grabbed my keys.

"I really appreciate this, Leonard. I would have gotten a ride from Emily, but Noah already packed half the team in her car, and since most of my friends are used to riding in with me, they filled up everyone else's cars fast."

"Oh, it's cool." I really didn't need her excuse and thought it really wasn't that big of a deal. I'd dump her off and bail out before anyone could see she'd gotten a ride from me.

We walked out, and I unlocked her door and went around to the driver's side.

When we were both in our seat belts, she reached up and put her hand on the dashboard, giving my car a pat like it was a pet. "I like your car, by the way. It's pretty cool, even with the dent."

My '86 Mustang SVO was my dad's last attempt at trying to help my social life, but so far, the only action it had seen was when I backed into Kya's mailbox. "Thanks. I wanted a new paint job anyway." The car, which was originally a much glossier red, had oxidized to an unflattering pink on the top half, making it a two-toned nightmare that had earned the nickname Pretty Pony.

I started her up, and we went down the street to the stop sign.

"Which way do I go?" I asked, revving the engine, which was the most impressive part of the car next to the clean interior.

"You don't know where Seth lives?" She made a face like I had just told her I'd never seen sunshine or a pencil.

"No, I haven't actually ever been invited."

Her face fell, and while I expected her next move would be to show how much she pitied me or change the subject, she gave me a nudge. "Well, you are now, so take a right."

I laughed not thinking she was serious. "Does that mean you want me to get out and walk you to the door? I'm flattered."

She turned in her seat to angle toward me. "What do you mean? You're coming in, right?"

"That would be a negative. I didn't even know about this party until you crawled in my window, and I'm pretty sure that was a deliberate strategy orchestrated by the rest of the senior class." It was like the other kids spoke a different language most times anyway, a language I wasn't supposed to understand.

"You have to. It's our senior year. This is not only the last party of the school year but our last party together as a class. We're all going our separate ways after next week, Leonard."

"I thought we did that our freshman year. Oh, wait, that was just me." I had learned to laugh at myself before anyone else could, and so far, it was a pretty good coping mechanism.

"You know what I mean. This party is for the seniors, though. And since you're a senior, you should come. I'm sure you'll have fun." She turned my rearview in her direction, straightening her eyeliner and lipstick with her finger.

"Look, I don't mind dropping you off. I'm used to not being included, so I promise I can handle it. It's not like I'm going to go home and hang myself."

She turned the mirror back in my direction and sat back in the seat. "Leonard Michael Pace. I'm going to be so pissed off at you if you don't go inside. You can't just dump me off and leave. How will I get home?"

"I tell you what. If you need a designated driver, I'll come back for you. But I'll wait for your call in my bedroom. I've got important shit to do anyway."

"Like what?" She didn't look convinced.

"Zombie killing. It's my favorite sport." For me, it was my only sport. I had outgrown everything but mock trials, and that was only because I had law school in my future.

"Take this street and then the next right."

I slowed down, following her directions, and finally pulled up to the house. "Here you go, curbside service."

"No, I'm not getting out until you park and promise me you'll come inside." She folded her arms and didn't budge, not even when I reached over and unbuckled her seatbelt and opened her door.

"Better hurry. Someone will see you in the pretty pony, and your reputation will be shot to hell."

"No. We're eighteen, Leonard. We've known each other our entire lives, and I want you to come inside and have a good time." She gave me a pleading look. "At least go in and have a drink with me. One drink, and if it totally blows, you can leave, and I won't stop you."

I looked across the lawn to Seth's house where every window was lit up, and music pulsed with a low thud. Laughter carried from behind the big privacy fence that led to the backyard, and there were so many cars in the driveway already, I was going to have to park around the corner.

"Fine. One drink. But only because this feels like every cliché teen movie I've ever seen, and I'm a die-hard Hughes fan."

"That's even more of a reason why you need to experience it. And I wouldn't tell any of the guys you see their killer party as the next teen movie."

"I'll remember that," I said as I pulled the car around the corner and found a spot to park, hoping I'd have an easy getaway if things went south.

She jumped out of the car and waited for me to unbuckle and reluctantly join her. "I can't believe I let you talk me into this." I raked my hand through my hair and smoothed down my wrinkled shirt wishing I'd dressed to go out.

"You'll love it." She walked with me to the front door, and we went inside, both blending quickly into the ocean of bodies that made up our school.

Kya was immediately swallowed up by her friends, and even though she looked back at me, she was helpless to stop them. She called out over Seth's head, "Thanks for the ride, Leonard."

Seth gave me a hard look. "You had Pretty Pony Pace bring you?"

"Yeah, so what? Leonard's a senior, Seth. Why don't you be a little hospitable?" I could hear them talking over the music a few feet away, and before I could make my way out again, Seth came over and handed me a shot.

"Here, Leonard. Have a celebratory drink on me." It was the sincerest thing Seth had said to me since I'd known him, but then I realized, other than "give me a pencil" or "give me your notes," it was the only thing he'd ever really said to me.

I took the glass, and after giving it a sniff, I turned it back, downing the liquid that was so hot, it burned my throat. The others whooped and cheered. And I smiled, certain my cheeks had turned the same color as my car.

Kya grinned big. "Have fun, Leonard. You deserve it." She mingled with her friends while I walked around, trying the punch and coolers and being stared at by many. No one talked to me, not even when they were passing me drinks, and I was okay with that. I tasted a few, especially the ones that smelled like a regular punch, and before I knew it, I was about to fall on my ass.

I found myself near the banister, looking up at the winding stairs and growing woozy. Suddenly, before I could hold it back, everything that had gone down made a violent climb back up. I turned in time to grab a vase that was sitting on the nearest table but dropped it, shattering it into a million pieces before puking all over the floor.

Heads turned, and everyone laughed even though most were trying not to hurl too. Seth and some of his other jock friends ran over and made a scene chanting Pretty Pony over and over, and though I was still woozy, I ran up the stairs and into the bathroom.

I washed my face and rinsed my mouth, preparing to go back

down and face the music before finding an opportunity to slip out of the party.

I couldn't believe I hadn't been able to hold my liquor, and I would go down as the guy who puked on everyone's senior party. I should have stayed home and not listened to Kya. I could have been leveled up on my game and chilling in my room content to be alone instead of facing traumatizing shame and mockery.

Being invisible sounded good at that moment.

"Leonard?" Kya's muffled voice came from up the hall, and then a soft knock sounded on the door.

"I'll be out in a minute."

The knob turned, and Kya walked in, putting the small pin she'd picked the lock with back in her hair. "I'm sorry that happened. I should have never encouraged you to drink, Leonard."

"It's okay. I just overdid it a bit. I guess Seth wants to kill me. That vase was probably pretty expensive."

"It was a cheap knockoff from the five and dime. Besides, Mrs. O'Haver's taste is so shitty, you did her a favor." Kya giggled and then reached forward to move my hair from my face. "I'm more concerned about you."

"No need. I'm resilient."

"You know, when you say that, you don't look as convincing as you sound."

"You wouldn't understand."

"Hey, it's me. Kya, remember? The girl who you used to tell all your dreams to. You've got a big future ahead, bigger than anyone else in this house, in fact."

"Yeah, and college is going to be great, right?" I feigned being enthused. "I mean, I can't wait for all of the parties and fun. I'm sure it'll be just like high school. Instead, I get to be invisible to a whole new group of people. But hey, at least that whole Pretty Pony nickname shit won't follow me, right? I guess they'll all have to make up something new, but I have a feeling they'll be able to see the invisible V on my forehead."

"V as in virgin?"

"Yeah, I'm probably the one guy in the entire senior class who hasn't gotten laid this year. I hoped it would happen. You know, I'd find a nice girl who knew and liked me, maybe who could even love me. I'd treat her like a queen, you know. Take her to senior prom, make out in my car, but there aren't any girls who would be caught dead in my car or with me for that matter." *Not only that but the only person I ever loved is you, Kya.*

"And yet, I came to a party with you in that car."

"Because you needed a ride. Not because you missed me as much as I've missed you all these years or because you really wanted me to have a good time."

She moved away from the door and walked to where I stood at the sink and took my hand. "Come on. Let me show you how much I care, Leonard."

At first, I thought she would walk me out, take me out the back exit, and walk me to my car on the corner. Instead, she walked me out into the hall and down to a bedroom at the end of the hall.

Before I could ask what was going on, she moved forward and put her arms around my neck, her tall boots making her even taller and nearly my height.

"What are you doing?"

"Showing you how much I care." Her mouth met mine, and my eyes rolled back in my head as she kissed me without any hesitation. I was thankful the O'Haver's had strong mouthwash, and even though she tasted like alcohol, the kiss was nice and turned me on.

By the time she walked me to the bed, I realized what was going on, and her hand on my hard cock was enough proof that I wasn't just imagining things.

I lay back on the bed, and she straddled my hips, taking off her shirt, and then she lifted my hands, resting them on her breasts as her eyes met mine with a look that told me it was all right to touch.

I played with her tits as we made out a little, her hips grinding mine through our clothes, which I couldn't wait to get out of. But I wasn't sure we were going to go that far. Surely, she didn't like me enough for that, and I'd take what I could get.

But then, she blew my mind. She slipped down and went to work on my jeans, and before I knew it, her lips were on my hard cock.

It was my lucky night, and all of my fantasies were finally coming true.

Kya

WHEN I'D FIRST CLIMBED up the lattice at Leonard's house, I never expected I'd be so bold, but I knew this might be my only chance to repay him for his friendship.

We'd gone our own ways in recent years, and while I knew Leonard wasn't the most popular guy in school, no one had ever really bullied him aside from the stupid nickname they'd given his car, and that was because they were all jealous. Considering that the girls outnumbered the boys in our school two to one, it was a little surprising he hadn't lost his virginity. But Leonard was probably too much of a gentleman, so I decided on a whim that he needed someone else to make the first move.

I had always thought he was a cutie and wondered what it would be like to do more with him. In fact, he was my first crush as a girl, and at one time, I could see myself marrying him. That was many years back, though, and once we grew up, we'd grown apart. The thought of that saddened me.

At nearly six-feet, he was a tall guy, and I was glad I'd worn my tallest heels. When I pulled down his pants, my jaw dropped. He was packing the biggest cock I'd ever seen. That along with his dark, bedroom eyes hidden by his glasses, and his perfect smile, courtesy of the braces he'd just had removed, made it hard not to be turned on by him.

I slipped down between his legs and wasted no time taking him into my mouth. He moaned, his body grew rigid at first but then relaxed beneath me. Taking half of him into my mouth had my jaw sore, but when I relaxed my throat and pushed myself down farther, I heard it crack.

I pulled off and turned my head, running my mouth from his balls to his head, kissing and sucking as I went along. I tongued the rim of his broad head, and then licked the tiny slit, tasting his salt, which only made me want more. I gripped him and stroked, my jaw growing tired, but I was determined to make him come.

I worked myself up to a fevered rhythm and moaned with a mouthful until I felt his head swell and twitch before his release filled my mouth.

"Sorry," he said with a strained voice. I swallowed and kept on it, sucking him until he was hard again.

I pulled my mouth away, my grip tight on him, steadily pumping to keep his erection as hard as possible, I wanted to feel the full effect of him buried deep in me. I undid my pants, and he pushed them off my ass with my panties, taking a handful of flesh as he pulled me closer. His cock pressed against my clit, and I moved my hips, humping his shaft. Our bodies moved together in a perfect rhythm, while he kissed my breasts. I gripped his erection and lowered myself, my channel walls stretching to their limits as he filled me up.

I rode him steadily, grinding against him, panting and moaning so loud, I wasn't sure we didn't have an audience outside the door. And at the moment, I didn't care. I was right where I wanted to be.

Being with him was way better than being downstairs with the same old shit going on, and there was no worry between us because we'd completely trusted one another since we were younger. Still, I leaned forward and whispered in his ear, "Don't forget to warn me so you can pull out."

He responded by flipping me to my back and taking charge, which I had to admit was pretty fucking hot.

I ran my hand up to stroke his hair, brushing it back so I could look into his eyes, which were his best feature, and I could see his potential. What might he be like years from now? But I knew it was probably the last time I'd get to hang out with him, much less be alone. He was going to move on and go to college, and with any luck,

I'd move on and follow my dreams to become a rock star. I wasn't going to let anything stop me.

My mind got back into the game as he hit my G-spot, thrusting his hips steadily until I came, my toes curling. I couldn't believe his stamina, or that I'd actually had a chance to finish for once. Both of the other guys I'd been with had only ever cared about their own pleasure.

As soon as the last wave of mine quaked through me, he pulled his cock free and shot his load all over my tummy.

"How'd you get so good? Are you sure you were a virgin?"

He smiled at the praise. "I'm glad you liked it, and yes, I'm sure. It's not like I've never, well, you know." He moved his hand to gesture beating off.

"Well, I'm thankful for all of your practice." I gave him a smile, and his cheeks were red again as he leaned forward and kissed me.

"I'll get something to clean you up." He rose up and found some tissues by the bed and then lay down beside me to kiss my shoulder while I tended to business.

We lay there for a quiet moment, and I thought about the times we'd lay in the backyard and look up at the stars. The popcorn ceiling made for a poor substitute, and the background noise of the party below us only served as a reminder that everyone down there would witness our walk of shame soon enough.

I wondered if everyone would know.

When I met his eyes, he had a dreamy look. "That was pretty amazing, Kya. I mean, I've always hoped you'd be the one, you know. I just didn't know you'd ever be with me like this."

"Really? You wanted it to be me?"

"Why are you so surprised? You're the hot girl next door, Kya. That's every man's fantasy."

"I might regret it later, but only because I won't be able to walk straight when I get up from here. You're really packing a monster."

He blushed and reached out to me pulling me close to him. "You felt amazing on it. Your mouth, your tight little slit. I could do that again and again with no regrets."

"Too bad we're graduating next week, we could have made a habit of this." If I had known the boy next door was hung like that, I'd have climbed through his bedroom window sooner.

"Why can't we?" He turned and met my eyes.

Unless he wanted to hook up again before graduation, say on Tuesday, there just wasn't going to be any time to fuck again. "You have college, and I have my dreams."

He rose up on his elbow and turned to face me. "It's not too late, Kya. We can support each other's dreams. I could come to your shows."

I couldn't help but laugh, but then I realized he was serious. "You have never come to any of my practices, and I live next door. The minute I found music, you stopped coming around. You don't seem to care much about my dreams, Leonard, and we don't even have the same tastes in music."

"That's not true. We have a lot in common, and I listen to rock now."

"Oh, you do, do you?" I rose up and met his stare dead-on. "I hear that rap shit blaring from your car when you drive away."

He glared at me defensively. "So, I'm a man of many tastes. I might surprise you." He let out a long breath and then took another. "Want to know a secret?"

I was growing a bit nervous, wondering if I'd done the right thing. "Go ahead and tell me."

"Those sunflower seed shells, I didn't dump them there. I sit there every other Friday night and listen to you sing, Kya. I think you're the most talented, beautiful girl in the world."

I had never known he did that and didn't understand why it was a big secret. "Why didn't you come down and join us? We don't bite."

"Your band name is Sabbath Sundae, and the guys in your band look like they sacrifice small animals for sport."

I had to admit the boys in my band, who were all nineteen to twenty-two, did wear a lot of black and might come across a bit scary, but that was just their images. "They're not that bad."

"Not only that, but I've seen the people who hang with you there. They don't even speak to me at school."

"Maybe if you came over and joined in now and then, you wouldn't have that problem. People would get to know you and like you like I do." I had never had any problems making friends, but Leonard, he had always been a bit socially awkward. He was just too damned smart for his own good, though, and most people didn't understand his sense of humor. "You're the only thing holding you back."

He sat up, and I joined him. "I didn't think you would want me around. I don't really fit in with your friends. But that's the beauty of it. School is over, and maybe we could really have something."

"Have something?" I knew for sure I'd done something I shouldn't. I got up and found my pants and shirt. "We do have something, Leonard. Friendship, a long friendship that means a lot to me, believe it or not."

"Look, Kya, I've always loved you. I've been too much of a coward to say it, but this night, it's everything I've dreamed of. Well, aside from the whole drunk and sick thing. But I promise, if you give me a chance, I'll make you happy."

"What are you saying?" I asked.

His voice had softened, and he was looking into my eyes with such conviction, I was caught off guard.

"I want to be the man in your life, Kya."

His words were so genuine, and they really tugged at my heartstrings, but I wasn't going to be happy settling down in any way. I had shied away from having a boyfriend for many reasons, but the biggest was that I needed my freedom to chase my dreams. I'd promised my band that once school was over, we'd book more gigs and travel. We had big plans. I was still young, and the idea of letting anyone be there for me other than to further my dreams felt like I had a weighted rope around my neck.

"I'm sorry, Leonard. I don't think that's a good idea. I mean, I care about you, but I cherish our friendship too much, and I don't want to ruin that. Things get complicated, and with what I want to accomplish, it just wouldn't work out." No one was going to like the fact that I'd be gone for long periods of time, sleeping in a van or motel room with five guys.

Leonard's eyes narrowed. "Then, I'm confused. I thought we just had sex, incredible sex. What just happened here?"

"It was amazing, but I just wanted to help, Leonard. I mean, I thought I was helping. You didn't want to go to college a virgin, and we've always trusted one another, I just thought—"

"You thought what? That I'd be okay with a casual thing? If I'd thought you didn't like me, that you were just giving me a pity fuck, I'd have told you to go to hell, Kya." He got up and found his clothes before I could find my bra.

"Leonard, we're friends. I just don't think it should be more, is all. And that doesn't mean this was a pity fuck." The fact that he'd accused me of that really pissed me off.

"What was it then? A favor? Forgive me if I'm not a fucking slut like the rest of you people." He opened the door and left, slamming it behind him.

I looked under the bed and found my bra, and by the time I'd run down to go after him, he was already gone.

I walked up to Seth and tapped him on the shoulder. "Have you seen Leonard?"

About that time, there was a lull in the music as it changed and tires squealed outside. "Sounds like he just left."

I leaned against the wall and sank to the floor. The friendship I'd tried so hard to rekindle was ruined.

1

LEO

Five Years Later

Law school had done wonders to change me, and as I looked in the rearview mirror of my latest Mustang, a black convertible GT, I made sure my hair was perfect despite the top being down and gave myself a smile to check my teeth. I straightened my cuffs and smoothed down my tie as my phone rang in the seat next to me.

I glanced over to see Bailee with two e's name and smiled. She was a persistent one, much more than Bailey with an *ey*, but instead of answering her call, I turned off the ringer. I couldn't very well have my phone blowing up under my graduation robe. It was time to walk the stage once again and make another transition in life.

The last time I'd done this, it was with a broken heart, and even though things had turned out much better than expected, with me not only filling out but finding a social life, I still felt rattled thinking of Kya.

I let out a deep breath and reminded myself that I didn't want to think about her, but with graduation on the schedule, she'd come into my mind a lot lately.

There came a tapping on my windshield on the passenger's side, and Jon, my roommate, who had driven his own car to the event, walked around to my side. "Come on, man. Are you going to stay in that car all day?"

"Hell no, I'm as ready to finish as you are, my friend." I opened the door, and while I stepped out, shutting it behind me so I could go to the trunk and get my graduation gown, Lacey, whose last name I'd never asked, hurried over, nearly knocking Jon off of his feet.

She threw her arms around me. "You look amazing! I hoped I'd get to see you before you took your place in line."

I pushed away, glancing around with the hope that no one else had seen her. "Yeah, I better get to it. I'm running a bit late."

Jon rolled his eyes and looked away while Lacey frowned. "Will you meet me after?" she asked. "I wanted to give you a graduation gift." She flashed me a wink, and from the way she said gift, I had a feeling she meant blow job. Lacey was a pro on her knees, but she still wasn't the best blow I'd had. Once again, Kya came to mind.

"I'm sorry, Jon and I already have plans to celebrate together."

"I don't mind gifting both of you." She winked at Jon, and he shook his head.

"As tempting as that is, we'll pass." I got my gown and shut the trunk, looking around the lot for my father's car. He was usually late to everything but a court date, and I wasn't one hundred percent sure he'd come to see me graduate.

"Fine. Call me if you change your mind." Lacey walked away in a bad mood, glaring at us over her shoulder as if trying to give us one more shot.

We made it to the back where the other graduates were still standing around talking and taking pictures. But before I could get too comfortable, Professor Templeton came over and got us to line up according to out last names. Finally, after minutes of working the others into their places, she called my name. "Pace."

As I took my place in line, I quickly wished I hadn't slept with

Samantha Overton or Patricia Patterson or any other girl who would fall in line near me. Each was giving me a different look, and all expected me to show them the same affection.

I had been a busy man, and Jon had once asked me how on earth I managed to keep them all straight. I wasn't sure myself, but it helped that most of the women just wanted a little fun. There were plenty of sluts around like Kya willing to throw themselves at you for a quick lay, and best of all, I didn't have to feel shit for them.

Once we got seated, after making our grand entrance, Samantha leaned over and licked her lips. "I'm having a party later if you want to *come*, Leo."

"I'll keep that in mind, sweetheart." I saw no harm in giving her hope and didn't care if she was upset later that I didn't show, but sometimes it was just easier to keep things simple and vague, no promises made, none to keep.

I sat through what seemed like a never-ending cattle call of everyone before me and finally got to walk across the stage. I had much more applause from the crowd than I'd had in high school, and that was because everyone was still stunned I had somehow managed to bag Kya Campbell.

Most of my applause this time was from the slew of friends I'd made and all of the hearts I had in my back pocket.

With my degree in hand, the world was mine.

After the ceremony, Jon met up with me, pushing the crowd. He had a lipstick print on his cheek and another half on his lips. "You look like you've been tagged," I said.

He gave a soft chuckle. "Yeah, Breanna and Casey. Both asked me where you were going after." Jon had his own fan club, but he could only manage one or two at a time.

"I don't know, man. Where are we going?" I clapped my buddy on the back.

"We are going to Rock Fest, my friend. I've got us front row seats for a night of music and hopefully a lot of tits and beer. One last night of fun before your father whips us both into shape at the firm."

"Speaking of the old bastard, did you happen to see him around?" I knew it was a longshot but thought I'd ask anyway.

"No, but thanks again for getting me a job at his firm. I can't believe he agreed to take me on."

"That's because I told him how competitive you are. He likes a competitive spirit. It's what makes him tick." The old man had always been wired that way, even when I was a kid in the science fairs and mock trials. He had wanted me to be the best, and he would always find the other overachievers to compare me with. Jon had that spirit, too, but he wasn't an asshole like my father.

I turned on my phone and found another call from Bailee. "This girl doesn't give up."

"Is that Bails?" He still called her by the stupid nickname he'd given her when they dated.

"Yes, and I don't think she's going to take no for an answer so easily." She had been a stage-five clinger for the past two months, and I'd somehow not managed to shake her off.

He followed me as I walked out to my car. "She's a nice girl, man. I didn't introduce you to her so you could treat her like all the others. I thought she'd be good for you."

"No, what you thought was that she'd preoccupy me while you moved in on my herd. You're a wolf in sheep's clothing, that's what you are. And thanks a lot for passing off your leftovers. She told me how she blew you in your car. I think she thought I'd appreciate the fact that you were experienced."

He belted a laugh. "Why would she tell you that?"

"She was comparing our cocks. Said mine was ginormous compared to yours." I liked to tease Jon even if it was the truth.

He nudged me. "Maybe we'll just have to find someone at this concert tonight to size us up. I've got nothing to be ashamed of."

"I think what you mean is, you have no shame. There's a difference." Jon was a hell of a lot more straight-laced than me, but he still knew how to have a good time.

"Slight but I'm okay with that too. I'm so pumped up to see this concert. I'm going home to change, and then we'll head out when you're ready."

"Sounds good. Who's playing?"

"The Deathgrips, Ocean's 666, Rock and Mayhem, Frankfurter Apocalypse, and Sabbath Sundae."

My pulse quickened. "Sabbath Sundae? They're still a thing?"

"Fuck, yeah. They have that song on the radio, Sacred Hearts. That lead singer is one fine piece of ass. They're really growing in popularity, considered one of the hottest new groups to look out for."

"I guess they finally paid their dues. Last I heard, they were hitting most of the dives across the state." I had only heard a few things from the occasional hookup from my list of chicks who wouldn't fuck me in high school. I'd met a few of them over the years, and when they noticed how much I'd changed, they all wanted to see what I was about, although two of them never knew, which was kind of funny too.

"You know the band?"

He imagined Kya going down on him, taking his cock into her sweet lips and sucking it for all it was worth. "I know that hot piece of ass you mentioned."

Jon's eyes lit with surprise. "No way. Maybe you can introduce me."

"If anyone is fucking Kya Campbell, it's me." And then I'd fuck her over as hard as she'd done me.

"Kya Campbell? You mean Kya Star?"

I had never heard the name before. "Don't tell me she's married." Even though I still held a grudge for what she'd done to me, I felt a sting in my chest that she had actually given herself to another man for more than a cheap hookup. I had always wanted to be the man in her life and had pictured what had happened between us ending in many other ways besides how it had. But the one thing they all had in common was us walking down the aisle and me taking her for my wife. I'd never been able to imagine anyone else in that position.

"Fuck, I don't know. Is that not her name?" He took out his phone and moved his fingers quickly across his screen. "Oh, I guess her name *is* Campbell. There are two others for me to choose from."

I breathed a sigh of relief that she wasn't off the market. "Then maybe you have a shot after all." I had thought the band was made up of a bunch of guys, but I guessed Kya had probably run them all off as well.

"Funny guy," said Jon. He started to walk away and turned back to wave. "I'll see you soon, man."

I waved as a hand fell on my ass. I turned to see Bailee had caught up with me. "I can't believe you won't answer my calls. I've been trying to tell you I finished up my last day at work early and decided to come see you graduate."

"That was nice of you." I didn't know what else to say.

"I know you're going to be busy, and I'm moving to Florida for the summer, but I thought we could keep in touch. Maybe when I get back in town for my last year, we can start again. Only this time, maybe you'd like to take things to a deeper level." She met my eyes, and I couldn't help but see the hope in hers. It was sweet but totally out of left field.

"I'm flattered, Bailee, but the truth is, I don't want to ruin our friendship. We've got such a strong bond, I feel like having anything more would tear it apart. I know you know I'm right. I mean, I'm not crazy. It's special, right?" I needed her to agree if I was ever going to get any peace.

"Okay, Leo. I understand I guess. Maybe when I come back, we'll talk again?" I could see her hope turn to disappointment, and I sympathized, I'd had my reality shaken once before too. Besides, better her than me. In the end, all of these girls were the same.

2

KYA

I arrived at the show hours early only to find that the organizers hadn't given us a room to get ready in. So after touring the stage, greeting the other bands, and running through sound checks, I returned to our tour bus to get ready and wait for our spot. We were right after Rock and Mayhem and were the third show of the night. With our song doing well on iTunes and actually getting some airtime, we were well on our way to success.

I heard footsteps at the other end of the bus and wondered which of my bandmates it could be. Mona Star had thrown a fit two days ago claiming she was tired of being overshadowed in the band by Sadie, who was one of my oldest and dearest friends. I was trying to keep the peace, but if someone had to go, I'd choose to keep my bestie over Mona any day of the week. It was truly enough drama for me for a lifetime, and all I wanted to do was get through the show without any issues and be grateful for the chance to open for some of the hottest bands out there.

We'd recently gotten some airplay and positive promotion, and it was a long time coming. I'd formed Sabbath Sundae, a hard-hitting rock band, the summer before my senior year of high school, and we were just now getting the recognition we deserved.

"You'll never guess who wormed her way into getting ready in Ocean's dressing room."

"You've got to be kidding me." I took a deep breath and tried to remain calm. "At least there's more room for me here, and I don't have to smell her fucking hairspray.

"No shit, but it's such an embarrassment. Mona is down there with her arm around Teddy Faith at this very moment like some cheap-ass groupie. Two days ago, it was Mud from the same fucking band, and before that, it was Brock from Rock and Mayhem. It's hard enough to earn the other bands' respect in this business without her fucking half the tour."

She had a point. A lot of bands in the industry were all men, and while some included a female or two and all-girl bands were making ground, females were still the minority. I reached out and took her hand. "I'll talk to her, okay?"

Sadie sighed. "You're too easy on everyone. You need to put your foot down. If you had done that before, we wouldn't be in this predicament. She's going to learn the hard way. None of those guys respects us, and she's making us all look bad."

"I agree. Where are Rob and Liam?" Our drummer and bassist were the only two remaining men. Sabbath Sundae had gone through some changes over the years already, and it was never easy.

"They're hanging out with Rex from Frankfurter Apocalypse. He and Liam are old friends, and they just came off the stage."

"Yeah, Rex used to come to my house back in the days when I'd practice in my garage." Liam had stuck with me since Sabbath Sundae had formed, and Rob joined right after I graduated. Sadie was the next to join, and then Mona was the most recent addition and probably the next to go.

"Rock and Mayhem are being announced any minute." She looked at her watch and then sat down to freshen up her face. We both wore more makeup than usual while onstage, but Sadie caked on the eye makeup a lot heavier than I ever could. By the end of the night, she would look like a raccoon, but somehow the smudgy look looked great on her.

"I'm stoked about this show, Sadie. We're taking off, and I feel like it's going to pay off in a big way." It had been my dream for years, and I'd paid my dues in dive bars all across Chicago and surrounding cities. I'd finally made the right connections and proved myself as a class act.

Sadie raised her mascara wand in the air. "The sky's the limit now, baby. We're headed for the stars." Sadie thickened her lashes even more and fluffed up her hair, and then we both held our breaths for the cloud of hairspray.

"Let's go make our way around. I don't want to stay holed up in here." I hated looking like I didn't want to associate with the other bands. I saw them as my coworkers, and I needed to make sure morale was high before I took to the stage.

Sadie straightened out her skirt and tossed her hair back over her shoulder. "Blitz said he wanted us to pop in and that he misses you."

Blitz was the singer for The Deathgrips, and he had been a friend of mine for years as well. I had always looked up to him as a father figure, and he was not only much older than anyone else on tour, but he was a legend. "I miss him too. He's the real reason we're here, so you better believe I'm going to stop by. I worried about him because he wasn't at the sound check earlier."

"He's fine. I passed him on his way to his dressing room. He's probably looking for you to make your appearance."

We left the bus and headed into the building, and thankfully, it wasn't too far of a walk and security had our backs. I did see a few fans sneaking around, looking for a backdoor, mostly groupies who wanted a chance to hook up, and those would be let in when the guys in the band requested.

Sadie and I walked down the hall and into the room where two of the bands had to share opposite sides of the room. Teddy Faith and Mona were nowhere to be found, and Mud, the bassist, was pissed, his nostrils flaring so much, his nose ring bobbed up and down.

He walked up to me as I made my way across the room to get to the door on the other side. "Where has that skank friend of yours taken Teddy? We've got shit to discuss, and that bitch is a distraction."

I wasn't going to let them get me riled. I had to keep a professional head, and I wasn't about to waste or strain my voice in a screaming match. "I'm not her keeper."

"You should be. You should keep a leash on that dog or keep her out back with the rest of the groupies." Some of his bandmates chuckled, and the drummer, Zac Marzen, stepped up.

"What do you call three groupies who try to be rock stars?" he asked. "That's right, my friends. Sabbath Sundae."

Before I could say anything in our defense, Mona Star came in with Teddy Faith, wiping her mouth. Her lipstick was smeared, and I had an idea where she'd left it. Teddy had barely put his dick away, and the guys started in, making a mockery of them both.

Mona seemed unfazed, grinning ear to ear as if she didn't have a clue how slutty she came across, or maybe she didn't really care. She was just dumb enough to think it gave her power. "Just having a little fun, boys."

The band riled up, everyone shouting and cursing, and I didn't think I could get out of there fast enough.

But when the door opened, and Blitz from The Deathgrips stuck his head in, you'd have thought the principal had just arrived to check on his unruly students. A hush fell over the room. "That's no way to treat my guests, Mud. Zac." Blitz waved me over, and Sadie followed. Mona stayed with Teddy as the others apologized.

"Sorry, Blitz," said Mud. The others mumbled their half-assed apologies until Blitz grunted.

Blitz shut the door, and when he turned around, he crossed the distance in what seemed like two bounds and picked me up to spin me around. "How's my favorite songstress?"

"Ready for the show and glad to see you. Thanks again for giving us the opportunity." He put me on my feet but held me tight, and if he were anyone else, they'd never be welcome in my space.

"Hey, it was the show's organizer, not me. You know I can't play favorites." He gave a sly smile and then a wink. I knew better. He'd gotten us on the schedule, and for that, I owed him big. Blitz had been one of the only front men to take me seriously enough that he had signed me on with his show.

"I can play favorites, though. You're definitely at the top of my list." I hugged his neck even tighter.

Sadie cleared her throat. "If you're done hogging all the good Blitz hugs, I'd like to get in on that." She moved forward as Blitz opened his arm and pulled her in.

"You girls can't let those assholes get to you. And if you have any more problems, let me know. I'll talk to their manager and get it to stop. There's no room for that kind of rubbish anymore. We're here to rock, and I know you two are class acts."

"Thanks, Blitz." He squeezed us both so hard before letting us go, I thought my eyes would pop out, and then he offered us a seat. I plopped down on the couch, and Sadie sat next to me.

Blitz walked over and poured three cups of tea. "I heard the organizers fucked up on your dressing room. I wish I'd known sooner. I'd have pulled you guys in with us. We have a private bathroom and everything, so if you want to hang out in here, feel free. And tell Rob and Liam. Those bastards owe me a visit too. We're going to have to get together real soon, the four of us."

"There's five," I said, taking the steaming white cup that was given to me. I didn't have to ask what it was. It was Blitz's very own honey-lemon tea. He drank it for his voice, and I knew it would do me wonders onstage.

"Yeah, I saw Mona. Look, sweets, and this is just my advice, you can take it or leave it, but she's the source of your problems. You two are never going to be respected as long as you're performing with her. She's been a stain on your band for a year now, and if it were me, I'd let her go."

Sadie met my eyes and then put her arm around Blitz. "Thank you. I just told her that like twenty minutes ago."

"And I know she's right, but I didn't want to rock the boat, not while we have all of this going on."

"Shit, do it now while you can. As soon as you sign with a manager as a band, you'll have less control over these things, trust me. Do it now. And when you sign, keep creative control. You'll be able to make decisions when needed."

Part of our trouble booking shows was that we didn't have anyone representing us. What little we'd done, we'd done under my watch. Sadie had been working a lot of long hours to help, and we were both ready for someone to help. "We don't even have anyone interested as far as I know."

"Probably because of Mona. She's like a stain." Sadie groaned. "Can we please do it before the next show?"

We didn't make any decisions without the guys, and I'd always tried to do things fairly. "I'll talk to the boys. I know you're right, Blitz. Thanks for the advice."

"As for managers, there are a few talent scouts sniffing around. You never know what can happen, but I'll tell you about good things. They happen all at once."

My heart raced. A manager seeing us would be awesome. I knew I couldn't make any decision in haste. Our money and our futures were both on the line. Not to mention getting into a relationship like that one was a huge deal. "It's a lot to think about before the show."

"Don't be stressed. We're here to unwind and have a good time. Remember, if it's not fun, it's work." Blitz gave her a wink and plopped down on the couch across from them.

The rest of his band filed in to get ready, the room filling up and taking on a heady smell of sweat and alcohol. After a while, Liam and Rob came in to join us, and I warmed up my vocal chords a bit while waiting for the call to perform.

Sadie leaned in closer to whisper so no one could hear, "Now, there's a man I wouldn't mind being a groupie for." I looked up, seeing she was referring to Stones Hunter, Blitz's bandmate and oldest son. He was gorgeous, to say the least, and he turned and smiled at Sadie who wasn't hiding her interest.

That was the very moment the organizers came in to give us a twenty-minute warning. "Well, it's too close to show time, so maybe you'll get an introduction after." If anyone deserved someone special, it was Stones, who was one of the hottest and sweetest guys around, and there was no one more special than my bestie.

"We better get to our stage. Liam, would you stick your head in the other room and see if you can find Mona." Liam was always our most diplomatic member, and he was a good guy at heart, but the look on his face when he stuck his head through the door was enough to put me on edge.

"She's not in there."

"Are you kidding me?"

"No. Looks like we're going to have to find her." Liam looked at Rob.

Where Liam was always diplomatic, Rob was a straight shooter. "Fuck her. We don't have time to go looking for her ass, and no telling who she's under. Let's do this without her."

Sadie threw her hands up in frustration. "See, Kya? She's making us look bad."

I couldn't do anything but agree. "Fine. We'll go on. If she shows up, we talk to her after the show. This is our big chance, so let's go out there and do this." All we had to do now was wait for our call.

3

LEO

The first two bands Jon and I watched were pretty good, but I knew Sabbath Sundae was coming up, and while I had the overwhelming feeling I should flee, I was there to have a good time. If I happened to rub that in Kya's face, even better.

She probably wouldn't recognize me anyway. I'd changed so much in the past five years, filled out, grown a beard, changed my hair, not to mention I had a much better sense of style.

"Leo!" I turned my head to see Breanna pushing through the crowd. "I thought that was you!" She was one of my friends from school, and when she saw Jon, she tugged her friend's arm. "I told you he had a hot friend."

Jon and I exchanged a look. Breanna wasn't going to give up easily, and she apparently already had plans for playing matchmaker. The way Jon looked the other girl up and down, I could tell he didn't mind one bit.

"This is Mindy, Jon. She's my best friend from high school, and she's down for the week."

"It's nice to meet you, Mindy. Are you enjoying the show?" The two made small talk while Breanna turned toward me.

"So, what are your plans for the summer?"

"Taking my bar exam and working."

"The same for me."

Jon overheard the subject and turned his attention to me. "I wish I didn't have to study as hard as some. This asshole is probably not even sweating it, he's so smart."

"I'm building up anxiety too," said Breanna. "That's why I hoped to burn off a little stress here tonight." I didn't have to speak slut to know what she meant. She was down to fuck.

"Then why are we here talking about the fucking test? We should be unwinding and enjoying the music."

We finished watching Rock and Mayhem's encore performance, and before it was over, Breanna had cozied herself up against me, her arm locked in mine as if we were on a date.

The band left the stage, and the two girls stepped over to whisper and stare, both seemingly confident they had found their hookups for the night.

All I could think about was Kya walking out on that stage, and soon enough, the band was announced, and the music started. The energy shifted around me as everyone screamed. It was pretty amazing to see it was all for her and her band, and when they took the stage, I could barely breathe looking up at her. While everyone else in the room stared up at her like she was some kind of goddess, all I could think about was the girl who ripped my heart out and stomped on it.

I had poured my heart out to her and told her my true feelings, given her my virginity, only to have her give me some bullshit line about wanting to remain friends. If our friendship was so goddamned important, then why did she not call me and try to make things right? Instead, we'd never spoken again.

The music was so loud, and her voice was even more powerful than it had been when she was younger. I could see how in five years, she'd really matured in her art. She worked the audience on the other side of the stage, reaching down to touch their hands, and it gave me an idea.

I would make sure she saw me. I stood pressed against the stage,

Breanna back at my side, and Jon and Mindy dancing and jumping to the beat, their hands in the air. When Kya made her way over, she reached down touching hands, and when she passed me, our fingertips touched a split-second before our eyes met.

Hers widened, and she flashed me a smile, not missing a beat as she got up and went back to the middle of the stage. After the song was over, she walked to the side as the band geared up for the next song and pointed me out to security. I waited to see if they were tossing me out or sending a message.

As the muscular guard approached, Jon leaned over and whispered to me, "I wonder what this is all about."

"I have a feeling I know."

Sure enough, he walked up to me with a backstage pass. "Hey, man, Kya Campbell said to give you this. She'd like to see you backstage after her show."

"Thank you." I glanced up to see Kya wave in the middle of her performance.

"I'll come and take you back." He turned and walked away, weaving through the crowd.

Breanna leaned closer. "You know Kya Campbell?"

"I grew up next door to her."

Jon patted me on the shoulder. "Wow, man. You going to go back?"

I felt a little strange not having a pass for him too. "If you don't mind, I'd like to."

Breanna pulled Mindy to the side, and I could tell by her hard glances, she wasn't happy.

"I thought I'd take Mindy home. You could see if Breanna wanted to hang with you. She's willing, and you know she's not the kind to be clingy later."

I'd been with Breanna before, and while she'd been good about us not forming a relationship over our hookup, she did seem a little put-off and entitled about the chance meeting. I had come to the concert alone, and now she seemed like I was obligated to leave with her.

"Maybe you could take them both home. I'm sure Breanna wouldn't care, and unless you're planning on making more than a one-nighter of Mindy, then what's the harm?"

"You planning on staying with Kya Campbell?"

"No, but I do want to catch up a bit, let her know what's changed, catch her up to speed." She needed a full course on the new me.

"Dude, I'm under enough pressure with the bar coming up." Jon smoothed out his shirt as Mindy came over and took his arm.

"You're more than capable of handling both." I turned to see that Breanna was standing next to me with a frown, and if any good thing had come from the invitation, it was that she had given up on me for the night.

By the time Kya's band left the stage, Jon had his arm around both women and was geared up to have what could turn into a better night than me.

I figured I'd go backstage and say hello, and we'd take a minute to catch up, and I'd have enough time to show her I wasn't that nerdy little boy she could manipulate anymore and that my heart had recovered quite well. She wanted us to remain friends. I'd keep it friendly.

A few minutes later, the guard came over. I shook Jon's hand and made a promise to call him later, assuring him it was okay to go and that I'd find my own ride home.

As I walked through the maze of halls that made up the backstage, I followed the bouncer who seemed like a nice enough guy and wondered how many had gone back to see her over the years.

"I suppose Kya sees a lot of men after the shows, so I'm probably not the first you've brought back, right?"

"Kya never sees anyone. She's a good girl, so you'll make sure to mind your manners or I'll rearrange your face for you." The guy opened a door, and they walked to the back lot where Kya's tour bus sat. The guard walked over and knocked.

"It's open."

"Thanks, man. And you don't have to worry about me. I'm an old friend." He turned and gave me a hard look that said he was still not impressed.

I stepped into the bus, and Kya was standing there to greet me. "Leonard!" She pulled me in for a hug and then stepped back to look me up and down. "You look great!"

"I just go by Leo now. You don't look so bad yourself."

She wiped her forehead with a pink towel. "I'm a bit grimy from the stage. It's always so hot out there under the lights."

"Yeah, well, you were amazing. You really have come a long way since the garage days." I always wondered how she'd turn out, and it seemed like she was doing well for herself.

"I've missed you. I tried to get in touch after graduation, but your mother didn't want to give me your number."

"Yeah? I didn't know. I left for my new life as soon as I could. It wasn't like I had any reason to stick around." I wanted to be bitter, but she looked so amazing, her smile still as beautiful as always, as sincere, that I had a hard time not falling under her spell.

"Right. Look, I've wanted to apologize for that night a thousand times."

"Please, Kya, that's in the past." I didn't need her apologies, especially for sleeping with me. That would only be another kick in the balls. I'd learned to get over it and move past it, and now so could she. She certainly hadn't had any trouble avoiding me that last week of school, but then I was sure it was easy with most of the class whispering about what had happened. The more space between us, the better.

"What have you been up to? You look like you spend a lot of time in the gym."

"That and law school. I graduated today."

"Wow, that's amazing. I guess we're all grown up now. You know, I haven't had a friend as close as you since we were kids. Not even in high school. You really knew me, you know."

"Yeah." I thought of how well I had known her, how I'd crushed on her all those years, only for her to forget about me in high school.

Then just when I thought I had her back, she went and turned me down.

"I know it's silly, but I wish things had been different, with what happened, you know. I was stupid and scared."

"Nothing to be afraid of now." She looked so vulnerable, and I wished I'd had the chance for a redo too.

I closed the distance between us and brought my arms around her. She stepped closer in my embrace, looking into my eyes as if searching for the boy she'd once known.

I didn't waste another minute and brought my lips down on hers as she relaxed in my arms as if giving in to the moment. The kiss had my blood pumping, and I moved my hand down to grip her ass and grind against her. I wanted her to know what she'd been missing all these years and how hard I still and always would be for her.

"Are you alone?" I knew her band had to be around there somewhere or at least on their way.

"Everyone else is inside celebrating with the headlining band. I told them I was meeting up with an old friend, so they don't expect me for a while." She ran her hand up my arm and rested it on my shoulder as the other dropped lower to my hip.

"Good." As if a gun went off to start the race, the two of us collided once more, this time in a frenzy of passion.

4

KYA

I hadn't been worked up as much in ages, and even though I'd been in a few go-nowhere relationships, I hadn't found anyone as special as Leonard had always been to me.

As we came together with so much passion, I couldn't help but wonder if I had a second chance to make things right between us. I'd regretted my decision not to let him be for me what he had offered and had wasted so much time in my life without him.

But he was here with me again, and this time, I wasn't going to waste a single moment. He had grown up so much, growing a dark beard that matched his brown eyes which smoldered when he looked at me.

I pulled back and took his hand, turning to lead him to the bedroom where I slept on the road. It was a smaller double bed but plenty big for the two of us as we groped and pawed at one another like two horny teens. But we didn't climb right in as I'd expected.

As we stood at the foot of the bed, he took my hand and pressed it against his thick erection, his cock just as long and thick as I'd remembered. I stroked it through his pants as he kissed me, and then I brought my other hand from his ass to undo his jeans. His cock fell heavy in my hands, and I wrapped my fingers around it, feeling his flesh growing hotter by the second.

A lick of heat went through my body, sending an aching feeling of need straight to my core. I had a hunger for him that drew me in, and I reached up and stripped off my top and made quick work of my bra, tossing it to the floor.

He brought his mouth down to my breasts, his large hands cupping them as he squeezed and kneaded them with his fingertips.

"I can't wait to be inside of you." He reached around and cupped my bottom, lifting me up against him and then turning me to the built-in dresser where he propped me up and nudged his way between my thighs, the head of his cock rubbing against my slit.

He reached down and drew his head in-between my folds, rubbing it up and down, sending chills through me every time it passed over my clit. I ground against him, and soon enough, he found my center and pushed his cock into me. He was only halfway inside of me, and I was already stretched to my limits, but he rutted deep and then thrust his hips hard, burying himself to his balls.

His confidence showed much more than it did when he was younger, and I noticed it most in his performance. He met my eyes and took charge once again, turning us around where he lowered us to the bed. Then he hitched up my legs, and I rested them on his shoulders.

He turned his head and kissed my ankle but never took his eyes off of mine. "I've wanted this. After what happened between us back at Seth O'Haver's house, how you climbed on me and fucked my brains out. I've wanted to return the favor."

Knowing he'd thought of me made me smile. "It's even hotter this time around, don't you think?"

He gave me a devilish grin. "Oh yeah, much sweeter, that's for sure." He brought his mouth to mine, and our tongues mingled, moving in and out, stroking one another as our bodies moved in a slow and sensual rhythm.

My first release had my toes curling as I moaned loudly, and the bus was shaking from our movements, no doubt making anyone outside wonder who was getting laid inside.

"How about you ride me as you did before?"

I didn't have a chance to respond or say a word before he rolled us over, and I fell astride, my tight channel still milking his cock from my orgasm. He filled me deeper as I settled on his base, and then I leaned back, angling him toward my G-spot, stroking it with his cock until I came again.

He moaned, and it sent a warm feeling over me to hear it. He whispered against my flesh, his breath warm against me. "You're getting greedy with those. You're a bad girl, aren't you?"

I played along, but only because I knew the truth. I wasn't one for random hookups, and I never slept with members of other bands. In fact, I had a pretty strict set of rules, most of which I didn't mind breaking to be with him. Leonard had always been special. "Yes, I'm especially bad with you."

He chuckled and then nipped at my tight nipples, his teeth closing on them, sending a delightful pinch of pleasure straight to my core that only turned me on even more. I gave a little moan. "They're so sensitive."

"Feels good, doesn't it?" He grazed his teeth along my breast, and I couldn't stop thinking how hot he was, his glasses and braces gone, leaving nothing but a tall, strong, handsome man.

My entire body was alive as a wave of pleasure coursed through every inch of me. "Yes, it does."

"Spin around," he whispered, urging me with his hands to do so.

I did as he told me because it was obvious he knew what he was doing and because I'd known him longer than anyone else in my life. I trusted him completely, especially with my pleasure. Neither one of us could ever deliberately hurt the other. We weren't wired that way.

I rode him reverse cowgirl for a minute, but then he sat up, shifting around behind me where he slapped my bottom and gripped my stinging ass, angling me upward as he thrust hard and fast.

Another orgasm had me screaming so loudly with pleasure that I put my face down on the bed to muffle it. He continued relentlessly until finally, he took one last thrust, hard and deep, and I felt a splash of his release soaking my insides as he pulled free, shooting what was left on my ass and back.

"Damn, that was so hot, I nearly forgot to pull." He found the pink towel I had used earlier and wiped up his mess.

"It's okay. I'm on the pill, and despite your average rocker's reputation, I don't sleep around." I didn't want him to think I was anything like Mona, who I still had to fire. She'd shown up to go onstage, but she had me worried up until the very last moment.

"Good to know we've both changed since high school." He rolled over and lay on the bed a minute to catch his breath. There was an image of us reflecting in the tacky mirrored ceiling. The band before us had it installed, and I'd inherited it.

We made a handsome picture, the two of us.

I reached over and brushed his hair away from his face. "Those rumors about me weren't exactly true, you know." I had the reputation of being a lot easier than I was, and aside from Leonard, I'd only slept with one guy and given a blow job to another. It wasn't half as bad as some of the other girls, especially considering I'd had as many chances.

"It hardly matters anymore, does it? But I will say, you're really amazing." He laughed, shaking his head as if he had something more on his mind.

I was content to lay there with him for a while and snuggled closer, hoping I might even be able to convince him to stay. It would be nice to wake up in his arms and have someone who wasn't going to wake up in the morning and forget all about me.

"This is nice, isn't it? It's like old times when we were kids, just lying here together."

"Yeah, we had some good times."

"You know, I finish up this tour in a few weeks, and I'm planning on heading back to Chicago when I'm done. It would be nice to get together, and maybe we could reconnect. You know, maybe give something a chance to happen for us?"

He smiled but gave me an overly sympathetic look. "Come on,

Kya. We both know that would be a mistake, right? I mean, you said so yourself five years ago. I think we should just keep things friendly. I wouldn't want to ruin our friendship by trying to date."

My face fell, and while I rolled over to find my robe, he got up and found his pants.

"I just thought things could be different, is all. I mean, we're both different."

"Are we, though? I mean, at my core, I'd still say I'm the same guy I was five years ago." With that, he walked out of the room and down the hall. I got up and went after him, hoping he'd talk to me instead of leaving upset again like he had before.

"Hey, wait up. Can I at least get your number so we can stay in touch? I mean, it's what we do, right?" I felt like a desperate fool running out after him that way, but I really wanted to stay friends.

He turned and looked down at me and then leaned over and gave me a kiss on the cheek. "See you around, Kya. Congratulations on getting everything you wanted. It looks good on you." The door slammed behind him, and I stood there stunned, unable to process everything that had just happened. He'd run out on me again.

5

LEO

The steady rhythm of Jon's headboard banged against my walls as I rolled over and tried to adjust my eyes. Without my contacts, I couldn't see a thing, but from the sounds, Jon was still entertaining from the concert.

When I'd gotten home, his music was on, and an unfamiliar car was in my spot out front. I'd showered and went to bed without bothering to let him know I'd made it home.

Not wanting to disturb the party, I dressed for the day and then went to the kitchen for something to eat. I made sure we still had milk before pouring myself a big bowl of cereal and was surprised we did. It seemed like when I didn't check, that's when we didn't have any. *Must be my lucky day.*

I had just finished my last bite when I heard the door open across the room and looked up to find Breanna and Mindy walking out in front of Jon who picked up the rear. "Hey, Leo, when you did you get home?"

"Last night. I didn't want to interrupt." I wondered how Kya was doing but tried to push her out of my head.

"You could have joined in," said Breanna, who seemed like she was in a much better mood.

I gave her a wink. "Thanks. I'll keep that in mind for next time." The two girls giggled as Jon walked them to the door, and while Breanna gave my best friend a simple kiss on the cheek, he practically stuck his tongue down Mindy's throat.

He saw them out and then joined me in the kitchen. He wore nothing but his shorts and scratched his chest like he was a bear coming out of hibernation. "I'm starving."

"I bet you worked up an appetite with those two. I'm proud of you, man. You're really coming along nicely."

"I learned from the best, and as it turns out, both of them enjoyed each other's company as much as mine, so let me tell you thank you, brother. You really left me in a good place." He grabbed the cereal and milk and poured himself a bowl before sitting with me at the table. "So, what happened with you and Kya Campbell? Am I the only one who got laid last night?"

"Come on, haven't you any faith in me, man? Of course, I got laid. Do you know she was my first?"

"Wait, that's the girl who fucked you and then broke your heart?"

"The one and only."

"Fuck, man. I wish I'd known that. I'd like to meet the woman who created The Legend." He had called me The Legend because of the way I'd become over the years, not only with my reinvention but my love 'em and leave 'em motto.

I got up and tossed my bowl into the sink, causing a loud clatter. "I wouldn't give her that much credit."

He grinned. "So, did she break your spirit again?"

I gave him a dead stare. "No, I broke hers."

"You mean she wanted more than a quick fuck?" He didn't look like he was buying it.

"She said she wanted to see more of me, but I made up my mind a long time ago that she'd never get another piece of my soul." I wouldn't give her the opportunity if she begged for it.

Jon gave me a sideward look. "So you walked away and haven't thought of her since?"

"Yep, who needs her? Besides, even though she claims she's not the same as she used to be, why should I believe her?"

"I don't know. You changed, so maybe she could have too? And I'm not convinced, by the way. You've spent the last five years waiting for this revenge of yours, and I bet it was a lot more than just that once you got her horizontal."

I had liked being close to her, and the sex was amazing, but Kya wasn't worth the pain I'd felt before. "Nah, I'm over her. It's not like she's still worried about it. She's got thousands, millions, however many fans now to stroke her ego, so she probably already forgot about me again."

I didn't believe she'd called my mom asking for my number. It was just a poor excuse for abandoning me all those years ago.

"Well, I'm glad you had a good time. I, for one, think I've found the girl for me. Mindy is incredible."

"And it helps that she likes sharing other chicks, right?"

"That's not a turn-off, but no, we actually have a lot in common. We talked for hours after Breanna crashed and even made love without her."

"Made love? That sounds serious."

"Well, I wanted to show her the tender side of me, you know, since I already baited the hook."

"Good job, man. She didn't even run from the house screaming."

"No, and she insisted that she and Breanna take care of my morning wood. I woke up in heaven, my friend."

"And you haven't mentioned the overwhelming fear you have of the bar exam since you came in here, so that's a plus."

"Fuck, you had to remind me."

"Yeah, but don't worry. I'll help you study when I get back from my old man's. I have to pick up some mail." I grabbed my keys and told him goodbye before heading down to my car.

It was a good day to put the top down, so when I started the car, I did just that. I pulled away from the lot thinking about Kya and how good it had felt to be with her physically. I wouldn't allow myself to feel the emotions, but they had been an intense battle of wanting to hurt her and wanting to rekindle and give her everything she wouldn't let me have before. But there was something I felt the moment she mentioned my mother. When the woman had passed away two and a half years ago, Kya wasn't there. Even though her parents still lived next door, even though her parents surely told her all about my mother's struggle, I'd never heard a word.

I pulled up at Dad's house, and even though he had enough money to start over in a much fancier home, he'd kept the house he'd shared with Mom. The only problem was, that day in and day out of coming home without her there had taken a toll on him and made him bitter.

I got out and walked up to the house, knocking and announcing myself as I opened the door, "Hey, Dad, it's me."

He didn't give me a response, as usual, so I went in to find him in his armchair, kicked back in the old recliner as if Mom were still in the kitchen cooking his dinner.

"I graduated yesterday." I walked to the kitchen and stared across the open concept room to see that he was still unfazed.

"You think I don't remember?" He barely took his eyes off the game he watched to give me a glance.

"Oh, so you remembered the ceremony but not that you were invited to it?" I didn't know why I argued with him. Nothing I said was going to sink in or make him understand he'd turned out to be a shitty father.

"Did you set up your bar exam?"

"Yes, Dad, I'm working on it." I wasn't the type who put things off, but I could never be good enough in his eyes. He'd never once been proud of me or any of my accomplishments, and even when I won, he always pointed out how the other kid did it better. Pretty soon, he'd be comparing me to Jon.

"As you should be. Instead of being out with your friends. That's all about to change, you know. I expect you and Jon to work hard and show me I didn't make a fucking mistake taking the two of you on together."

"Yes, sir. That's the intention." I walked up the stairs to my room and sat on the bed. My mom had kept it just the way I'd left it, and Dad hadn't bothered to mess with it either. I looked over to the window and remembered all the times I used to sit out on the roof and listen to Kya's band while I ate sunflower seeds and dreamed of having sex with her. Now, I'd gotten that privilege twice and screwed it up both times.

I heard footsteps, and my father walked into my room. "When are you going to clean this shit out of here?"

"I don't know. Mom always wanted me to leave it alone. She said I'd always have a home here."

"Yeah, well, that's not happening, so you may as well pack up what you want and take the rest of it to storage. Looks like a lot of it could be thrown away, if you ask me." He walked over and stood in front of my trophies and ribbons, none for anything he'd have called a great achievement. "Who the fuck keeps second-place trophies? So you can be reminded you're the first loser? Take this shit down."

"Yeah, I heard you. I can't do it today, but I'll come by this next week and get it out of your way." I wanted to tell him that maybe he could use the room and adopt a son he could be proud of, but I'd had enough of his shit, and if I wanted to keep the peace at work, I'd bite my tongue. I heard my mother's voice, whispering like a ghost in my memory, *choose your battles.*

Dad walked over to the mock trial banner. "I remember this. Best thing you ever did with your extra time in high school. Too bad they don't hand out trophies for that." He turned and walked over to the window. "I'm thinking of selling the house."

The reality of his words settled deep and heavy in the pit of my stomach. I couldn't stand to think about anyone else living in my mother's home. She'd always been so particular about everything, and it had taken her years to get everything the way she wanted it. She had done a home improvement project every summer, and since I was out of school, she'd recruited me to help every chance she got. We'd painted nearly every wall, and there was that time we'd installed the wood floor in the kitchen. It was the first time I'd ever heard my mother curse. "I understand, Dad."

"No, you don't. You never will." He started out of the room. "Whatever is left at the end of the week, I'm tossing to the dump."

I went ahead and went down to the kitchen to get a few garbage bags and made a sweep of things I might want to keep and other things I knew I definitely didn't want.

When I was on my way out, my father, who had returned to his chair and his game, stopped me. "Make sure you're on time for work and don't embarrass me down there. I've built that firm around my reputation and my name, and I'm not having you come in to do your usual half-assed job and make me look stupid."

I was starting to think I should have taken a job elsewhere. It wasn't like I didn't have other offers. Of course, none were going to be better than my father's. His firm was the most prestigious in the state. "Right, Dad. I'll try to remember not to be such an embarrassment." I rolled my eyes and headed out to my car, slamming the door behind me for what might be the last time. I threw the bags over the door and into the back and looked up at the door. *If I ever have a kid, I will not be a shitty father.*

6

KYA

I had slept all night in the tour bus, which was still parked behind the venue, even though my parents only lived twenty minutes from here. Most of the out of town bands had done the same, and those who hadn't stayed in their buses had slept in hotel rooms and partied until the sun came up.

Sadie came dragging in around eight after having spent the night with Stones Hunter and looked at me with a dopey grin as I drank my coffee.

"What?" I asked, knowing she wanted details.

"Nothing. Just can't believe you didn't jump at the chance to tell me all about your hookup. I came out and saw this bus a-rockin'." She moved her hips in a twerking motion.

"You haven't offered up any saucy stories, either, so I guess we're even." Normally, when we met someone new, we'd compare notes, but I didn't feel like reliving the last moments of the night with Leo.

He had changed, and now he was nothing but a player, an egotistical asshole who I had wasted time thinking about all these years wondering if I'd done the right thing by rejecting him.

She slid into the seat across from me at our little tour bus booth and turned on the Keurig to make her own cup. "Fine, I'll go first.

Stones is incredible. We got our own hotel room, and we talked all night."

"All night? So, you didn't hook up with him?" I gave her a sidelong look, and she shook her head.

"Nope. If Stones wants to get with this, he's going to have to work for it. I'm not a skank like Mona who sleeps with men she barely knows." She met my eyes and pulled her lips in tight like she regretted her words. "Oh, I'm sorry. Did you know your guy?"

I gave a half-hearted laugh. "Yeah, I did. I slept with him before in high school."

"Wow, an old flame. That's hot."

"No. More like the one who got away. He was such a good guy, a little socially awkward and a virgin, so we were at this party just before graduation, and he mentioned how he didn't want to go to college a virgin. I had a little experience and had always had a little crush on him, so I offered to help him out."

Sadie picked up her steaming cup and turned off the coffee maker before she took her first sip. "You popped his cherry. Jesus, Kya. So, what happened?"

"Well, he was really hung, and the sex was amazing, but then when it was over, he was so over the moon, he wanted to hook up and be a couple, which scared me to death."

Sadie brushed her bleached hair back. "You were scared of virgin boy? He must have really been something." She waggled her brows. "Or was it the big penis?"

I reached across the small booth and nudged her. "It was him. I've known him since I was six. He stopped coming over when I discovered music, and I thought he wasn't interested. So, by then, I had made my plans around my dream and didn't want anyone standing in my way."

"Ouch." She rubbed her arm to feign injury. "What did you say?"

I sank back in my seat. "I said I didn't want to ruin our friendship, which was the same thing he said to me last night when I suggested we get reacquainted."

Sadie's jaw dropped. "Oh no, he revenge fucked you."

"Right, and in a very *in my face* kind of way, which really sucks. I mean, I guess I didn't think he was capable. He had always been so sweet, but yeah, I'm still bleeding a bit." I rubbed the tender flesh over my heart.

"Damn. That sucks." Sadie reached out and took my hand to offer comfort. "Almost as bad as what we have to do next."

I took another sip from my warm mug. "Which is?"

Sadie gave me an apologetic look. "Fire Mona, hello? Did you forget?"

In honesty, I had forgotten after the previous night's drama, but I couldn't put it off any longer. "I guess I need to call a meeting."

Sadie smiled big and held her chin up high. "Done. And for your information, they'll all be here any minute. I told them it was important."

I realized I needed to get my head out of my heart and pay attention to what mattered. "Where did Mona stay last night?"

"I'm not sure, but it wasn't with Teddy. He was at the party that Stones and I went to before we got our room. Blitz asked about you, by the way. He said there was a manager asking questions about us, and he was supposed to have given them your number. The man said he's local, so he'd be around."

"Awesome. Did Blitz say if he's any good?" It would help if this guy had a solid reputation in the industry. There were too many wannabes as it was. I needed someone who could work well with others to get the best for us.

"Nope, but you can ask him all of that when you call him. But don't tell him I spent the night with his son. He's really funny about that shit, and Stones doesn't want his dad or the band to know."

"And if I know Blitz, he already knows. He keeps his boys on a tight leash, from what I'd seen and heard."

Before we could continue the conversation, Liam and Rob came into the bus. "Good morning, ladies," said Liam. "I brought doughnuts."

Rob sat on the makeshift couch across from the little booth. "Is Mona here?"

"No. She's probably going to be fashionably late like that shit she pulled last night." Liam's tone showed his distaste for the woman.

"I guess we're all still in agreement, which is good. It'll make things a lot easier. I need you guys to have my back for sure." I knew getting rid of her was the right thing to do, and though I'd never had any problems getting rid of troublesome people in the past, Mona was different. She'd given me a place to stay when I needed it and been there when shit had gone south with my parents. The only reason Sadie hadn't been around at the time was that she'd been in a relationship, and her controlling asshole of a boyfriend wouldn't let me stay with them. I just needed to suck it up and stick to business.

"We're definitely in agreement. We never needed her in the band anyway. Don't take this the wrong way, but you two are more than enough eye candy, not to mention, you guys actually have talent." Liam took a seat and kicked his feet up, his heavy, chain-decorated boots resting at the edge of my seat.

The door to the bus opened up, and Mona strolled in carrying her spiked boots in her hand with her hair a mess and something crusty on her shirt. She smelled like a mixture of cigarettes, sweat, and booze, and the circles under her eyes were way too deep for a young woman her age.

"What's up, bitches? Was that a fucking killer show or what?" Her excitement fell flat in the room. "What's the problem now? Was I late for the meeting?" She leaned against a small partition. "Well, is anyone going to tell me what this is about?"

It was time I spoke up. Being my band, it was my responsibility. "It's about you, Mona. We just can't work with you anymore."

"You're shitting me, right? I make this band fun. If it wasn't for me, you wouldn't know half of these people."

"Wrong. If it wasn't for you, I'd still know them, only I wouldn't know who they were fucking and who has the biggest dick."

"So now you're jealous that I get all the guys?"

Liam cleared his throat. "You're not getting the guys, Mona. They're getting you. You're a fucking joke to these guys, and you're making us look bad."

"Shut up, Liam. Always the fucking kiss ass. We all know why, too, but Kya's never going to like you that way."

Liam laughed and shook his head. "You're such a bitch."

Liam and I had been friends forever, but the only love we had in common was music. The guy was like a brother to me, and that kind of loyalty was something people like Mona couldn't understand.

"Right, I'm a bitch, so I'm just out, just like that?" Mona turned her attention to me. "I was such a bitch to take you in when your parents got sick of your lifestyle and kicked your ass out on the streets."

"I appreciate you helping, but at the same time, I should have never let you talk me into putting you in the band because of that. You're not professional, you're making us look like a joke to the other bands, and you don't have any respect for us."

"Why, because I don't sit around with you before a show? I made it to the stage."

Rob cleared his throat. "Which you shouldn't be on." A hush fell across the room as his words registered. "You don't have what it takes, Mona. You aren't serious about your instrument, you barely know how to play it, and half the time you don't."

"I'm part of the show. I add flair." She shrugged like it wasn't a big deal. "And I do know how to play, thank you. I've been playing since I was a kid."

"And you haven't improved much. Look, I'm done arguing. You're out. It's time to move on." Rob got up and moved into the back room and shut the sliding door.

"You'll regret this." She went to the back to gather her things.

I looked at Sadie and let out a long breath. I was glad that Rob had spoken up, but he had cut her deep and said a lot of things about her talent that I wouldn't have. But it was time to move on.

As Mona walked through with her bag, I felt I had to say something. I got up and walked to the door behind her. "Take care, Mona. I sincerely wish you the best."

She narrowed her eyes at me. "Fuck you, Kya." As she threw open the door and stormed out, she nearly ran over a man who still had his hand up to knock. "Out of my way."

"I beg your pardon, miss." He stepped aside and watched her as she rounded the corner. "Did I come at a bad time?"

"That depends. What do you want?"

"I'm Whit White. I manage young talent like your band and would like to talk to you about representation." The man was dressed in a suit and had a bright smile, but I'd always been taught not to trust anyone based on looks alone. But I knew in my gut that this was the man Blitz had mentioned. Had to be.

I stepped back and waved him over. "Please, come on in."

"Thank you. I thought I better make a move on you guys before someone else did. I guess my first question would be, have you been approached by anyone else?"

We hadn't, but I didn't think we should tell him that. "Maybe a few."

"A few?" He gave a smile that told me he was onto me. "Well, then, it looks like I came just in time."

Rob came out to join us, and once we got Whit settled at the booth and offered him some coffee, we got down to business. "What is it that you can offer us?"

"Here's a contract I'd like to offer along with some of the people I've worked with in the industry. It's standard terms, but feel free to look it over. With your talent taking off, it's going to be important to have someone handling your schedule and making sure you get paid."

Sadie nudged me. "Hell, I'd be happy to have a proper dressing room."

We gave a collective chuckle, and Whit joined in. "That's the easy stuff. You've got the talent, and I think performing is all you really should be worried about. Let someone else haggle with venues, coordinate your schedules, book your shows and interviews. You should really have a meet and greet after the shows too. You've built quite a fan base. Now, let's use it to take this into the stratosphere."

"Can we have a minute?"

"Take all the time you need." He got to his feet and walked to the door. "I'm leaving town today, though." He disappeared out the door, leaving us there to decide.

Sadie pointed to the door where the man had stood a moment before. "I don't think we should let this guy get away. Blitz is the one who told me there was someone scouting us, so if there was some red flag, he'd have said so."

"I'm good with it," said Liam. "He's got some impressive connections, and the numbers are spot on to what I hear the standard is. I don't think we should be too petty. Let's take what we can get, and after the five years, renegotiate if we need to."

Rob leaned in, keeping his deep voice low. "Five years is a long time. I say we ask for three, cut it down a little. If we take off, and we don't like this guy, we're stuck for a long time."

I had looked over the contract and hadn't found anything about keeping our creative freedom. "I say we rock the boat a little for creative freedom. It's the only thing Blitz really warned me was a must. I don't want some stranger coming in and telling us what kind of image to have or what to include in our songs. Besides, that's supposed to protect us down the road. It might not be a bad idea to have a lawyer look this over."

Sadie nodded. "I'm with Kya. Let's see what he says."

We called Whit back in, and he joined us, taking his previous seat at the booth. "Did you come to an agreement?"

"We're a little concerned about the length of the terms, and I'd like to keep creative freedom as the band's founder."

"Of course. I will say, the terms are standard and, in my opinion, creative freedom is a given. It's not like I can tell you what to do when it comes to your music. I can spell it out if you want, but reworking the contracts will take time. I've got a couple of other prospects, too, and I'd hate to sign them before you. I mean, it only pushes you farther down my list of priorities."

We all exchanged looks. Sadie's eyes were pleading with me, Liam and Rob nodding in agreement. "Should we have a lawyer look over this?"

Whit let out a casual laugh. "Look, I get why you would think that, but I'm representing you, so naturally I'd have your best interest at heart. And if you want to spend money and time on a lawyer, I'll just leave my card, and you can get back to me. But if I sign someone else, I'm going to be busy making their dreams come true by then."

I felt so much pressure with the others looking at me. I didn't want to disappoint them, and Whit seemed so sincere.

Sadie leaned over and squeezed my hand. "This is our big shot, Kya." She nodded, her eyes widened, and she bounced in her seat, and even Rob and Liam were smiling like they wanted me to give the word.

I smoothed the contract out on the table and then looked across the table at Whit. "Fine, let's do this." I held out my hand, and Whit reached into his coat to get me a pen.

7

LEO

Five years later

Mondays had never been my favorite day of the week, but walking into my office to see Tabatha Holt bent over made up for it.

She looked up from the pile of sugar packets she'd spilled and gave me a warm welcome. "Good morning, Mr. Pace. How was your weekend?"

She'd always called me Mr. Pace, even in the bedroom, which had been as much of a turn-on as anything else about her, and she was a beautiful girl. She picked up the last of the packets and stood, smoothing out her skirt and fluffing her hair.

"It was good. Too short as usual." I glanced up to see a stray sugar packet had wedged itself in the pleat of her blouse and walked over to save her from future embarrassment. "You missed one." I pulled the packet off her shirt and gave her a wink. "Better put that one in my coffee. It's extra sweet."

She giggled and turned to fix me a cup as I walked into my office and placed my briefcase on my desk. She walked in with my steaming cup of brew, placed it on my desk, and ripped the packet open. Once she poured it in, eye fucking me the whole time, she stirred it with a red swizzle straw.

"Just the way you ordered." She licked the stick, her tongue stroking it before her mouth closed on it, exactly the way she'd tasted my cock, and then with a wink, she walked away.

"You sure make my mornings brighter, Tabby." As she closed the door, I mumbled to myself, "And my dick harder." I knew I shouldn't encourage her so much, but the game between us was the only thing that kept me sane around the office.

My father hadn't ever made working for him pleasant, and with him being such a hard-ass all the time, putting me and my best friend Jon against one another constantly, it only made working for him worse. Lucky for me, I had proven myself to be a vital asset to the firm, and my undefeated title was still strong thanks to my latest win.

I heard a knock and wondered if Tabby was going to come in and offer more of her services, but then Jon opened the door and walked in, killing my boner.

"There's the golden child. I heard about the case Friday. Congratulations, man. I don't see how you do it, but you're on fire. I hope you celebrated over the weekend. I didn't hear from you."

"I might have had a little fun. Or two." A brief image of the two women I'd spent my nights with came to mind and got my blood flowing again.

"Oh, yeah? What were fun's names? New fun or old fun?"

"Names are unimportant. You know I'll never actually hook up with anyone for more than a night or two."

"Right. But you do realize that one day, you're going to have to settle down. You can't keep juggling your job and all the women."

"That's just the thing, man. I don't waste time juggling. I tell them right up front what I want. If they don't want to play my game, they don't have to. Maybe if you'd quit trying to put your energy into finding Mrs. Right, you'd stop losing cases. Get your head in the game."

Jon chuckled. He hadn't been on a date in months, but every time he found someone, he wondered if he should marry them. "Just because your father gives me all the losing cases, doesn't mean I'm not focused. And we're not getting any younger. I thought I'd be married by now."

"You and Mindy practically were. Which reminds me, did you ever get your balls back from her purse?" He'd dated Mindy for almost four years before they finally broke up, but because of a home they'd bought together, they'd remained friendly. I hated the way she walked all over him, and I'd offered to represent him in suing her to force her to sell so they could pay it off and he could recoup his money. Instead, being the gentleman, he'd given it to her.

"Very funny." He gripped his sac and held up his middle finger, and that's the precise moment my father walked in.

"Jesus, what the hell is going on in here?" My father clenched a file in one fist and waved the other hand out like he couldn't believe what he was seeing.

"Jon's checking for a hernia. He said the cases you're giving him are too much to carry."

Jon pulled his lips in tight to try not to smile. "Actually, I came down to congratulate your son on another victory, but I was just leaving."

Now it was my turn to hold up a middle finger. It was just like him to rush off when my father showed up, and even though he'd tried to get the old man to acknowledge that I'd done such a great thing for his firm, he knew as well as I did that it would never happen.

My father huffed, looking at us both with a scowl. "Stop making those obscene gestures. You're professionals. Act like it."

Jon hurried out and left me alone with him. "So, Dad, what's up. You rarely come down the hall to my end of the building." I offered him a seat, but he shook his head. The old man liked to posture over people. It made him feel like a big shot.

"I've signed you on another case. It's high-profile, and a lot of money is on the table."

I eased back in my chair and put my hands up over my head. "Naturally, you want the best on the case?" I gave him a wink and figured he'd know I was kidding. Any normal father would. Hell, a normal father might have kidded back or acknowledged I'd never lost a case and maybe been proud of that.

Instead, he shook his head and looked at me like I couldn't disappoint him more. "That ego is what's going to knock you on your ass one day. Now focus, would you?"

"What's the case about?" I never knew what type of case he'd throw my way, and I was waiting for the one that might come in and blow my streak.

"You'll be representing Whit White. He's a manager in the music industry, and he's being sued by one of his bands."

"Is it a strong case? What's he being sued for? Breach of contract? Sexual harassment? Misuse of power?"

"They claim he was stealing their money. He seems to think the contract is ironclad." My father walked over and placed the folder on my desk.

"Who's the band?"

"Some hard rock garbage, Bloody Sunday or some shit. I can't remember. It's in the file."

"Sabbath Sundae?" The blood rushed from my head, and I felt like melting into the floor.

He snapped his fingers. "That's it. Sounds like it will be pretty cut and dry."

I got to my feet. "Dad, I can't take this case."

"Why the hell not?" He stepped closer. "Is there some kind of conflict?"

"You remember our neighbors the Campbells back at the old house? Kya is the lead singer and founder of that band. They used to practice right next door to us."

"And you haven't been friends with her since she grew tits, so what's the problem?"

"It's a conflict." I didn't need to tell the old man I'd slept with her twice and that I'd been pretty shitty about how I'd treated her the last time I saw her.

While I'd meant the whole friendship thing, I actually never thought I'd see her again, but this was going to put me seeing quite a lot of her, and she'd never forgive me for representing some asshole who was out to get her money more than likely.

"You'll take this case. I'm not losing this money because you knew some kid back fifteen years ago. Be ready to meet your client tomorrow." He turned and walked to the door, and I plopped down in my chair, knowing, case aside, I might have just taken on a situation I couldn't win with Kya or my father.

8

KYA

I had just cracked the first of three eggs into the skillet when Addison walked in with her hair a mess and still wearing her kitty cat pajamas. "I don't want eggs today."

"Too bad. I'm not a short-order cook, and you better hurry up and get ready for school or I'm going to take away your TV privileges." At four years old, she was too strong-willed like me. Add that paired with her father's smarts, and she was a tiny force to be reckoned with when she wanted to be.

"I want to stay home." She lifted her chin, her little round face staring up at me with eyes from the other side of her gene pool. She was a tiny duplicate of me, yet her eyes had always been like her father's.

"You can't stay home. You're almost done with this year, and then you'll have all summer to sleep in." I couldn't believe she was complaining. She never had before. "You usually like school. What's this all about?" I hoped this wasn't a new phase that would bleed into her teenage years. Surely, it wouldn't start this early?

"I want to go to Aunt Sadie's house." She smiled and batted her thick lashes. "I haven't seen her all week."

"If you get yourself ready, we'll go over after school. I promise."

She hesitated, but I didn't back down. "Go. I have a lot of stuff to do today." I didn't want to tell her I'd be spending time with Sadie.

"Okay, but can I bring her some of the cookies we made last night?" I realized that was the real issue. She'd asked about sharing the night before.

"I'll tell you what. I'll bring her a baggie of these and then let you make a special batch the next time we go over for dinner."

"Okay." Addison seemed satisfied and ran to her room to finish getting ready.

I breathed a sigh of relief and finished cooking the eggs. I had too much on my mind with the recent blowup with our manager, and this time, it was the final straw. I thought back to the day we'd signed him and wished I could take it all back. Not only had we shit-canned Mona Star that day, but we'd signed our souls away to Whit White who had talked a smooth con.

I had later found out that not only had he pissed a lot of people off in the industry, but he wasn't the man Blitz had wanted us to meet. We'd only assumed he was. And to make matters worse, Mona had hung around outside to wait on him to come out of the bus, and she'd propositioned him. They'd been together ever since, and he'd taken every opportunity he could to skim from us. I didn't know what was worse, knowing he was taking more than his fair share or that he was spending it on Mona.

Addison and I ate our breakfast together, and then I drove her to school. She'd started her education a little early because of my tour, and she'd had enough tutoring on the road that at four years old, she knew how to read at a third-grade level. I tried to keep her life as normal as possible, but there were times it was a challenge.

With my parents still not talking to me, especially now that I was not only a heathen rock and roll singer but because I was an unwed mother, Sadie and the rest of my rock tribe was my family.

Sadie and Stones had gotten together and were still in a complicated relationship, and since Blitz was in the picture because of that said relationship, he had taken on the role of grandpa to Addison when he was around. Rob and Liam had been like uncles even though Liam was expecting his own little one.

We were a very motley crew indeed, but I wouldn't have it any other way.

I pulled around the circle drive and stopped at the drop-off point. "Here you go, little one. I'm sure you'll have a good day." She turned and gave me a hug and then stopped to hold out her finger.

I held out my own finger, locking it with hers. "The two of us," I said with a wink.

"The two of us," she repeated with a giggle.

It was our special way of saying I love you, and though we'd said those three magic words many times, too, this had been our thing.

Her teacher walked over and took her hand, and after giving me a warm good morning, she shut the door and led Addison inside.

I drove away and went to the diner for my meeting with Sadie, hoping traffic wouldn't be terrible. The last thing I needed was to be late again. She was already on me about the last time.

I found a parking spot outside the diner and then went inside to find her looking at her phone. "Not too bad. You're only a minute late this time."

"Like you have anything else to do, and I was only three minutes late the last time." I knew she was just having fun with me, and she reached over to give me a nudge.

"I know. I was getting a little worried, though. I went ahead and ordered your usual. Didn't want it to get too cold. How's Addie?"

"She misses you. God forbid we go a few days without you." I sometimes thought she loved her aunt Sadie more than me.

"You should have brought her along. She's too young for school anyway, and what's she going to miss? She's already reading."

"Which is why she's in a special school. It's important she stays grounded while she can, and you know if this lawsuit goes anywhere, it could be a while before we tour again. I can't keep her out that long." Sadie had always argued that she needed to be a kid as long as she could.

"Fine. And that reminds me, we have a meeting tomorrow." She took a sip of her coffee and gave me a pointed look over the top of her cup.

"Who with? And don't tell me it's that slimewad, Whit White." Thinking of him made my skin crawl. He was the worst decision I'd ever made, and I'd made some doozies.

Sadie shook her head. "No, it's our lawyer. I've finally found one who looked professional, and she's supposed to be fierce in the courtroom. I think we need a strong woman to put little Whit in his place."

"Has she seen many cases like ours?" I didn't want a newbie with no experience.

"She's no rookie, but I guess we'll have to ask her tomorrow." Her phone rang, and she glanced down and made a face she only reserved for Stones Hunter. It was somewhere between excited to hear from him and unsure of his faithfulness. She turned the phone down, but let it ring.

"Are you going to answer him?"

She sighed. "No, he can call me back later."

"I'm sure he misses you."

"I'm sure he does, but we talked like two minutes before you showed up. We had a fight, and he hung up on me. The band signed on for six more shows. You know Blitz, always taking the opportunity where he can find it."

"Don't we all?" I could hardly blame the man for wanting to make a living for himself and his band and crew.

The waitress arrived with our food and topped off Sadie's coffee. She stirred in extra sugar and looked up at me. "I'm scared if he doesn't come home soon, he never will."

"That's all the more reason to answer his calls, Sadie. I know it's been a rocky relationship, but he loves you." The guy had written sappy songs about her and treated her like a goddess on most days. One could only be so lucky.

"I know. I just don't know if it's enough. Blitz is nonstop and expects him to be in his shadow, and it might be fine when I'm on the road, too, touring the same venues, playing the same shows, but the distance makes me wonder if we'll ever be a real family or have kids of our own. I mean, look at Blitz and Addie. He loves her like she's his own."

"And spoils her like it too," I added.

Sadie laughed. "Right, but you'd think that would make him understand our need for a little time to have the same." Her smile faded, and her lips turned down to a frown. "Stones and I want kids, too, but at this rate, we'll never have time to get married, much less start a family. And he won't stand up to his father."

I cut up my waffles and passed her the only knife on our table to do the same. "I'm sorry." I took her wrist and gave it a squeeze.

She gave me a half-hearted smile. "Yeah, me too. I hope this lawsuit doesn't drag on. It's only going to make things worse before it gets better."

I hoped that wasn't true. I didn't want any ugly legal battles ruining the peaceful life I'd built for my daughter. It wasn't easy, but we'd managed, and it helped that without all the stage makeup and spiked heels, I could look normal. Most of my tattoos were hidden, and I had lost my red streaks for a tamer look over a year ago.

I raked my hand through my hair and sighed. "I just want us all to get our money. It makes me angry every time I think of how we just listened to that asshole like a quartet of morons. Maybe if we'd gotten a lawyer then, we wouldn't need one now."

Sadie took a bite of her waffles. "I'm just glad you finally figured it out. I mean, I thought things were good, but a little short, you know."

I took another bite of waffle after swirling it in syrup. "I know. We should have known that any asshole who'd fuck Mona Star, much less keep her around for five years, was up to something. I want back everything that asshole skimmed. And I want something for all the shows he cost us."

We shared a collective sigh and busied ourselves eating. After a moment of silence, Sadie looked up and dropped her fork to her plate. "You know what the scariest part of this is?"

I lifted a brow and shrugged. "All of it?" I knew I couldn't think of one silver lining if we lost. Our reputations would be ruined, no one would want to work with us, and getting future representation was going to be hard as hell. Not to mention he controlled all the work we did, and while we would still get our cut, he'd continue to profit from it as well. With me having Addie, I didn't have time to start all over at the bottom. "Or the fact that if we lose this fight, we might all have to get regular jobs?"

"That's a pretty bad one, but I was thinking about having to see Mona's smug face."

"I just want to get back to making music. I'm not really alive unless I'm in the studio or on tour. This could ruin everything I've worked for since I was seventeen years old, Sadie. I can't see it end this way, not by some asshole who was taking advantage of us."

"Look, it's going to be okay. We'll get through this. Let's go meet that woman tomorrow and annihilate Whit White." She stabbed a piece of egg and popped it into her mouth. "We'll hit him so hard in the wallet, Mona will feel it."

9

LEO

I had just about given up on my meeting with Whit White when Tabby called to say he'd arrived. She walked in with a pissy look on her face. When he turned to her, looking her up and down, I understood. And then he told on himself, proving what an ass he was. "You're a lucky man getting to look at that peach all day."

I rose from my desk and offered him a seat as Tabby rolled her eyes and shut the door.

"I didn't think you were going to show."

He waved his hand dismissively as if it were me who'd made him wait. "Sorry. I had some shit to do. You know how it is living the busy life, I'm sure." He glanced back at the door and pointed. "Tell me, are you tapping that? I still see nothing but tits and ass. And those legs, I think she could wrap them around my neck lying flat on her back."

I ground my teeth and decided that instead of scolding him, I'd change the subject. "Let's get down to business, Mr. White. My time is just as valuable as yours, so if you'd like to tell me what this is all about, I'd appreciate it."

Whit's face fell. "Right. Well, it's really cut and dry. My clients are threatening to sue me. The band signed with me five years ago to be their manager, and just before time for renewal, they're accusing me of skimming money. They said I needed a lawyer, and I want the best."

"Have you been skimming money?"

Whit seemed offended that I'd ask. "No. I've only taken what's rightfully mine. Anything they say falls under skimming is perfectly legal, and furthermore, they have breached their contract many times by not moving forward with ideas that could have made them millions."

"Such as?"

"Such as reuniting with their old bandmate, Mona Star. The fans loved Mona, and they got rid of her for no reason. I wanted to call it a reunion tour, which would make a great deal of money, but like my many other ideas, Kya Campbell got in the way."

I steepled my fingers and leaned in closer. "She's the band's founder, is she not?"

He smiled, his eyes lit with surprise. "You've done your homework."

"A little. But wouldn't it be the band's call if they take a job or don't?"

"No. That's why they hired me. I've also tried to offer other services, all denied."

I'd read through the lawsuit, so I knew what Kya was accusing him of. "What is this about misuse of funds? It says you collected money for refunds, and you never gave any of it back to the band's account. They claim you spent that money on personal vacations."

"I was out looking for venues. I can't help it if I have to take my girlfriend along and want to stay in a hotel. Those are all expenses for their benefit, so I feel they should pay for them."

"The band book a lot of shows in Cancun?" The man was a swindler, and I could already tell I wanted nothing to do with him.

His phone rang in the middle of our meeting, and he cursed under his breath. "Excuse me. I need to take this." He got up and went to the window as if I couldn't hear everything he said.

"I can't talk now, Mona. I'm in a meeting with the lawyer now … Yes, he's the best, undefeated, so he cares more about his record. He isn't going to want to lose, so don't worry about it … Okay, yes, I'm on my way. Tell them to wait." He ended his call and returned the phone to his pocket. "I'm afraid I need to be going. I can call you later with the rest of the boring details, but I'm sure you can see this should all work out in my favor. The contract was signed and agreed upon. They really don't have a leg to stand on. Bunch of bitches anyway. Especially that Kya Campbell."

My fist clenched. Even though I'd had a negative thought or two or three about Kya, I didn't like hearing the words come out of his mouth. I took a deep breath. "I'm sorry. I couldn't help overhearing your conversation, but were you speaking with Mona Star?"

"Yes, she's my girlfriend, well, fiancée for as long as I can keep her on the line. God knows I'm not the marrying type."

I had to agree with that. I couldn't see why anyone would want to marry the guy. "So you have a conflict of interest?"

"No. They released her from the band *before* they signed me. Before we were ever together, actually."

If he couldn't see why his ideas for a reunion with their old bandmate was a conflict, then I was in trouble. I had to get out of this case. It was too much of a shit storm, and I didn't want my record fucked up because of someone like him. "I actually have a few more things before you go, and one very important thing is that we'll be holding a press conference. I've already had a few calls asking questions, and I think we need to be prepared. The media will be all over this."

He laughed it off and waved his hand dismissively once again. "Don't worry. I know how to handle the press. I represent people, too, you know."

I'd dealt with his type of ego before, and I was still wondering why I'd won that case. This wasn't going to be easy. "I'm well aware, but I need you to understand, this isn't going to be like usual. I'll do the talking."

"You?" He looked me up and down as if I were a bug.

I squared my shoulders. "Yeah, do you have a problem with that?" I could already tell he despised the fact that he wasn't going to be in charge.

"Fine," he said with a huff. "If you're done here, I really should go."

"It was nice meeting you, White. I'll call you later, and we'll finish when we both have time." He got up and shook my hand, which I wiped on my pants as soon as the motherfucker was gone.

I walked out to make sure he hadn't upset Tabby and found her sitting with a look of shock on her face. "Are you okay, Tabs?"

"Yeah, he's the not first man who talked to me like I was a piece of meat, and I'm sure he won't be the last."

"If he says or does anything inappropriate, you let me know. I don't like that guy."

"If you don't like him, why are you going to defend him?" She spun her chair away from me and got back to work, her fingers flying so fast on her keyboard, you'd have thought it was on fire.

"You're right. I'm going to tell my father I can't do it."

She gave a short chuckle and glanced over her shoulder. "Good luck with that."

Jon walked in about that time and stopped to lean on Tabby's desk. "What do you wish him luck for? He's got the best record ever. Even his old man hasn't gone on an undefeated streak like this one."

"This is different. I don't want this case. The guy's an asshole."

"So? We defend assholes every day. It's our motto. Get a magnifying glass. It's printed right on our business cards." He laughed but met my eyes. "You're serious. You're really bothered by this guy."

"It's not the man as much as the case."

"Well, you can't drop a case just because you think you're going to lose."

"I'm not sure I'd lose. I just don't know what could happen if I win, but my guess is, nothing good."

"Jesus, is this guy being sued by the mob or something?"

"No, not hardly. Look, I need to get to my dad's office before this goes any further. I have to get off this case." There were no ifs, ands, or buts about it, and with any luck, he'd see it my way.

I walked past Jon toward the door, and he put his hand out to stop me. "Hey, you know as well as I do, he's never going to let you drop a case. If he wants you on it, you're on it."

I thought of Kya. I couldn't face her on an opposing side knowing the person was probably guilty and most likely needed to serve some time in prison. It was bad enough I'd been such an asshole to her the last time we'd hooked up, but I didn't want her to hate me even more. Besides, I'd said I wanted to be friends. It was time I proved it. It was the least I could do despite a broken heart. "I've got to try."

I headed down the hall to the opposite side of the suite to my father's office and stopped to talk to his secretary, Edith, who was three times the age of mine and not as fashion savvy. The dress she wore was one I'd seen her in when I was in high school.

"Hello, Leo. You can go on in. Your father just got back from a meeting."

"Thanks, Edith." I walked in and found him practicing his golf swing. He kept a putter and a return in his office, and when he was really stressed, he would spend his time there, focused on the ball and the hole.

"Hey, Dad."

"How did the meeting with the new client go?"

"I need to talk to you about that." I scratched my beard, which I kept trimmed short, and took a seat. "I don't think I can defend this person."

"Not this again." My father swung his club too hard and sent the ball over his return. "What's it this time? Not your type of music?"

"Dad, you know as well as I do that this is a conflict for me. Kya and I were friends. We graduated together. She was my first, for fuck's sake."

"Well, if we stopped taking cases based on every woman you fucked, we'd never take any clients." He stormed to the door and shut it all the way. Then he walked to his desk and plopped down in his chair.

My father flattened his palms on his desk. "Let me put it to you this way, son. This client, the one you want to pass off, he chose us because of your record. He is also willing to pay us a butt-load of money, and I don't have to tell you that a high-profile case like this one is just what we need."

I met his eyes. "*If* we win. I'm not sure I can defend him without wanting to kill him."

He slapped his palms against the table. "That's your immaturity talking. Do you think I've liked every client I've defended?"

"No, and neither have I, but this is different. I don't want to upset a friend."

"But you're perfectly fine to upset your father?"

"That's not it, Dad."

He eased back in his chair. "Did you tell him about the press conference?"

"Yes, and he didn't seem too happy that he couldn't put on a show."

"That's just how his type is, son. It's our job to steer them where we want them to go, to make them show the side of themselves to the public that we want them to and nothing else. It's an art form all its own and one I know you're good at."

"Well, I'm not sure he has a good side. He showed up late, he sexually harassed Tabatha, and he's just an overall arrogant asshole. And all of that is aside from the fact that he's most likely guilty of stealing from my oldest friend." I hoped he would see I was serious, but he cleared his throat and sat up in his seat.

"Are you finished?"

"Dad, listen."

"No. We keep the case. You do the best you can, but I didn't raise a fucking quitter. This case is way too important. Change your attitude before the press conference. I need them to see you confident."

I got to my feet and left his office already feeling like I'd lost.

10

KYA

On the way inside the lawyer's building, Sadie stopped and checked her reflection in the door. "We clean up nicely, don't we?"

I glanced at myself, smoothed down my blouse, and fluffed my hair. I'd worn simple boots and jeans with a silky blouse while Sadie had donned a skirt and heels. Her top was much more conservative, but her bleached blond hair was enough to keep her edgy reputation as a rock diva intact. "Yes, we do. Too bad we won't win this case on looks alone." Whit White looked like a slimeball with beady eyes and a sly smile.

Sadie squared her shoulders and tucked her handbag under her arm as she opened the door. "Let's just hope he hired some loser for his lawyer. Someone who's like him."

Even though Sadie seemed sold on this person, I hoped our lawyer was someone who could make Whit White squirm.

We walked to the front desk, and Sadie approached the receptionist as I glanced around the room. The place was drab, and it looked like everything in the room could be packed up in about ten minutes for a quick getaway. Then I noticed there was a box on the floor behind the desk. They seemed to be just moving in. Perhaps they'd gotten a new office?

"Holy shit. You're Sadie from Sabbath Sundae."

"Every day of my life," said Sadie.

"I'm so sorry. My mom didn't warn me she had such awesome clients. I have both of your albums, by the way. I've been a fan since your song. *Liar* broke the charts. Wow, Kya Campbell."

"Hello," I said giving her a warm smile.

Sadie looked over her shoulder and grinned. Being recognized never got old but always seemed to happen at the strangest moments. "Yeah, we're here for our appointment."

The girl gestured to the office door. "You can go on in." She looked like she had only been out of high school for a year at most and was dressed too casual for an office environment. Things already seemed off, but I followed Sadie back.

She opened a door, and a short, mousy-haired woman stood up from behind a desk that was surrounded by boxes and waved us over. "Come on in. I'm sorry we have such a mess around here. My daughter, Darci, she's the one out front. We just moved across town, so I got this office closer to home."

That explained the young girl behind the desk. The woman extended her hand. "I'm Susan Costanzo."

Sadie slapped on a big smile and reached for her hand. "I'm Sadie Boyd, and this is Kya Campbell."

"It's so good to meet you. Please, have a seat, and we'll get down to business."

Once we'd all settled, Susan pushed some papers around on her desk, and after what seemed like ten minutes of searching, she finally found our file. "Here we are. I'll be so glad when this move is over." She went quiet for a moment while she read over her papers. "Okay, so from our phone call, Sadie, I know you two are seeking a lawyer on a suit you're bringing against your manager?"

"Yes. I mean, we're hoping you can help us."

"I'll do my best. Let me look over my notes. So, you claim that your manager, whom you've had for five years, has been embezzling money and booking false shows?"

Sadie eased back in her chair. "Yes. He's costing us quite a bit of our money, and we hope to get it back."

"This says you believe he's been falsifying documents as well?" She raked her hair back and rested her chin on her hand.

"Yeah. We found out he took some money for a deposit and then when that event fell through, he never put the money back. After bitching for him to let us see the books, we finally got to and found three occasions where he'd done that, and the most recent, he tried to put back after we asked to see."

"The others had been so long ago, we think he hoped we wouldn't see them, but I did a thorough check. I also found where he claimed to be paying a roadie for a year and a half after he quit working for us, and more recently, we found a name of another employee he paid who doesn't even exist. When I asked him about it, he tried to make an excuse, said the person had made a few threats, and it was hush money. But we haven't had any problems with any of our staff. In fact, the only issues that ever come up are because of him."

"And since you were in such a long contract, you never could get out of it."

"We tried to fire him, but he came at us with talk that we would have to compensate his salary, and none of us wanted to do that."

"Sounds like he's been a real pain in the ass. The good news is, your contract is expiring in a month, so you won't have to deal with his shit anymore. This should be a cut and dry case as long as we can show our ducks are all in a row, so if you want me on it, I'm going to need your help. He's going to try and drag you through the mud since he'll soon be out of the picture and won't have anything to lose."

I glanced at Sadie and shrugged. "He's already threatened that."

She nodded in agreement. "Yes, he has, many times. It's his go-to threat. He doesn't have anything truthful on us."

"Are you sure? I mean, don't take this wrong, but you're in an edgy business. There's drug abuse, drinking, sex, and parties."

"Yes, and that's what he's banking on. But we've never been your stereotypical band. We have a strong, drug-free family of rockers who do this for the passion of creating music and celebrating the art."

Susan looked like she didn't buy my story. "Nothing, not a sex tape, not a drug addiction, no alcoholism?"

I would hold firm on it. "Nothing that would warrant a scandal. I'm not going to say there isn't pot smoked here and there, a little drinking, but we fired people, including Whit's girlfriend, for being a pain in the ass who would give us a bad reputation."

She held up her finger. "Ah, so he has a motive. You fired his girl. And she could have secrets, could she not?"

"No, not on us. We fired her before we signed with him, but I can see how she'll try and be a problem."

"Yeah, you can count on it, and all he has to do is get her to say things happened."

"But that's slander. We could sue, right?"

"You have to prove it to be untrue when it happens, and let me tell you, it will happen. I just want you to be prepared."

"We're ready for a fight," I said. "I have a daughter to worry about, and this asshole stole enough from me that I could pay for her college." It wasn't like I didn't have money for her college, but that was beside the point. I wanted the best for my daughter, and I shouldn't have to stand by while some greedy asshole stole my hard-earned money.

"I don't blame you. I'd feel the same way if someone took money from me and my daughter." She leaned in and gave me a reassuring smile. "Don't worry. Hire me, and we'll make this man pay." She sat back in her seat and then grabbed her pen to make a few notes.

Sadie turned and gave me a nudge. "Do you think we need to look any further?"

I didn't want to waste time finding anyone else, and she seemed to be on the same page as me, and being a single mother, which I assumed from her earlier talk of moving across town with her daughter, she seemed to understand my situation. "I think we'd like for you to represent us."

"Excellent," said Susan as she smiled and reached forward to shake our hands. "Now, I'll need the copies of the financial records and whatever other paper trail he's left, and once the suit is officially filed later today, we'll schedule a meeting with him and his lawyer when he gets one."

"He may have already. We've let him know he needs to and that we intended on taking him to court."

"Then you can bet he has one in his pocket. Don't worry. With my experience, you're in good hands. I'm going to recover your money if he still has it."

My shoulders dropped, and I turned and looked at Sadie. "You mean we could win and not get a dime?"

Susan shrugged. "Happens every day. You have to go into cases like these prepared for that."

"I see." I already felt defeated, but I had to consider that even if I didn't get a dime, I would at least have proven he was the thief we thought he was, and maybe if he ever tried to sign another act, they could learn from our mistakes and not hire the douchebag.

We ended the meeting, and as we walked out of the building after signing a couple of autographs for her daughter, Sadie flashed me a confident smile. "We're going to kick Whit's ass."

"I don't know. It seems like an awfully big risk. We're gambling with our reputations for what? The chance that we might but most likely won't get some money back? You heard her. Our contract is nearly over. We'll be done with him soon enough anyway."

"Yeah, but don't you get it? If we can prove he was crooked all along, it could break the contract, and we could be free to make decisions not only about the existing material, but maybe he'd stop making money on it too." She gave me a nudge. "Come on, Kya. Let's go get a coffee or ice cream and celebrate."

Coffee sounded great, but I didn't have time. "I have to go pick up Addison."

She pulled me in for a quick hug. "Cheer up, at least. We're doing the right thing."

I released a deep breath and adjusted my handbag on my

shoulder as I pulled away. "I know. It's just frustrating. It seems that fucker always wins."

"He won't. We're going to kick him in the balls with this lawsuit. You'll see." She gave me a smile, and then as she started away, she turned back. "Call me. We'll talk about it later."

I went to my car and hoped we'd made the right decision as I headed to get Addie.

I slowly made my way around the pick-up line at her school, and when her teacher opened the door, she put in Addie's bags, situating them in the floorboard, and then helped her climb into my Escalade. "Have a good day," she said, after helping my daughter with her seat belt. Then, she closed the door, and we drove away.

I reached over to brush the hair from Addie's face. Her ponytail had gotten messy through the day. "How was school?"

"Good. We got to use the smelly finger paint. Mine smelled like a banana." She gave me a big smile. "Did you and Aunt Sadie make more songs today?"

"No. I'm taking a little time off from recording. I want to spend more time at home with my favorite girl."

She smiled really big, her little face turning pink with a blush on her cheeks. "I like that idea, Mama. You have enough songs anyway for now."

I sometimes wondered if I didn't have enough songs for a lifetime. It wasn't easy staying in the game with so much more I wanted out of life. I'd made some money, and with the investments I'd made, the savings I'd managed to put back, and the fact that I hadn't gone too crazy with a fancy apartment I couldn't afford or outrageous cars, we could live a while without me having to be away all the time if I wanted to take a permanent vacation.

But that would never happen. I'd be like Blitz, rockin' out until I was in my fifties as long as people were still buying my music and coming to my shows. But maybe the lawsuit would end all of that, and then I wouldn't have to worry about anything. I looked into Addie's eyes and knew those were things I couldn't tell her. It was best she didn't know.

11

LEO

Tabby's hands were amazing. "That feels so good," I said, letting a small moan follow.

Her voice vibrated in my ear. "I know how much you like this, how much it eases your tension. And boy, are you tense." She dug her fingertips into my shoulder, and I rolled my head as I let her ease me with the massage.

"You're the best. Thank you so much."

She leaned close to my ear and whispered in a seductive voice, "Anytime."

Sometimes fucking your secretary actually worked in your favor, and it helped that Tabby was a good girl who liked her fun and didn't have jealous tendencies.

Jon rapped on the open door as she moved from behind me. "Am I interrupting something?" He liked to tease me and Tabby for our past, and she wasn't bothered that he knew, or at least she had never acted like it.

"I was just getting a massage from the best hands in the world."

"Lucky. When do I get one of those massages, Tabs?"

She smiled and walked over to grip his shoulders. "How's that? Feel good?" She whispered seductively in his ear as I chuckled.

"As a matter of fact, it does. You have magic fingers, doll. Now I know why he's winning all the cases. If you calm him with this every time he gets stressed, no wonder he's Mr. Cool in the courtroom."

"That's right," said Tabby. "It's all me." She looked over and gave me a wink and then walked out, pulling the door closed as she left.

"Damn, I'm jealous. She's pretty fucking amazing, that one. I should ask her out."

I shook my head. "You shouldn't. I've got her trained to me. I don't want to have to hunt her down in your office when I want a massage or a blow job."

"Greedy fucker. What the hell do you want anyway?" Jon rolled his shoulders and walked over to join me at the desk. He lowered himself to one of the two chairs in front of me and eased back, resting his leg on his knee and showing off his argyles.

I pulled my chair up closer to my desk. "I've got a high-profile case, and I need you on my team as co-counsel."

"Really?" His eyes widened in surprise. "Fuck, yeah. It's about time you ask for some help, and clearly, you knew to come to the best."

"I'm the best, but yeah, this called for next best." I laughed as he threw out his middle finger. "I'm glad you're willing to help, and I hope you're available today."

"Today? Wow, thanks for the notice." He turned on his phone, and I had a feeling he was checking his calendar.

"Sorry, I have a press conference, and I really need you here, man. This client is a pain in the ass, and I'm really hoping he isn't going to be hard to keep on track. I want to make a strong front, too, let the world see he's being represented well, and hopefully, he won't say a fucking word with one of us on each side of him."

He gave me a hesitant look. "Great, you got a loose cannon? I wish I'd known that two minutes ago."

"You'd have still said yes, and this is the guy I tried to get away from. I told you about him the other day."

"Fuck. I knew your father would say no. You just had to drag me in, huh? To the losing case? Thanks a lot. And here I thought you threw me a bone."

"The band suing is Sabbath Sundae."

"Fuck, that's why you wanted out. This is your girl."

"Yeah, but my father doesn't give a shit. So, having you on the case will make things a little more balanced. At least, I hope."

"I'll be a human shield, you mean?" He chuckled.

"It's high-profile, so on the off-chance it does well, we'll be doing our careers one hell of a favor."

"Or a hell of a lot of damage."

"Come on, trust me." I checked my watch and cursed.

"What?" He seemed alarmed.

"He's late for the fucking meeting I scheduled. I told him we need to prep. If he does open his mouth, I want him to know what to say."

"Fucking great. The guy can't even be on time for meetings. How late is he?"

"Ten minutes when you walked in, but now it's fifteen. I hate people who are late. The press is going to be gathering at any minute, and they'll be chomping at the bit and better prepared. I tried to get him last night, but that fell through."

About that time, there was a commotion outside my door, and as I rose from my seat, Tabby opened my door and stuck her head in. "Mr. White is here to see you."

"Send him in," I said as Jon got to his feet.

Tabby pushed the door open and in strolled Whit White looking like he had the world on a string. Tabby stomped out and shut the door behind her.

"You're late again."

"Yeah, this traffic is a bitch. Sue me?" He shrugged and then took the chair next to Jon who still stood in front of his.

Jon extended his hand. "It's good to meet you. I'm Jon Hanson."

I spoke up. "Jon is going to be working on our team. I want to show a strong front for your case."

"Nice to meet you," Whit said with a shit-eating grin. "I didn't think I'd get my very own dream team."

Jon took his seat, and I did the same, clearing my throat. "Yeah, well, in cases like this, it looks good. Now, we should get down to business. The conference will go on as scheduled. We can't be late to that, especially if we want to make you look good." I hoped it sent him a message, but he was a clueless bastard, so I doubted it.

"These bitches better think twice before they fuck with me anyway. I have enough dirt on them that I think I can make them back down or at least shut their mouths."

Jon covered his mouth and turned his attention to the window over my shoulder. He could probably tell I didn't take too kindly to the comment because I felt my face heat up.

"Let's take it easy on the name-calling. No sense in starting off on the wrong foot before a press conference. You need to keep your attitude to a minimum and let me answer the questions. I'm going in with a prepared statement. Just the basics, denying the allegations and letting the other side know we're ready for this fight, we've got evidence to support our side, and we're a strong defense."

"It sounds good to me. I'll kick back and follow your lead."

"I wish it was as easy as all that. If you're asked a question directly, you need to make sure you don't react emotionally or physically, rather."

"Pretend you're in a card game," Jon added. "You don't want them to know anything but that you're confident."

I felt the need to add, "And don't be cocky. You're going to want to be well-liked in the public eye. You already have a tough job of not looking like the man who took advantage of a beloved rock band."

"Their shows were declining." He shrugged. "Not many people wanted to book them." I had a feeling that was only true because he was such a colossal pain in the ass to deal with rather than Kya or the band being a problem.

"Let's just keep it professional above everything else." If I could get the fucker to agree to that much and abide, I'd be okay. That was, if his idea of professional was on the same level as mine. "Better make that above professional."

He took out his phone, and his thumbs moved over the keypad. "Just a quick tweet before we go out then?"

"No, don't tweet anything. Stay off social media." Jon looked over at the screen.

"Oops, too late. I just thought a friendly warning would be okay. I mean, it's not like the conference has taken place yet."

Jon took his phone and read the tweet. "It's show time, bitches?"

"Hey, give that back." Whit reached out, but Jon didn't let him have his phone.

"No," said Jon. "I'm deleting the tweet. This isn't your chance to get in one last dig. Professionalism starts now." Jon looked up at me, and I was glad he was sitting right there. Hopefully, he didn't have many followers, and no one saw it. Those who did, probably already knew he was a douchebag.

"Look, I'm all for your advice, and that's fine and dandy if you want to control my social media, but let me say, I think we're going about this all wrong. We need to use scare tactics, get these bitches shaking in their boots."

Jon stepped in again as I tried to calm my nerves. "Yeah, that's not how it works. They filed a suit, so they obviously aren't afraid of you. And let's limit the whole name-calling thing."

"Let's," I said.

Before I could make another comment, my door opened, and Tabby stuck her head in as if she didn't want to show Whit White too much of the short skirt she'd worn.

"The conference is in five." She disappeared as fast as she'd popped in.

I got to my feet and straightened by pants, cuffs, and tie. Jon raked his hand through his hair and did his tie as well as Whit sat in his seat like he had nowhere to be.

He finally got to his feet. "Let's get this shit over with."

I lead the way, and Jon followed behind Whit to show that we had his back. I went down the hall to the room where they had the conference set up and was surprised at how many outlets had shown up.

The microphones crowded the podium, and we crowded around them with Whit in the middle.

We were making a strong front, all right, and the worst part about that moment was knowing Kya was about to see me there, defending this asshole against her.

12

KYA

As Addison ran back and forth through the house, singing and shaking her booty, I couldn't help but wish I had her energy. She held her play microphone up to her mouth and didn't miss a lyric of Sacred Heart as it blasted from the radio, and she'd lined her stuffed animals up along the couch to be her audience.

"Addie, let's turn that down and have some lunch. I don't want your ravioli to get cold." She dropped her mic and ran wide open to the table and climbed up into her chair.

"When I grow up, I'm going to sing, too, Mama."

"Are you?" I thought of the lifestyle I'd had before she came along and cringed. Before Blitz had truly taken me under his wing and helped me. Before the slimy manager. I wanted better for her. I wanted her to pursue her own dreams and hoped that by the time she was truly old enough to make that decision, it was a different one.

"Yes, and I'm going to give front row tickets to all of my friends at school so I can call them up onstage."

"That sounds like fun, sweet pea. You can do whatever you want. Whatever you put your mind to. You remember that." And I will love you, all the same, no matter what path you take, because you are my daughter, my flesh, my bone, my blood, and unlike your shitty grandparents who still don't know what they're missing out on, I will love you forever.

I wanted to say all of those words. To tack them on so she'd know that my love was unconditional.

It had been a long time since I'd sat down and talked to my parents, and while I didn't really miss my father too much because he'd always been an asshole, I missed my mother. We'd been close, and she'd encouraged my musical abilities. Of course, if she'd known where that would lead, she probably wouldn't have. When I was just singing with my friends in the garage, they both had laughed it off and claimed it was an impossible dream. But when I booked my first show at the local pub just out of high school, the fight was on. They'd believed nursing was my true calling, even though I'd never expressed any interest and had never even liked to go to the doctor, much less give shots or take blood. But because my mother had always wanted to be one and her sister, my aunt Jodie, had become one, then I was supposed to follow in their footsteps. No thanks.

I'd never want to be like anyone who didn't want to see their grandchild, who could write off their family because I chose to be successful in a different career. But they were convinced my music was blasphemous, that it was an affront to God and the church, and that the neighbors would look down on them for raising a drugged up, sexed up, devil music singing, unwed mother. Who needed them? Not me. I had made my own family, and they were a hell of a lot more loving.

I'd get by on my own as I always did.

Addie stabbed her ravioli and then wiped the sauce onto her lips. "Look, Mama. I have lipstick."

"Eat it. Don't wear it."

"But I look good in makeup, don't I?" She batted her eyes and looked into her spoon as if it might reflect. "I'm upside down." She giggled.

"Yes, the curve of the spoon reflects that way. And you look pretty without makeup too. I've already told you, when you get a little older, we'll talk. Until then, it's Chapstick and clear lip gloss."

"And nail polish?"

"Yes, nail polish is fine." I couldn't take away her and Sadie's fun. The two loved to paint each other's toenails.

"But nail polish is makeup, Mama." She had been trying to find a decent argument for her case on wearing makeup over the past two weeks, ever since she'd watched Sadie and me make YouTube makeup tutorials for our channel. Sadie had found out we could use the platform to have a little fun with our fans, and so far, it was going well, and we were actually making a nice chunk of money. We had plans to launch our own makeup line as soon as we got rid of Whit.

"Then maybe you shouldn't be wearing it." I gave her a pointed look, and she frowned.

She changed her tune fast, shaking her head. "No, it's not really the same, is it?" She licked the sauce off her lips and then bit into the noodle.

The phone rang, and I glanced over to see it was Sadie. I answered. "There's the woman whose bones I need to pick."

"What did I do?"

"Nothing. But my daughter is sure putting up an argument for painting her face."

"So? Let her. It's not a big deal. Look, I don't have time to debate. You need to turn on the TV. Like, now."

I got up and headed across the room to find the remote on the side table. "Why am I doing this?"

"Channel four and because Whit's having a press conference with his lawyers."

"Are you fucking kidding me?" The screen lit up and answered my question.

...manager for the hard rock band, Sabbath Sundae is being sued. Sources say the band came out with the lawsuit earlier this week accusing their manager of embezzling money and reportedly misusing funds for lavish vacations. We take you live on the scene where the press conference is about to kick off after some technical difficulties.

The video changed, and my heart dropped like a stone to the bottom of a dry well. Not only was Whit the worm standing behind the display of a hundred mics, but Leonard Pace stood next to him.

"Kya?"

"I'm here."

"I saw a clip earlier when they were trying to sort out the technical shit. I thought you'd want to know Leonard was the one representing him."

Sadie had grilled me about who he was for the longest until I had finally shown her a few pictures on his social media and some from the many charity events he'd been to with his father and the slew of girlfriends. "I can't believe it. This has to be a nightmare."

I went quiet as Leonard prepared to speak. I couldn't wait to see what the asshole had to say for himself and that crooked fucker he was representing.

"Good afternoon, and thank you for this opportunity today. I'm Leo Pace, representing Mr. White. I'd just like to say the allegations made against my client are absolutely false. Mr. White, as the band's manager for the past five years, had certain rights, and all monies in his care were properly distributed. My team and I will prove there was no mismanagement on his behalf."

Despite the fact that he was one of the absolute hottest men I'd ever laid eyes on and nothing like the young nerd I'd deflowered in high school—and much more mature and handsome than the young, cocky asshole I'd slept with in the tour bus five years ago, I felt like crawling through the TV screen and ripping his head off. "No mismanagement? Are you fucking kidding me?"

"Mama?"

I turned to see Addie standing behind me, one of her stuffed animals in her hand and a look of worry on her little face.

"Go finish your lunch, sweet pea."

"You said a bad word, Mama." She walked over and hugged my leg as if my cursing told her something was very wrong.

Sadie spoke in my ear, "I don't see how they think they can prove that, Kya. The records are clear, and we have them. We have the proof. You should call Leonard and tell him that. There's no telling what Whit's said or done or what kind of fake evidence he's providing. The man has to be being used, right?"

"He's really crossed the line this time. I mean, it's one thing to treat me the way he did, but I understood, you know. I chalked it up to him getting back at me, but this. It's the ultimate betrayal."

"Careful you're not throwing stones in glass houses, Kya. You let him down first."

I looked down to my daughter and felt the pang of guilt knowing exactly what she was referring to. Addie grabbed one of her stuffed animals and carried it back to the table as I continued with Sadie. "That's different. I didn't set out to deliberately hurt him or anything. I did him a favor."

"Well, he must really hate you."

My ass hit the couch, taking out half of Addie's crowd. "Thanks. That's such a comfort."

"I'm just saying. This is, like, unforgivable."

"Not to mention, that's not the biggest problem with all of this. Leonard works for his father's firm, which happens to be the biggest and most well-respected in Chicago. If I know him at all, he's going to eat us for lunch. Even with the evidence we have. He's the smartest person I know, Sadie."

She growled through the phone. "I'll call Susan. Who knew the asshole would use our money for the best legal team in town."

I pulled a purple bunny from under my butt and held him tight against my chest. "I can't believe this is happening. I'm going to have to face Leonard, aren't I? Whether in a courtroom or a meeting, it's going to happen."

"You knew you'd have to face him again sooner or later, right?"

"I mean, I guess I knew living in the same city, it could happen, but I stay on my side of the tracks, and he stays on his."

Sadie let out a deep breath. "You grew up next door to one another, and for all you know, he could be living down the street, and you'd never know it."

"We're in different worlds. I'm sure he graduated to a life of charity events and stuffy courtroom action, while I'm down at the arena performing for a much different crowd."

Sadie gave a half-hearted chuckle, the way she did when I'd overreact. "You're both eating lobster, Kya."

It wasn't the same, though. "Only right after a show, and then by the time I get to book another one, that's gone. If I didn't scrimp and save, I wouldn't have what I have. He hasn't lived in a bus or slept in a single motel room with five other people. He's probably never seen the inside of a tattoo parlor or smoked a joint."

She chuckled a bit louder than before if only to lighten the mood. "You don't smoke weed, and your only tattoos are barely visible when you're not half-naked on stage."

"See? I'm sure when he gets in front of his courtroom crowd, he's not half-naked." The whole half-naked thing was an exaggeration anyway. I was always completely covered, even if it was see-through lace or satin. I always had on my underwear, a bra, a tank top, something. I did have a child to be an example to, and I would never have her looking into my past and being embarrassed by me. There'd be no sex tapes or amateur footage of me on stage on the internet looking like a fool.

"We're going to rip this guy a new one in court, Kya. Don't stress about it, okay? I'll talk to Susan about the situation with Leonard. We need to make sure this won't hinder us, and if it helps in some way, even better."

"I don't see how it could help." I'd been content to let him live his life, and I live mine. But this, it was the worst betrayal. And as hurt as I was, I knew with certainty that all those years ago, I'd made the right decision to steer clear of him.

But now, nope. Now, I was going to have to face him, and whether or not the lawyer ripped Whit apart in the courtroom, I was going to give Leonard a piece of my mind. So much for friendship.

13

LEO

As Monday finally rolled around and I drove to a diner across town to meet with Whit, I tried to put it all into perspective.

I'd expected to hear something over the weekend from Kya's lawyer, Susan Costanzo, who was known as a hot mess in my circles because of her recent divorce and the way she'd handled it by losing her fucking mind in the courtroom, suffering a mental breakdown at one point. Rumor had it that she had relocated her office across town and that she was trying to start over. I had no idea if Kya knew any of that, and it didn't seem likely she'd have hired the woman if she did.

But it seemed odd that other than filing the suit, Susan hadn't reached out or offered some kind of counter announcement. Unless she thought this was a strategy or perhaps she needed the weekend to get over the trauma of the press conference? Considering her past breakdown, it was entirely possible. I knew it had to come as a surprise, which was the point.

I hated to do Kya that way, but if I was going to please my father, I had to do things the way I'd normally do them, all feelings aside. I did wish I could warn her about Susan, but then again, I didn't know what the hell that was all about, and if the woman was a friend of hers, I certainly didn't want to insult her.

I pulled into the small lot of the diner and went inside. The place had been one of my favorites for years, and being close to the courthouse and my office, it was convenient.

Being early, I found a booth and slid into it. If I was lucky, Whit would show up on time for once, and I could get this meeting underway.

Aside from not hearing from Susan Costanzo, I had gotten my accountant to look at the numbers from the band for me. Despite being ripped off, the band had been making a healthy profit for a number of years, and Kya should be very proud of herself for that, but there was evidence that some of the numbers didn't add up. He was pinching money and doing a poor job of covering it up.

I ordered a coffee and doughnut, and when the waitress came to bring it, the bells on the door sounded, and I looked up to see Whit had shown up right on time. At least that was one improvement made. *Baby steps.*

Whit slid into the seat across from me. "How's it going?"

"I wish it was better."

"That bad, huh? Sucks to be you, I guess. Always having to sort out other people's problems."

"Yeah, and from what I can tell, it's not a good day to be Whit White either. I had my accountant go over the financial records, and you're guilty of theft."

"So what? Your job isn't to tell me that. It's to find a loophole to get me out of it, right?"

"Well, no, not exactly. My job is to defend you within the limits of the law. If you're guilty, it's going to make my argument a hell of a lot harder to convince anyone else otherwise. Not to mention, it makes a fool of me and my firm."

"Do you think I give a shit?" He raked his hand through his hair and leaned in across the table. "As long as I look good, what the fuck do I care how you and your firm look? It's my reputation that's on the line, not yours, so the next time you call me down here, remember that." Whit looked over his shoulder to see if anyone was listening. "This is your job to get me off, so do your job. I had legit reasons for doing what I did. Those bitches made this hard on themselves. They'd already told me they weren't going to keep me around, and I needed to make sure my ass was covered. You can call it a retirement plan if you want to, but I had that coming to me."

"You can't just set that kind of thing up for yourself. And quite frankly, if I hear you refer to those women as bitches again, client or not, I'm going to put my foot in your ass." I might not have always respected women like some kind of saint, and I'd fucked a few with no intent on calling them back, but I didn't treat them like trash or call them bitches. And okay, maybe I was a little partial because I knew Kya, but still, I got pissed every time I heard it come from his mouth, and it wasn't doing us any favors with our professional relationship.

After a moment of awkward silence, Whit White turned his chin up in the air and looked down his nose at me. "Are you threatening me?"

That didn't sit well with him. He glanced over his shoulder again and narrowed his eyes at the only waitress who had been brave enough to stick around our section of the diner. Then, he turned his attention back to me. "You find a loophole. Do what you have to do. You work for me, remember? Not the other way around."

As he slid out of the booth and stood, adjusting his belt and glaring down at me, I knew I had to watch my tongue. As much as I wanted to get up and walk away from this abomination of a fucking client, I knew my father was going to hate me if I did. His approval was the only thing keeping me in my seat.

Whit left without another word, and I wished I'd put him in his place, told him how I didn't have to fucking work for him and what a laughing stock he'd be if I just up and quit on him.

I took a sip of my coffee and bit my doughnut. The entire case made me itch, knowing he was not only the asshole that I thought he was but also guilty. Forget the fact that he was going to ruin my perfect record, but he had villainized me going up against Kya, and she'd probably hate me forever.

My bite of doughnut went down in a hard lump, and not even the coffee could wash it down. I had to get out of there. I left half of it sitting on the table along with enough money to cover my bill and bring a smile to the face of the waitress who'd served me. The bells on the door chimed when I pushed it open, and after stepping out into the sunshine, I walked to my car. It was too pretty a day to be in such a pissy mood.

I had just hit the unlock button on my key when footsteps brought my head around. The call of high heels was always a head turner.

Kya stopped a few feet away. Her arms clenched tight around her handbag which she held to her middle, her sultry lips turned down in a frown, and her eyes narrowed like a predator's.

"How could you?" Her voice was so acidic, I was surprised it didn't burn my ears.

I held up my hand to stop her from killing me, which looked like something she might try at any moment. "I'm sorry. I can't talk to you here. I can't be seen in public with the person suing my client."

"A fucking asshole who shouldn't be your client!" She stepped closer, her hand coming away from her middle to point at me like she wished to stab me with it.

I looked around to make sure no one had seen or heard her. Luckily, there wasn't anyone paying attention to what might have been no more than a lover's quarrel.

"I agree, but I can't do this right now, Kya. Walk away." It would endanger the case if we were seen talking together, and it would also not be good if the media saw it and published something. Not to mention, Kya was a well-known musician in the area. She'd done decently for herself and had a following. If one of her fans rounded the corner, I could be in serious trouble.

Her eyes widened. "Then why? If this is some sick way to get back at me for high school when I didn't want to date you, then you've already gotten your revenge when you slept with me five years ago."

I looked around again just to make sure Whit wasn't still around sitting in his car. "I can't talk. Here." I handed her my card. "Text me your number."

She recoiled and shook her head, her eyes regarding me like I was a piece of trash that had blown across her fancy shoe. "My number? Hell no! I want to look into your eyes while I chew your ass! How could you do this to me?"

Her voice broke on the last syllable, and I tightened my jaw, not wanting to show any emotion or say anything that would have me pulling her into my arms and holding her to make it all better. No, that's not where we were with each other. We'd one refused the other, so we were even. Square. Owing nothing.

But I still wanted to see her. I wanted a chance to explain my side of things, and like it or not, she'd listen. "I'll call you after I arrange a private dinner for us. You can chew my ass over wine and at a low tone if you want. But not here." I opened my car door, and she took a few steps back.

As I sat in my seat, she pointed her finger in my direction, shaking it like a mad woman. "Fine! You better show up, Leonard. This is not over!" I knew better than to think it was. Kya had never been the kind not to speak her mind or to let things go without doing so.

I slammed my door, and she shook her head and walked away, and as I watched her go, her hips swaying as her long legs taking her away from me with the speed of a runway model, I resolved that she had to be the sexiest woman on the planet. It took everything in me not to go after her, to stop her and tell her how sorry I was. But that wasn't how it needed to be.

I had to explain how I didn't have a choice, and as a professional, sometimes I had to make decisions that were best for the entire firm and not just myself. I'd have to speak my father's language, and boy, how I hated that.

14

KYA

After I picked up Addison at school, we went to the market for a roll of cookie dough big enough to choke a horse and a few other things I needed. We'd gone home, and I busied myself baking cookies and tried not to think about Leonard. He'd call when he called, and all the pacing in the world wasn't going to make it happen any faster.

As the timer went off, he'd called, and I'd been so distracted by his invitation and his refusal to listen to my bitching, I nearly burned the last batch.

Addie had fixed a basket of cookies, which she now held in her lap as we pulled into Sadie's driveway. Though it wasn't unusual for us to bring dessert when going to Sadie's for dinner, I had also hoped the sweets would work as a bribe.

I shut off the car, and we had barely made it out when Sadie opened the door. "Just in time. I have dinner almost ready."

Addie ran over and gave Sadie a big hug. "I've missed you. Mama let me bake you some cookies!"

"I see that." Sadie looked at the cookies, and then her eyes turned up at me and widened. "Wow, I didn't realize this was a special occasion." She got a suspicious look on her face, and I knew I wasn't going to be able to do a dump and run so easily without explaining myself first.

"Yeah, well, I was hoping you and Addie might want a little time to goof around together."

Addie went inside, leaving the two of us behind as she hurried into the kitchen.

Sadie led me in, and we stopped in the living room. "That depends. Do you have a date?" Her narrowed eyes met mine. "I didn't know you were seeing anyone."

"I'm not. And this isn't a date per say. More like a business meeting with an old friend."

Sadie folder her arms across her front. "Business? As in band business?"

"Yes. Look, don't make a big deal out of this, but I had to see him."

"Him? Oh shit, you mean Leonard?" She looked over her shoulder, and I glanced over it to see that Addie was in the kitchen putting her cookies on the table where she'd climbed up in her usual seat.

"Yes, I went down to chew his ass out, and he wouldn't talk to me. He gave me his card so I could text him my number, and he wanted to have a private dinner to talk. I think he just doesn't want me to beat his ass."

"Please. He probably wants to ride yours."

I shook my head, determined. "Not going to happen."

Sadie wasn't buying it. "Ha! Tell me, was he handsome?"

I thought about how he looked and other than the shock of my being there, I had to admit, "He was gorgeous. He looks even hotter now that he's matured even more. It's like he's better with age. He still has the facial hair that I loved the last time I saw him."

"You're getting that sound in your voice. The one where you're mooning over a guy. And if you can do that after just a moment talking about him, you're going to end up back in bed with him. He's your kryptonite."

"Fuck that. He's just a man, someone from my past, and you're the one who wanted me to tell you what he looked like. He can't help but be handsome." I couldn't help thinking of him in that way. His eyes were so brown and deep set that they were permanently shadowed and dreamy, and his body, that big package combined with his strong, muscular frame, it made me grow warm inside.

I came around and turned my attention back to Sadie. "So, will you watch her? I've got to be down there in half an hour. I don't want to be late."

"What are you going to say?"

"I'm going to keep it simple. He doesn't need to know shit about my life. But I'm going to ask him why he's doing this to me."

"That's not a good idea, Kya. It's like a conflict of interest or something. I'm sure our lawyer is going to flip out when we tell her you know Leonard on a personal level."

"Which is another thing I'm going to cover. How this is even possible. He should excuse himself from the case on that basis. Instead, he's making press conferences and sticking his nose right in it. I want to know why. I'm not going into this not knowing."

"Fine. But tell me what happens." She pulled me in for a hug. "We're going to eat your share of the cookies and do our nails. You have fun."

"Save me one," I called out to Addie as I headed to the door. "I love you, sweet pea."

Addie came around the corner eating one. "Bye, Mama."

I shut the door and headed to the car, hoping I was doing the right thing. I didn't need this to be a date or any kind of rekindling. What I needed was for him to explain himself and us to get the shit from our past cleared up. I had always thought of us as at least friends, but this had been the worst thing a so-called friend had ever done to me.

I got to the address he told me about and found it to be a small yet classy place. I gave my name to the hostess, and she led me back to a small area with a private table all alone.

My waiter came right away, and I ordered a glass of wine, which I drank, and then checked my lip gloss a few times and then my phone for any messages from Sadie or Addie, but there was none.

I was just about to ask for my check when Leonard came into the room dressed like a million bucks in his tailored suit and joined me at the table. "I'm so sorry I'm late. I got caught up in a meeting with a prospective client."

"It's fine." I didn't need to hear his excuses. I could barely look at him. I turned my head and tried to focus across the room.

"You look beautiful, Kya."

I glanced over and found him staring at me with a longing in his eyes that was the same one I felt.

"Please, save it. I want an answer, Leonard."

"Call me Leo, please. And I will give you an answer, Kya, but it's not going to be enough."

"You're right. It won't unless you can make me understand it because I can't think of any good reason you'd do it."

"My father expects it."

"Your father? Jesus, I've known him my whole life too. I guess that's why you think it's okay to shit on someone you've known your whole life because the old man taught you it was."

He met my eyes. "It's not about you."

I fought the urge to kick him under the table. The two of us had grown up wrestling around in the backyard back when I thought I needed to be tough to hang with the boys. I'd taken him a time or two then, and I wished I could make him eat a handful of dirt for dinner. "How can you say that? You're defending the man suing me."

He held his hand up, his palms facing me like he needed to hold me back. "I mean that this has nothing to do with our pasts."

I wasn't about to go there with him. I sure didn't need to talk about my personal life. "Are you sure about that?"

"I'm positive. Look, you have your life, and I have mine."

"Right. And never the two shall meet. I get it. I got that when you ran out the last time like your head was on fire." And he didn't even care to ask me about it, not that I'd want him to. And it wasn't like I cared what kind of skank he was seeing.

"I just mean it's been a while," he defended. "We're different people."

"Yes, we sure as hell are. So I need to know, the private dinner, the panic earlier—if it's not such a good idea that we're seen, why not excuse yourself? There has to be some law against defending someone against me."

He nodded. "Normally, I'd excuse myself."

That sounded good to me. "There. Do that. Excuse yourself."

"No, I cannot do that. I already tried to get off the case, and my father said no. He needs me to take the reins. I did pull another member of my team over, so if it makes you feel more comfortable in the courtroom, I'll have him speak directly to you."

I feigned laughter and rolled my eyes. "Oh, thanks for making me comfortable while you're trying to ruin my life. You're such a fucking prince."

He stopped and stared at me a moment. Then, his jaw dropped, his face turning red. "I don't want to do the case any more than you want me to, trust me."

"Whatever." I sat back in my chair as the waiter came and brought more wine. Then, Leonard ordered us food despite me saying I wasn't hungry. Like he had to help me keep up my strength or something.

"You need to eat. I don't want you to go hungry." He gave me a warm smile, and though it made me want to smile, I fought the urge.

"Like you care."

"Look, Kya. I was young and stupid the last time we saw each other. I admit, refusing you felt good for a few hours. You broke my heart. I just wanted you to know what I felt. I'm sorry."

I looked down into my wine glass. "I went after you, you know. But when I got downstairs, you were gone. I wanted a redo with you and had always dreamed I'd get another chance. When you showed up that night, I hoped I could."

"I was miserable if it helps."

"It doesn't. That young man is a memory, and the thought of you going up against me makes me sick." I looked up from the glass and shook my head. "He's guilty, you know. I'm not sure if he's told you. But I have proof that—"

He waved his hand. "I can't even talk about that. No details." He cleared his throat and straightened his tie. "I shouldn't even have met you here. I just wanted the chance to tell you it wasn't anything personal."

"Drop the case."

He turned his eyes away. "I can't. I won't."

The words stung. "For me?" There was a time when he would have done anything for me, and I liked to think that when it came right down to it, he still would.

He shook his head and then took a long pull from his drink.

My heart filled with anger and grief. He may as well have been dead to me, and it wouldn't have hurt any worse.

"I can't believe the day has come when you're back to letting people bully you. I thought you'd changed." I got up and stepped away but turned back. "The old you was a hell of a lot easier to like." While I walked away, he made no attempt to come after me, which was good because I'd probably turn around and knee him in the nuts.

I made it to the door before I broke down in tears. Of all the people in the world I thought would be big enough to put aside pettiness and help me, he had proven me wrong. But then, I'd never asked him for anything, so maybe I'd known deep down all along that was a lie.

15

LEO

I'd thought about Kya all morning, and it didn't help that she'd looked so hot the night before. After she stormed out, I wished I'd gone after her and made her listen. She had to understand my side of it, even though it was the wrong side. It was all I could do. My hands were tied.

As I walked back into the office after lunch, I knew I had to go down and talk to my father about the new evidence in the case. This was not only going to make us look like assholes, but we'd never win.

"Hi, Edith," I said, greeting my father's secretary.

She glanced up from her computer screen. "If you're looking for your father, he's in his office. I don't even think he's busy." She returned to her work as I walked inside.

I found my father behind his desk, his head down focused on his phone in front of him. "How do you get this damned thing to turn back on?"

"Hey, Dad. What's the trouble?"

"This piece of shit, for one. I tried to turn up the volume so I could hear my conversations, and for some reason, the damned sound is gone. Even my games, my ringtones. Piece of shit. I remember the good old days when we thought a cordless was the key to all our problems."

"Here, let me look at it. I need to talk to you anyway." I took the phone, and in two seconds or less, I had his phone fixed. "That should do it."

He looked at the screen as I sat down across from him and hoped my fixing it had put him in a better mood. "I know you probably don't want to hear it, but there's bad news with the White case."

"What kind of bad news?" His voice was rough and suspicious.

"Well, for one, the evidence shows he is, in fact, guilty. The numbers, the withdrawals made by him. He didn't even bother covering it up most of the time. Then there's the whole Kya thing. I know it doesn't matter to you, but it sure does to me, and it could to anyone else who wants to point it out, like the plaintiffs." I didn't think telling him about my dinner date would do anything to help my case, so I kept my mouth shut about that. I'd made sure I'd gone to the one restaurant in town where I could depend on discretion.

The old man sat quietly a minute, almost as if he hadn't heard me. "Is there any way you can spin it. Make it look like he had the right?"

"No. Not unless I could prove he spent it on the band, but he didn't. He took countless vacations, spent money on toys and parties, none of which the band was even invited to, much less for their benefit."

"See if you can find anything else in the contract between them, a way to make it seem as if they're mistreating him, something that might deflect a little."

I couldn't believe what I'd heard. "I don't see why you're so hell-bent on defending a man like this. He's a piece of shit. He's disrespectful, has no care of his reputation, or much less how he makes us look."

"It's the name of the game, son. Try to find a spin. It's there. There's always one in every case."

"If not, then what? I can't believe you're making me do this. I wish for once you'd just be my father and understand where I'm coming from. This man stole millions from Kya, and you're okay with that? Doesn't it affect you at all?"

"And we could lose millions if this case goes wrong. Get yourself together and see if you can't spin it. They are bound to have done something. There are always two sides, son. Find out what they've done on theirs, and let's get this case resolved."

I had to go. I had to get away from the man. I walked out of the office and didn't even look at Edith as she said a farewell. I stormed my way back to my office, past Tabby, and slammed the door.

I went to my desk and took my phone out of my pocket and dialed Kya's number. I needed to talk to her, not just because I hated being on the case, but because I didn't think I'd stand another minute without hearing her voice.

She answered with a pissy tone, "I don't want to talk to you."

"Please. Let me see you."

"See me? Leonard, you're the one who said we couldn't meet up."

"I could come to your place. I mean, if you'll have me? I'd like to talk. I have some information I think you need to know about."

"Fine, but I'm not talking to you about the case from our end. If you want to show all of your cards, I'll let you."

I breathed a sigh of relief. "Thank you. What time?"

"I could see you around seven thirty. Don't be late." The forceful tone really turned me on, and I was glad I'd convinced her to see me.

She hung up the phone without a goodbye, and I realized I was going to have to try my damnedest to make it up to her. She was right to be angry about the situation, but I wanted her to put that angry energy to better use.

I spent the rest of my afternoon counting down the minutes until time to get off work. Then, I spent the rest of my evening getting ready to see her, hoping I could bring her out of her mood. I stopped off at the store for a bottle of wine, and when I got to her house, I still had ten minutes to spare.

I knocked and waited, hearing footsteps on the other side, and then she opened the door looking like a million bucks. I could see why so many adored her, knowing only her songs and the beauty that was only a small part of who she really was.

"Come in."

"Thanks for seeing me." I held out the bottle of wine. "You look beautiful." She wore a blush-colored cotton dress and flats that were just a shade darker. Her hair was swept back from her face, and a couple of tattoos peeked out from her sleeves.

She looked at the bottle like I was offering her a bug and then shrugged, taking it from my hand. "Yeah, I'm still not sure it's the best idea for me."

"Come on, Kya, don't be pissed off at me. It doesn't suit you." I stepped past her as she held the door and looked around her home as she shut the door.

Her place was small and pretty, not too flashy or strange or even what you might expect a rock diva's house to look like. But it was clean, and there weren't signs of a wild party or even another man in her life, which was good. "Nice place you've got here."

"Thank you. I've spent the last hour cleaning it, so if smell like lemons, it's the furniture polish." She walked to the couch, offered me a seat, and then placed the wine on the kitchen counter.

I lowered myself to the cushion, never taking my eyes off her. "You didn't have to clean up on my account. I used to see your bedroom, remember?" Of course, that was at a time before the two of us had any interest in sex. And once we got old enough to, her father had stopped letting me come over and hang out in her room. We had to go the garage or the backyard.

She seemed like she wanted to smile, but she didn't. She took a seat on the far end away from me but angled her body toward me. "I remember that, but I'm sure you didn't come here hoping to tell me about old times. You said there was some information about the case, something you needed to show me." Nope, just as cold as she could be.

I tried to think of something to tell her because, in truth, there really wasn't any newfound evidence. I'd just wanted to see her again, but there was no way I'd tell her that. "I found the proof, so I know you've got a case."

She rolled her eyes, and the smile on her face wasn't her usual pleasant one. "That's it? Tell me something I don't know. But I have a feeling I know way more than you. Like the fact that he tried to pay salaries to people who didn't even work for us? Have you found that little piece of evidence yet?"

My mouth hung open like a fool. "I haven't. I thought you weren't going to show your hand."

"You look like you need a little help." She got up and went to the kitchen.

I looked over, my eyes following her to the other room. She took the bottle of wine and put it in the fridge, and then she pulled out another that had been chilled and found two glasses. "I need a drink, and since I never drink alone, I'll pour you one too."

"Thanks." I got up and walked to the counter. She handed me the glass, and I took it, hoping a drink would ease us both. "Look, Kya. I lied." That brought her head around, and she narrowed her eyes. I held my hand up to let me finish. "I just really wanted to see you."

"But you're still helping that man?"

"Kya, there's no letting up for my father. I know I was a real dick last time, and what happened between us at Seth's party wasn't an excuse for it. I just wanted to say I'm sorry, and I hope we can start on a better foot."

She stared at me, her eyes wide and clear. "Thank you for saying that. And for my part, I'm sorry too. You know, for a moment, you were still that sweet boy I loved."

I searched her eyes and hoped to make myself clear enough. "I'm still in here, Kya."

She moved closer and reached out to put her arm around my neck. "Let me see if I can find you." Her lips found mine, and I kissed her deeper, bringing my hands up, stroking her shoulder with my fingertips. I reached up, my hand moving into her hair, and I brought it out only to release the clip she'd had it pulled back in and then tossed it to the table in front of us.

She pulled back and looked into my eyes. Then she trailed her gaze down across my body, pausing a moment on the bulge that filled out the front of my jeans. Then her hand moved down and landed on the throbbing length, stroking it up and down. "You're still there," she whispered close to my cheek before she kissed me, and I moved my hand down to cup her breast, the other playing with the zipper on her dress.

I wanted to slip it down, to peel the soft cotton from her shoulders, to run my mouth along her bare flesh and taste her.

She brought her hand up into my hair and took a handful in her grip, her hand pulling my head back as she looked directly into my eyes.

"I want you, Kya." Without a word, she kissed me once again, hard and deep, and then she moved forward into my lap.

"I'm right here, Leonard." She undid the button on my pants, and her hand slipped into the folds of fabric where she gripped me, her hand closing around my hard cock, stroking it up and down. "I want you too."

16

KYA

I couldn't believe I was with Leonard again, and even though he'd already betrayed me the last time I'd given myself to him, I was a different person now. I wasn't the same young woman, hoping to find someone who could take care of her. Nope, I didn't need that. I wanted his companionship, his friendship, and if it led to more, so be it. I wouldn't refuse him this time, and if he refused me, then I'd be okay, no better off, no worse than before.

His hands searched my body, one on my breast pinching my nipple, the other rubbing his flattened palm against my mound. I breathed out a moan as he created enough friction to start a small fire in my panties. I needed him to quench that heat.

As if reading my mind, he moved me off of his lap, and I lay back, his hands pushing up my dress, bunching it around my waist and exposing my panties. "May I?"

I nodded, giving permission, and I knew if I spoke, my voice would crack anyway. He moved up and kissed my lips and then moved down between my legs, his mouth covering my silk, breathing warmth against me that had me aching for more.

His fingers moved over the elastic, pulling it aside, giving his digits access to penetrate me. They sank into my folds, curving up to rub my tender spot which made me cry out again.

"It feels amazing, Leonard."

"Leo, please," he corrected. And I knew it was time I started to oblige.

"Leo," I whispered. "Don't stop."

"Oh, don't worry, baby, I'm only getting started." He worked his fingers against my G-spot and then his tongue moved across my center, licking my clit with a sharp flicker of his tongue.

My orgasm crashed over me like a tidal wave, and I could have sworn if I'd closed my eyes, I'd have seen fireworks bursting in a night sky.

"That's right, come for me. I want that little pussy just right for what I'm about to give you." He stood, and while he made quick work of dropping his pants, which exposed his thick cock, I slipped off my dress. He lost his shirt, too, but before he could move back atop of me, I moved to my knees and took his cock, giving it a firm grip that had him hissing through his teeth.

"Be good to it. It's going to love you." He smiled down, and I opened my mouth and licked my lips. "That's a good girl. Take it."

I closed my lips around his head and moaned as I worked it over, twirling my tongue along the broad tip, tonguing the rim of it as a taste of his salt splashed my mouth. I didn't stop. I wanted more, and I gripped his balls causing him to whimper and moan as I kneaded them in my fingertips.

"You're so good at that, baby. I've never had better."

I smiled with pride but didn't believe a word from his pretty mouth when it came to the best he'd had. I knew he'd been with a lot of women. There was no way anyone had refused him.

"Oh, fuck." Another splash of salt hit my tongue but just a taste. He rocked his hips, fucking my mouth and watching me as I stared up at him, gripping his ass. I relaxed my throat and pushed myself closer, taking his cock deeper.

He held my head, and I held my breath. When I gagged, he pulled back and then he came forward again, but this time, when he went deep, he didn't hold me as long. "I'm close. Tell me where you want it."

I looked up at him and pushed myself back down, and he cursed as he unloaded in my throat, and I pulled back only a little, gulping all I could, the rest rolling off my chin.

"Fuck, I warned you." He looked down, and I was smiling, wiping my chin. "That was so hot, but I'm not at all finished with you." He brought me up to my feet and pulled me close, kissing me deeply, the taste of him still warm on my breath. "I can't wait to get inside you."

"Do you want to move to my bedroom?" I had shut the door to Addie's room and spent an hour walking through the house to make sure her toys were put away, ensuring there were no signs of me having a child. That was a conversation for another time. I had to admit that deep inside, I'd known where this visit would lead or at least where I wanted it to lead.

Leo picked me up against him, and I wrapped my legs around his waist. He took to the hall, and I left my bedroom door open for easier access. "This is the one." I gestured. He brought us into the room and placed me back on the bed.

"Now, it's your turn to come again." He moved down, and his mouth closed on my sex, licking and penetrating with a feverish motion. He lapped and licked, and his fingers explored, eventually working their way down to stroke against my tight ass. The feeling of his finger there sent me squirming. I needed to feel him inside of me and fast, and I didn't care where he put it.

"Fuck me, Leo. Please. I need you inside me." The words were rushed off my lips.

He rose up and stroked his cock as I spread my legs wide. He moved into my hips and nudged his head against me, pushing it between my folds and barely into my channel. I was so wet, I soaked the tip of his cock, and he nudged slowly, which was good because it had been a while since I'd been with anyone, and I was already intimidated by his girth and length.

"Relax, baby. I'm going to go slow." He looked down into my eyes, and I calmed my breath as he sank his cock home. "That's a good girl.

You feel so fucking good wrapped around me." He thrust his hips, and I swear I didn't think the man could have grown anymore, but he had. He pumped his cock deeper with every thrust, and as another orgasm ripped through me, coating his cock, lubricating our motion, it became easier, and soon, he was fucking me so hard and fast, my tits were slapping together.

He gripped one and stopped the motion and then brought his mouth down to my nipple, sucking so hard, it sent a pinch of pleasure to my core. I felt another rush from my release, and even though I had come, he didn't slow down.

He finally breathed in deeply and then pulled me up against him. He sat down, and I fell astride him, riding him in a slow rhythm.

He stroked my cheek, and my eyes lifted to meet his. "I've missed you so much, Kya."

"I've missed you, too, Leonard." I couldn't help it. He was always Leonard to me. And I finally felt like I had him back, if only for a little while. I had no idea what would come of this, and I dared not think too hard about what I wanted it to be. That dream would have to wait. For now, I wanted to cherish the closeness we shared at the moment.

He gripped my ass as I moved against him, and now and then, he would kiss me, or brush my hair back. I milked him with my core, and he met my eyes. "I'm close."

"I'm covered." I had barely gotten the words out when he held me down hard on his cock and filled me up. He met my eyes and pulled me close, kissing my mouth deep and hard, nipping my lips with his teeth gently as he pulled away.

He held me tight. "That was so good."

I couldn't help but blush and giggle like a school girl. "Made my toes curl." He let me loose, and even though we were still joined together, I brushed my hands down his chest and looked into his eyes. "Promise me you won't go away this time?"

"Third time's a charm, right?" He shrugged, and I smiled big as I fell against him. "I'm not going anywhere, Kya. Not until you send me away."

I nuzzled against his neck, my head resting on his shoulder. "But this is bad, right?"

He stroked my hair. "For the case, you bet your sweet ass. This is trouble, and if anyone found out, I would have to recuse myself from the case."

I lifted up and met his eyes. "So, you're still going forward with it?"

He held my face in his hands. "I think I have something up my sleeve. Don't worry, okay? I'll handle it. We just shouldn't say anything to anyone." I wasn't going to tell him that Sadie knew, and I knew she wasn't going to tell anyone.

"So now what?" He squeezed my ass and ground his hips up against me, his cock still stiff inside me.

"You're insatiable." I thought of the handful of men I'd been with and how they'd either passed out, gone limp, or fallen asleep just moments after an intimate encounter, which sometimes I may or may not have gotten off during, but not Leo. He was so much hotter than any of them combined, and he knew how to use his cock to pleasure a woman. I couldn't even count the number of orgasms he'd delivered. "I can't believe we're still going?"

"It stays hard for you. Always has. You wouldn't believe how many times I had to take care of it after being around you. I fantasized daily about you, baby."

"I never knew. If I had, we'd have done something about it." I could imagine our teen years a lot differently when I thought about us together then.

"I always wanted to shower with you." He wiggled his brows. "That was the ultimate fantasy and the reason we kept running out of hot water at our house."

"Shower with me now?"

As if to answer, he picked me up against him, and we walked to the shower where he set the spray and put my back against the wall where he slow fucked me. "I want it to feel good for you."

"It does." I could already feel my next release on the horizon.

"Good. I'm spent, and my balls are fucking drained, but it can't get enough." He moved his hips a little faster, and I came hard. He captured my mouth and held me, the two of us seeming to rest in one another.

"I don't want to leave, but I know I need to get going soon."

"There's no rush." I knew all I had to do was make one call and Sadie would watch Addison for me all night. But with Leo and I not supposed to be seeing each other at all, going this deep, it was dangerous enough without a sleepover.

"Good because I haven't even pulled out yet." We shared a laugh, and he moved inside me, and I felt another wave from my last release quake through me.

He finally did pull away, and we spent a tender moment washing each other, the two of us lathered up and stroking each other, his hand slipping between my legs and washing me with care, as I worked my hands over his chest, my front brushing against his, his cock hitting my tummy, still a monster, even when it wasn't standing at attention.

I thought of all the years we'd missed out on and felt the nostalgia creeping up on me. Even though it seemed like we were doing well, I knew there was a long road to travel before being together, and I feared that once he learned of my life and family, he might not want to travel it with me.

Our future was only a glimmer.

17

LEO

The one Monday I decided to take my time and showed up for work a little late, I ran into Jon who was walking Susan Costanzo from his office and into the hall. I'd worked with the woman many times, and there was no love lost between us. I'd also been in the courtroom the day she'd had her rant and was carried out kicking and screaming for contempt. She had become a laughingstock overnight, and someone had even made a meme about it.

She stepped out and gave me a withering glance. "I do hope your professionalism will improve by the time we have our meeting. I know you men like to be casual about things, but we're gearing up to hammer your balls to the floor."

"Is there a problem, Susan?" I looked her right in the eyes and wished I'd have told Kya how much I hated her attorney. She was a man-hating hard-ass with no soul.

She narrowed her eyes and turned up her nose. "Other than you strolling in late. I had hoped to come down and meet with you both, but I suppose you forgot I sent a text and wanted to see you about our upcoming client meeting."

"No, I never got the memo. You could be a little bit more professional and maybe call me sometime. You know those texts can be undependable. At least you'll know when a call goes through." I had gotten her stupid text, but it had slipped my mind to put it in my phone calendar. I would never apologize or admit any wrongdoing. I'd been on too many cases for that. "What meeting is that again? The one you're just now arranging? So, I'm a little late to work while you're late to the game."

Jon covered his mouth and tried to keep from laughing.

Susan's eyes widened, and somehow, her nose got even higher. If I kept it up, would I have her smelling her own ass? "I do hope you make better use of my client's time."

I wanted to tell her so badly that I'd put her client's time to very good use and how many orgasms I'd delivered, but I couldn't rat me or Kya out.

I gave a little wave. "Have a good day, Susan. I'll see you then."

She stormed away, and Jon turned to me, dropping his hand so I could see the full effect of his grin. "What's gotten into you? Rough weekend? I mean, I get it. I hate the case too. I hate the client, I hate Susan, but we have to do our jobs."

"You looked like you had it under control. Besides, how many Mondays do I get to sleep in?" And not to mention, I needed the extra sleep. I needed it to refuel from all the energy I'd pumped into Kya. It had been so hot. I was torn between wanting to tell Jon about it but glad I had to keep it all to myself. She was a hot little secret to keep.

"Susan didn't mention anything about a conflict of interest with you knowing her client, so I guess Kya Campbell must not have said anything to her. Do you think Kya's figured it out yet? Maybe she doesn't realize it's you representing?"

"Oh, yeah, she knows." I turned and walked to my end of the hall, and he followed as we rounded the corner and passed Tabby's desk.

"Good morning, boys." Tabby looked up and gave us a smile.

"Good morning to you as well, Tabby." I didn't even stop to ogle the woman or take a peek at what she wore, but it didn't stop Jon.

"Looking beautiful as usual, Tabs," he called out behind me. I turned to see that he had the biggest, dopiest grin on his face.

Once we were in my office, Jon took a chair as I went around my desk to sit. "Has she been in touch with you?"

"Who? Tabby?" I had a feeling he didn't mean my secretary, but I thought playing dumb would be best for the moment.

"No, not Tabby. Kya." He gave me a look that told me I had to be cautious how I answered him. He was my best friend and old roomie, but he clearly, judging from his hard expression, didn't approve. "Shit, she did."

"What? Give me time to answer you." My voice got a little high and defensive, and from the look on his face, I knew he knew.

Jon shook his head and waved it off. "No, don't bother. You took way too long answering me, and I don't want to hear it come out of your mouth. At least then, when anyone asks, I can be honest that you never told me."

I sat there a moment trying to decide what to say. "I think its way worse on our side than we know."

He let out a long breath. "Yeah? Don't tell me how you know that. Just tell me, what's our course of action?"

There was only one course of action I could think of when it came to this case. "We need to get this guy to take a plea deal. If they make an offer, he needs to just take it."

Jon raked his hand through his hair. "Wow. That bad? I never thought I'd hear those words come out of your mouth." I had to agree. I hadn't expected it, either, but my hands were tied.

"Yeah, well, my father is a fool for making us stay on this case." I sighed and picked up my phone. "The only thing to do now is call Whit and explain. It's the best course of action."

"Fuck. He's not going to be happy."

"Like I am? Are you? I tell you, man. I hate this guy, so I really don't care what he likes and doesn't." Ever since I'd been with Kya, all I could think about was how shitty he'd been treating her and stealing her hard-earned money. If I could get him to take a deal and go away, that would be worth it.

Jon eased back in his seat as I dialed the number. "And the long morning gets longer."

I chuckled as the phone began to ring, and I put it on speaker for Jon to hear too.

"Good morning, Pace. Please tell me you're busy nailing Kya Campbell to a cross." I couldn't help thinking he had it half right. I was nailing her all right but not to any cross.

"I need you to be prepared for a meeting. As soon as I get the time pinned down, I'll let you know. We'll be meeting with the other side. Kya and the band will be present as well as their lawyer, so I want it to be respectful."

"Yes, I'm aware. You like to play nice in the sandbox. I'll try and remember not to piss in the sand."

"There's one other thing. It seems the other side is building a pretty strong case. If there is anything you haven't mentioned, say, paying yourself an extra salary or anything of that nature, then I'd suggest you come clean now." I looked up in time to see Jon's expression. He looked like a fish gasping for water.

"I had a few tricks. What does it matter?" As always, Whit sounded indifferent.

"If they bring them up before you do, I'll be blindsided in that meeting, and it won't go well. Did you pay a salary to someone who didn't exist?"

Jon's eyes widened. "Fuck," he mumbled under his breath.

"I may have kept paying a person or two, but they weren't fake people. I had some debts, and it was easier to just stick them on the payroll and pay them a salary with the others. Once the debts were paid, I took them off. We paid lots of people, crew, roadies, lights, sound. It all comes from somewhere, and people come and go. I didn't think they'd noticed."

"Well, apparently, they did," said Jon, who looked like he was about to go through the phone to punch the man in the face.

It was time to drop the bomb, and I knew it wasn't going to sit well because Whit was already in a defensive mood. "Here's what I suggest. You need to go to that meeting, and when they offer you a settlement, you take the deal."

"You want me to bargain? Why should I have to pay? I worked twice as hard as they did."

"Stop being so entitled. You had a deal, and as far as I can tell, you broke your contract right off the rip. So, yes, trust me, take the deal. You're not going to win in a courtroom, not if they go in dragging up people's names who you paid who didn't even work for the band."

"You can't possibly think you're in the right, or you're an even bigger narcissist than I thought," said Jon.

I continued, not giving Whit the chance to speak what I was certain would be nonsense. "God knows who you owed and who could get dragged into this. But I have a feeling the only person you paid was yourself, and if that comes out, and you don't take a deal, you're going to be in trouble."

Whit growled. "I'm not taking any fucking deal. And if you assholes want to be paid, you better fix this. Come up with something. I don't care what, but I am not about to bargain with those bitches or pay them a dime! I worked my ass off for them, and they owed me."

Jon cleared his throat and spoke up. "Mr. White, you do realize you could do prison time? This is a serious crime, and while we want to help, there's only so much we can do with what we're given. If there is anything else, I suggest you tell us now. If we're blindsided and can't come up with a reasonable explanation to your defense, then the judge is going to put you away. And that's the reason we're talking about a plea. You're less likely to serve any time and could probably just pay a fine."

"We're on your side," I added. I was losing my mind wanting to strangle the man. He had to be the absolute worst piece of shit on the planet.

"It sure as fuck doesn't feel like it," said Whit. "You want me to give them my money."

"No, we want you to give back some of what you stole. Tell me, Whit, did you do anything else?"

"I did a lot of shit. If I think of anything else, I'll call you, but I'm not going down for this, and I'm not making any deal. And furthermore, I'm only going to pay you if you do your job." There was a click, and suddenly there was a silence in the room as Jon and I stared across the desk at one another. Whit had ended the call.

"What the fuck just happened?" Jon took the words right from my mouth.

"There's no helping people like him. He's mental."

"Fuck, now I know why you wanted off this case. And you're fucking her, aren't you?"

I wasn't going to dignify that last part with a response, and he should have known better than to ask. "I caught wind of it, but I had a feeling it was true. When that little nugget is displayed in our meeting, he's going to have to either take a deal, which we know they'll offer, or this goes to court, and we'll lose to Susan fucking Costanzo, the courtroom head case."

Jon took a deep breath, looking like he wished he'd never agreed to be pulled into this mess. "Should we try to counter?"

"Well, like always, we should see what they offer him, and then we'll decide. If it's fair, he should take it without insult, but we'll decide. I don't want to push back too hard, or we're going to all land on our asses."

18

KYA

My lawyer's office was an even bigger mess when I arrived for our morning meeting. She had called me in to discuss the amount of evidence piling up, and I was certain, from the looks of things, she knew a lot about piles.

As her daughter, Darci, sent me back, I walked in, took a chair, and stared at the mounting stacks of boxes and paperwork. I was sure Susan had a system, a method to her madness, but it just looked like she'd dumped out boxes everywhere.

I was startled as she popped her head up from behind a stack that was three boxes high. "Jesus!" I held my heart, which seemed to do a backflip in my chest.

"Sorry about that. I got lost in a book." She smiled as she got to her feet. "Good morning. Sorry for the mess." She walked to her desk and tried to straighten the stack of papers, but when they were too much, she put them over on one of the boxes. I hoped there wasn't anything important there, like my case files. I was suddenly a bit nervous about her having the case. She seemed to have too much going on in her private life to be professional. I liked order.

"It's fine," I said, waving my hand, "Moving can be a pain." I tried to be sympathetic, knowing she was going through an adjustment in her life, but I hoped this wasn't a sign of how unprepared she would be.

"You have no idea. It's been just awful. My ex is a complete dick and didn't leave me any time to get out. I had to rush, and rushing is no good. Most of this stuff came from home. I'm a bit of a packrat. Love my books, and well, I need to keep records." She gave a little giggle, and suddenly, she winced and held her arm.

I noticed she looked a little pale, and her skin had a glossy, clammy sheen. "Are you okay?"

"I think I just got up a little fast. It happens." She took a tissue and wiped her brow and her upper lip, and soon, she was fanning herself. I wondered if she'd had a hot flash. "Let's get down to business," she said, straightening out her collar. "I talked with the other side, and they've agreed to meet. That Leo Pace is a hard hitter, but he's also an immature man-whore. I'm hoping his professionalism suffers, and we can take him down. The daddy's boy is usually a golden child in the courtroom. All the judges love him, especially the lady judges, but I'm unimpressed. He's always an asshole to me."

How could anyone hate Leonard? "He gets around, does he?" I found it interesting she seemed to know so much about Leonard and wondered if she could offer any more clues as to who he was on the job. It was no wonder that the ladies all loved him, but I wondered if there was any validation to the whole man-whore accusation. I mean, I had thought that was probably the case, but to hear it firsthand? I was curious.

She rolled her eyes, clearly unimpressed with Leonard. "He's got a reputation."

"I would think his reputation in the courtroom would be the one we need to worry most about, right?" It seemed she had some kind of personal vendetta, and I wondered if it was because he'd turned her down or hadn't shown interest in her.

She shrugged, her face turning even paler. "True, but he was so rude to me." She held her arm and then wiped her brow again. "Excuse me. I think I'm having gas pains. This job is so stressful. I'm probably getting an ulcer." She opened up her desk and scrambled for a roll of antacids, which she finally pulled out and placed on her desk. She fought with the wrapper but eventually popped one into her mouth.

I was beginning to worry she was coming down with something, and I hoped it wasn't something even more serious. "Do you need me to get your daughter?"

She rubbed her shoulder. "No, I'm fine. As I was saying, I think we're going to be able to settle this thing out of court, and I wanted your take on that. I'd like to offer him a settlement in exchange for an admission of all wrongdoing, and then hopefully, we can wrap this thing up early."

I didn't mind a settlement as long as it was clear Whit had cheated us, but I also wanted a healthy settlement. "Do you think he'll take it?"

She eased back in her chair. "If we make him think he's getting a deal and keeping him from going to prison. If we save him from some embarrassment, the trouble of going to court, the time it will take. You see, you're most likely not going to see every dime he took anyway, but if we can recover a good portion, something he can most likely afford, you have a better chance of seeing it."

That sounded good, but I wanted to cover all bases and be done with him for good. "And what about the contract we're in? Can we prove he went against it and get back all our past rights?"

Susan closed her eyes, and her face scrunched up. "Yeah, I think we can. Excuse me. Water." She rose and before she took two steps, she fell headfirst into a stack of boxes, and as they crashed to the ground, she landed on the floor and rolled to her side.

I jumped to my feet. "Susan!" I reached for the phone and dialed 911. I called out to her daughter. "Darci, help!"

I walked around the desk, and the operator answered. "Nine-one-one. What's your emergency?" As Darci burst into the room, I answered, "I need an ambulance to 405 North Plaza. I believe my lawyer is having a heart attack."

"Mama!" Darci leaned over her mother, who was not responding.

"They're on their way," I told her as tears filled her eyes. "It's going to be okay, sweetie." I couldn't believe it had all happened so fast, but now, selfishly, I had no idea what it meant for the case.

Darci and I stayed with her until five minutes later when the EMT came and took her. Darci went with her in the ambulance after locking up the office, and I got in my car, shaken by the whole experience.

I put my head on the steering wheel and cried for a good five minutes, the stress of everything, the lawsuit, Leo, and Susan lying on the floor while her daughter cried over her. I didn't want to ever put Addison in that position.

After wiping my eyes and checking my mascara, I got out on the road headed home and dialed Sadie. I had to explain what was going on.

She answered the phone with a chipper attitude. "How's my bestie today? Did you get to talk to Susan?" She hadn't been able to join me because Stones was supposed to be in town for a visit.

I took a deep cleansing breath. "Yeah, that's why I'm calling."

"Have you been crying? Don't tell me Whit pulled one of his stunts. Is everything okay?"

I checked my rearview to make a lane change. "No, it's not Whit. Susan had a heart attack. Right there in our meeting. Right in front of me."

"Holy shit! Is she okay? Are you?"

"She's been taken to the ER in critical. Darci went with her. Seeing that poor girl, it scared me to death. It's got me a little shaken, but I'm fine." I was getting better now that I was able to talk to Sadie, thankful for a friend I could count on.

Sadie breathed into the phone, and I could imagine it had all come as a shock to her as well. "I can't imagine," she said. "But I'm glad you're okay. I don't want to sound insensitive to Susan's fate, but what the fuck does this mean for us, for the case?"

"I don't know. She was just telling me she met with Leo about arranging a meeting, and she says she thinks we're good. She also wants to figure out an offer we can make Whit. She is hoping he'll take a settlement. He would plead guilty, let us out of our contract, past and present since he breached it, and then he'd pay a portion back to us."

"A portion?"

"We're never going to get it all, Sadie. If this goes to court and we win, we may never see any of it. I agree with Susan on that. I think it's a good idea."

"If she pulls through, it will be wonderful. Until then, it's just an idea." Sadie had a point, and no telling how long we'd have to wait now for something to be done. Our only choice was to get a different lawyer or see who she might want to step into her shoes on the case.

"We'd have all of our rights back that way too. Like he never existed," said Sadie. "That would be good for us having full creative freedom. We could finally do more social media. He's really hit us in that market because he didn't know shit about it and didn't want to."

Whit had done a lot of things to damage shit for us, and now it was time to hopefully move on and heal. "So, do you agree?"

"Hell, yeah. Now, we sit back and wait, I guess. Hopefully, it won't be too long, especially since we've already paid her."

"If she can't go forward, do you think we get a refund?" I felt horrible even thinking it since I'd been the one to watch her fall out, but we'd already lost enough money in this deal.

"Fuck, I don't know, Kya." I could hear Stones in the background, strumming his guitar.

"Shit, I didn't mean to bother you while Stones was over." They didn't have a lot of time together, and I wondered if I'd interrupted them in bed.

Sadie gave a half-hearted laugh. "Considering the circumstances, you better be glad you called. I would have been so mad if you didn't. But don't worry, you're not interrupting anything. He's on the phone with Blitz talking about the next stop."

"How's the tour?" I wondered if they had a big crowd. Sales had been down all around with the recent shootings. People were afraid to be in crowds, but luckily, it would improve.

Sadie lowered her voice. "He said he's ready to be home for good."

I wondered exactly where his home would be? There with her, or with his daddy. "That bad, huh?"

"You know how it is, burnout. He's begging me for a home-cooked meal. I guess I'm going to have to put on some clothes so I can fry him some bacon."

I shared in her laughter, though I was still feeling a bit out of sorts. "That would be wise. Darci is supposed to call me and let me know how her mother is."

"Call me back. I want to know how she is too."

"Will do, and be careful frying up that bacon. I don't need you in the hospital too." I ended the call and pulled into my driveway.

I walked into the house, and as I saw Addison's stuffed animals scattering the floor, I couldn't stop myself from crying. It was times like this that I needed Addison to know her father. If something happened to me, she'd be without a parent. I knew Sadie would take her in, but I also knew that wouldn't be fair, not when her father could be in the picture.

19

LEO

Jon and I had just stepped off the elevator after returning from the parking garage where he showed me his new car stereo and speakers when Tabby rounded the corner. "There you are. Edith is looking for you. I told her you were around here somewhere."

"You should have called me," I said, patting my coat for my phone, which a moment later Tabby held up.

"You mean this phone? You left it on your desk."

About that time, Edith rounded the corner from my father's end of the hall. "I thought I heard your voice. Your father wants to see you."

"So I hear," I said, giving Jon a pat on the back. "It must be important. I better get down there. Oh, and I loved the speakers, by the way. Great choice." He had wanted to improve his system for a while now, and I knew it meant a lot to him.

Jon stepped away. "Thanks. We'll have to take it for a spin and see how loud we can stand it."

I hurried off to Dad's office wondering if I was about to get my ass chewed or if he was going to ask me a million questions I didn't know the answer to. Edith gave me a blank look as I walked by, and I wondered how long she'd been looking for me. I noticed three missed calls, but I didn't think Jon and I had taken that long.

I knocked on the door and stuck my head inside. "You wanted to see me?"

"Yeah, where the hell have you been?"

I walked in and helped myself to a cup of coffee from his private Keurig. "Sorry. Jon and I stepped out for a minute, and I forgot my phone on my desk."

He shook his head and didn't wait for the coffee to pour. "Tell me how the case is going. Did you find anything useful that could help the client?"

"Actually, no. It's just like I said, a total nightmare, and in fact, the other side has enough fraud for him to do quite a long time in prison when we lose the case."

"That's not very optimistic talk."

"No, it's realistic talk, Dad. I've tried to warn you. It's so bad, I suggested that if offered, he take a deal."

My father's face turned as red as his tie. "A plea deal? Are you out of your mind? I want to get this man off the hook."

As my coffee finished pouring, I turned off the machine and brought my cup with me to the closest chair in front of his desk. "It's a pretty big hook, Dad." I'd done all I could to warn him, but he was always so damned determined.

"I didn't put you on the case to take the easy road, and we're not throwing our client under the bus so we can. There's always an angle. Dig up some dirt on that Kya girl. See if you can find if she was somehow involved or knew about it. Paint her as a jilted partner in crime for all I care, but make this happen!"

His phone rang, and while I let what he'd said sink in, holding back the urge to kick the old man's teeth in, he answered it. "Hello?" His face fell into a somber expression. "I see. Well, is she going to make it?" I could tell it was bad. Perhaps dead relative bad. But then my father hung up the phone and was suddenly frowning again.

"Well?"

"That was Edith. Word just came in that Susan Costanzo had a heart attack earlier. She's in the hospital in intensive care, and her condition is critical."

All of my anger subsided for a moment, and as much as I hated Susan, I never wanted anyone to be hurt or in danger. "Shit."

"Yeah, so we'll have to see how we can work this to our advantage. If someone comes in, say a rookie, to take over the case, there might be one hell of a communication gap, and hopefully, we can turn this around. I want you to figure it out as soon as you find out who's replacing her."

"You're kidding, right? After the shit you said a minute ago, I'm not even sure I know who the hell you are, and now a woman, granted a complete asshole of a woman, but a human being is in the hospital and the first thing you think about is the next angle." I got to my feet and put the coffee on his desk. I couldn't stand to look at him, much less sip coffee and conspire with him.

Dad leaned forward. "I think you're overreacting."

"No, I think you are, Dad. I have tried to talk reason to you about this case from the start, and for some reason, you don't want to hear it. Are you trying to ruin my record? Can't let me get ahead, right? You only want to me to look good enough to make you look good, but when I start to look way better than you, you can't handle it."

"You're out of line." His face was back to deep burgundy, and any moment, he might start pumping steam from his ears.

"Did you even hear yourself a minute ago? Throw Kya, our neighbor and my oldest friend, under the bus and make her look like an accomplice?"

"I barely knew her."

"I know her better than anyone else in this whole fucking, sick world, and I'm not going to do her that way. Furthermore, I'm done with this case." I walked around the chair, and he stood up behind his desk.

"Get back here, son. You don't want to do this."

"Yeah, Dad. I so fucking want to do this." I had looked for a reason for years to tell my father to shove it, and today was the day.

"I mean it, Leonard, if you walk out that door, you can kiss your job goodbye. You can clean out that office and take your ass to the house!"

"Bye, Dad." I walked out and found Edith standing behind her desk, her mouth wide open and one hand on her heart.

But I didn't stop to say anything. I continued out the door, around the corner, and down to my end of the hall. When I passed Tabby, I stopped and took a deep breath.

"What's the matter, Leo?" She got up and came around her desk so quickly, I didn't have time to tell her to stay seated. I didn't want to deal with her and the whole packing my office just yet. By law, I had a little time to get out, and I'd get her situated somewhere else with me.

"It's fine, Tabs. We may be changing our address is all. Don't worry."

Her eyes widened, and she nodded. "Okay, Leo. Is there anything I can do?"

"No, but since I'm leaving for the day, you can leave too. Tomorrow, you can start looking for listings and see if we can find a new place."

"I'm sure whatever is going on with you and your father will resolve quickly, Leo, and then we won't have to go anywhere."

"I don't know. Maybe it's time I go on my own." I gave her a pat on the back, and she hurried around her desk as I went to my office. I needed a moment, so I shut the door and took out my phone.

As Kya's phone rang, I tried to collect my thoughts and my breath. I had gotten so angry, my blood was pumping, and my adrenaline was through the roof.

"Leonard?"

I smiled, wondering if she would ever call me Leo. "Hey, Kya. How are you?"

"Let's just say, if you've called to give me bad news, I could do without it."

"I heard about Susan. I guess they called you already?"

"Called me? No, I was there when it happened. She looked so frazzled and pale, I knew something had to be wrong, but she kept insisting she was fine right up until she dropped right in front of me."

"I'm sorry you had to go through that. I hope she's okay."

"Me, too, but I got another call that they're looking for a replacement for me. No one wants to take her cases because her life is a mess and so is her office. There are files everywhere. She fell right into a stack of them. Thank heavens the top two were empty, and they kind of cushioned her fall."

"Damn, that's rough." I hated to think of her on her own in this, and worse that Whit was going to team up with whoever my father left in charge and try to drag her through the mud with him. "Look, can I come see you?"

She hesitated a little, a humming sound bubbling from her throat like she had to think about it. "Are you sure it's a good idea? I mean, with this case falling apart, I didn't think you'd want to keep complicating things even more by seeing me again."

I let out a long sigh. There was nothing I wanted more than to be with her at that moment. "Trust me. I can't wait to see you again. I meant can I come now?"

"Now? Sure."

"Good, I have something to tell you. I think you're going to like it."

She gave a soft laugh. "If you want to tell me in person, I like it already."

"Give me twenty minutes."

"You got it." She ended the call, and I hurried out of the office, not bothering to stop and tell anyone, not even Jon, what happened. Even though I owed it to him, I'd have to tell him later.

I got to my car and hauled ass out of the garage and went even faster once I hit the freeway.

Making it to her house in what I was certain was record time, I got out of the car, and she met me at the door. I greeted her with a kiss and kicked the door shut behind me as I walked her backward into her front room.

She pulled away and searched my eyes. "Are you okay?"

"Yes, I'm more than okay now." Over the moon was more like it, or maybe since it was daytime, walking on sunshine, my head in the clouds, I could think of a hundred different ways, but mostly I was relieved. The dark cloud of the case had dissipated, no longer looming over my head.

She lay her head against my chest. "I'm glad you're here. My day has sucked up until now. I don't know what I'm going to do. I guess I can't exactly ask you for any advice. That would be weird, right?"

I gave a soft laugh, so relieved I could in fact help. "Actually, I'm all yours."

"Thanks, but I don't want to put you in a strange position. You could tell me what's on your mind, though. I know you have something to tell me."

"Yes, and what I'm trying to tell you is that I'm all yours. I'm off Whit's case."

"You are?"

"Yeah, I told my old man I quit. I couldn't go up against you, Kya. Not when I care so much about you. It's not only a conflict of interest but impossible. I told my father I didn't agree with his ideas and bailed."

"Holy shit. So that means that Whit's out of an attorney too?" She still wasn't getting it.

"Well, he's the only one. I'd like to represent you."

Her face shadowed with uncertainty. "Leonard, is that even possible? I mean, for you to switch teams like that?"

"Yeah, it's not usually done, no, but in this case, I don't give a shit. I can take over for Susan. I already know the case, so you won't have to worry about anyone coming in and fucking things up, and more than that, I already know their tactics. So if you'll let me?"

She backed away and walked over to the back of her couch where she leaned with her head down.

"What's wrong? I thought you'd be excited."

Her shoulders sloped. "It's just that I can't pay you, Leonard."

"Don't worry about that. I'll do this one for free."

"I can't let you do that, either."

I walked over and brought my arms around her as I straddled her legs. "You can make it up to me in other ways like kisses for instance."

I brought my mouth down on hers. "Mm. Yes, pay me in kisses, Kya. Your money is no good with me anyway."

She stood, bringing her arms around my neck. "If you're sure?"

"Yes, I'm sure."

Kya smiled wickedly. "I might need a little more convincing." She took my hand and led me to her room.

20

KYA

Leonard had me so turned on, and all he'd had to do was tell me he'd quit the case. I had started to have my doubts if he'd do the right thing, and I didn't want to be hurt by him again, but he'd really surprised me.

Now, it was time to make him as happy as he'd made me. "Just how much is this going to cost me?" I asked, moving in for a kiss once we reached my bedroom door.

"Hm. I'll have to feel you out and get back to you." He kissed me hard and deep, his tongue sliding in along mine, taking it deeper.

I pulled away and opened the door. "I have a lot more to give?" I walked him to the bed and stopped at the foot to kiss him again.

He pulled away after a quick peck. "Do you? Let's see what you've got." He unzipped my dress, and it fell off my shoulders and pooled at my ankles leaving me in my white, lacy bra and panties. We shared a smile, and I was enjoying the game. It made me feel naughty and turned me on.

I fluttered my lashes. "Mhm, please Mr. Lawyer, I need your help. I'll do anything." I reached down and rubbed his hard length through his pants.

"Then show me what a good girl you are, and I'll see what I can do for you." We both busted out laughing, and if we weren't so turned on, it might have been a distraction. Instead, he dropped his pants and took me into his arms and cupped my soft mound rubbing me through my panties.

I panted hard and moved against his hand as I stroked his bare, rigid cock in the same rhythm. I wanted to show him what a good girl I was still, and so I moved to my knees and pumped my hand, working him over as I opened my mouth and placed his head on my tongue.

"Fuck. You are a *very* good girl." He gave a sultry laugh, and as he hissed through his teeth, he rested one hand on my shoulder, the other on my head where he stroked my hair.

I focused on the task at hand and pulled off to lick his shaft from base to tip and back, then I planted soft kisses along the side of his cock and looked up into his eyes. His were barely a sliver, so deep and sexy, I felt a hot ache between my legs for him.

"Touch yourself, Kya." His voice was so commanding that it made me wet, and I wasted not another moment and brought my hand between my legs. I parted my folds, stroking beneath my hood on my sensitive little bud where my pleasure bloomed. "That's my girl. You look so hot doing that with my cock in your mouth. It makes me so fucking hot for you." He rocked his hips gently as I relaxed my throat and took him deeper, and then he threw his head back as I held myself there.

"Do you trust me?" he asked.

I nodded. More than ever, I wanted to say. Instead, I kept working his thick flesh, the taste of his salty skin tickling my tongue as his hand went to my throat, the other wrapping around the back of my head.

I relaxed as he pushed himself deep, holding me there for a good minute, and then I gasped like a dying fish as he pulled away and shoved it back in. I swallowed, gagging a little as it pulled him deeper. He moved away and smiled down at me.

"That's so hot. Do you want to taste it?" he asked. I nodded. "Good girl."

He held me down on his cock one last time, and then I felt my mouth fill with his release. He moaned loudly which caused me to moan as well. He let go of my throat and grabbed the sides of my head to pump in and out as I gulped and swallowed.

He pulled out, and what had rolled onto my chin, he gathered on his head, and I sucked and licked until it was all clean.

"Now, it's my turn to make you moan." He laid me back on the bed and moved his hand to stroke my soaking channel. "And you're going to taste so sweet, I can already tell." He brought his fingers to his lips and tasted my honey.

He dipped down between my legs, and his mouth closed over my mound, his tongue penetrating me, the pleasure so intense, I cried out and gripped his hair to hold him in that one spot that felt amazing. He didn't let up, either, and his tongue kept right on flicking, tickling the spot until an orgasm rippled through me, the waves of pleasure overtaking me as I released him and he licked and dipped his tongue into my channel to taste me.

He rose up, stroking his cock and moved between my legs, centering himself at my core, and nudging himself inside me, nice and slow, inching and retreating, little by little until he reached my depths.

He paused a moment, and I felt his eyes on me, and only then, I realized mine were closed. "You're so slick and tight, so perfect." He rocked his hips, slowly fucking me, rutting deeper, stretching me until I thought I might rip apart, but then I felt a pinch of pleasure lick my center, and another orgasm came, taking me over the edge as I writhed beneath him.

"That's right, Kya, soak my cock." He began to pump harder, his thrusts becoming more and more steady, more deliberate as he angled up and aimed for my G-spot. I tilted my hips to make it easier, and when he found the special place, I moaned and soaked his cock again. Once I began to milk him, my walls clenching and releasing, tugging on his dick, he tensed and unloaded deep inside of me. "Fuck."

He collapsed on me and kissed me hard, taking my breath away. I gasped and kissed him back. Feverishly, our lips collided, and I wasn't sure we'd ever be able to slow down, much less stop.

But soon, it subsided, and we lay curled up beside one another. "How can I not help you after that?"

"Only if you're sure, Leonard."

He sighed. "I tell you what. You can pay me."

"Yeah? Did you think of something else?"

"Yes, I want you to call me Leo."

"I know. It's just so hard. You'll always be my Leonard."

"I'm not that same little boy anymore, though, Kya, and I want you to see that."

"Oh, I do, but I happened to like that little boy, Leo. He was handsome and kind and my friend for as long as I could remember. How could I not?" He rolled his eyes up and stared at the ceiling away from me. "Fine. Leo, it is. But don't hold it against me if I call you Leonard at the moment. You make me so hot, I can't help myself."

"Fair enough." He stroked my shoulder and closed his eyes.

"So, what happens now? I mean, you quit the case. I can't imagine your dad is very pleased."

"I don't care if he is or isn't. He's always tried to put that firm ahead of me, and today, well, let's just say he really showed me it's what's most important to him. I could handle being around when I thought he had an ounce of integrity, but now that I know he has none, there's no way I want to be a part of what he has cooking."

"That's sad. I really hoped the two of you would lean on each other when your mother passed away."

"Normal people might, but we're not normal. Dad's a hard-ass. He always has been. No, it's all better this way. I'm going to try and lease a place, turn it into my office. I have to keep Tabby employed. Why should she be out of a job because Dad and I can't get along."

"Tabby? That's quite a name. Is she pretty?"

"Yes, she's gorgeous. But that still makes her only the second prettiest girl I know. You're the prettiest." I blushed, and he leaned over to kiss me. "Don't worry about anything, Kya. I'm not interested in anyone else."

"Good. I'm not either." It was nice to hear that come from his lips, and I wondered if this could finally be the time for us. It had been a long time coming, and if anything could work out between us, maybe it just needed time.

I sank back against the pillow thinking of Addison. I needed to figure out what I was going to do about her. He had the right to know I had a daughter, at the very least, and it wasn't like I could keep shoving her things in a closet forever or pawning her off to Sadie whenever he came around. Nope, I'd have to make an introduction soon enough. The thought of that made me nervous. What if they didn't hit it off?

I had always been careful not to get too deep in relationships because I didn't want to confuse Addie, but this time, it was different. This was Leonard. Leo. *Leo. Leo.* I wasn't sure I'd ever get used to it.

"What are you thinking?" His voice had me opening my eyes.

"Just about this case. Part of me wishes I'd never filed suit, that I'd just let it be and not have disrupted so many lives with it, and then the other part of me, well, I'm glad I did it. I've missed you." I leaned over and kissed his lips.

"I'm glad you did it, too, not only because you deserve justice, but because I've missed you too. I hate that we wasted so many years upset with each other."

"You were upset with me?"

"I was upset with myself, honestly. I know it was easy to blame you for what happened before, but I wanted to kick my own ass every day I was without you for how I handled things."

"Did you ever want to reach out?"

"At times, but I figured you were better off without me."

"I used to think that, too, about you." I had wondered many times if I should reach out to him and tell him all about my life and what I'd been up to. "I always thought you'd probably moved on to someone new."

"I've never found anyone like you, Kya. I won't even lie and say I never tried, but I guess I've known in my heart for ages that you were the only girl for me."

The words were all too much, and for the second time that day, I had tears overtake me. I wiped them away quickly and then turned over on my side to face him. That's when I caught a glimpse of the alarm clock by my bed. "Oh, shit!" I was late to pick up Addie. I jumped up and looked for my clothes.

He sat up and quickly found his shirt. "What's the matter?"

I gripped my forehead with my fingers and knew I couldn't tell him everything. At least not yet. "I've got to be somewhere. I nearly forgot. I am so sorry."

He shrugged on his shirt and then stepped into his pants before doing up any buttons. "It's cool. I should go anyway. I need to take a look at this case from your side. We'll get together soon and talk about our options."

"Awesome. I can't wait to tell Sadie and the rest of the band. She's going to be excited."

"Good. Glad I could help." He kissed me and then found his shoes and slipped them on.

I grabbed my sandals and a pair of yoga pants. I got a T-shirt from the top drawer, and after one more kiss goodbye, he left.

I couldn't believe I nearly forgot all about my daughter. I was a horrible mother.

21

LEO

A few days had passed since I promised Kya we'd get together, but at least I'd gotten settled into a new office, and Tabby was pleased with the location.

"Thanks again for choosing this place. It's so close to my house, I can go home for lunch."

I didn't mind, either, because it was not only closer to my house but Kya's as well, and with any luck, I'd be spending a lot more time at her house. The sex we'd had the other day had been amazing, and it had motivated me to get things all set up away from my father so I could focus on the case.

"I'm glad you like it. I was afraid you wouldn't. We didn't have a lot to choose from, and it's going to cost a small fortune to keep us here, so we'd better get to work." I gave her a wink and went to my office.

I sat behind my desk as I answered, "Hello?"

"Leo, don't hate me."

I smiled at the sound of her voice. "I could never hate you, Kya."

She groaned. "You might. I've had something come up, and I'm not sure I'm going to be able to make it today."

"Oh no, that is bad. I need to nail things down and get our information over to my father's office by the end of the day."

"Okay, I'll come."

I heard a quiet cough in the distance and wondered if that had anything to do with it. "Is it Sadie? I really need her to come too, baby. I've got to have your signatures as well as Liam and Rob, who already made other arrangements, but I can't continue without this meeting, and besides, I've already made reservations for us for lunch." I thought having lunch would be a much more laid-back environment.

"No, it's fine. Don't worry. We'll be there." She hung up the phone, and I hated that something had come up. If it weren't important, I'd have never argued, but as it was, getting things to my father in a timely manner was going to be beneficial to our case. We didn't want him making any moves first.

I tidied up my new office for the next hour, and when it was time to leave, I found Tabby putting my law books on their new shelf.

"I'm heading out to lunch. If you go home, don't forget to lock up. Do you remember how to set the alarm?"

"Yeah, I've got it. Good luck." She gave me a warm smile and followed me to the door where she locked the door behind me.

I headed to the restaurant and found the private table was ready. I ordered a drink while I waited, and Sadie showed up on time without Kya.

"Hi, you must be Leonard Pace. Kya's told me so much about you. I feel like we've already met." She extended her hand, and I gave it a shake.

"Nice to finally meet you." I looked around for Kya, hoping she'd be right behind her, but she wasn't. "Please have a seat."

She looked me up and down, her eyes lingering on mine a minute as if I were familiar in some way. "Wow, you're just as handsome as she always said. But then, I know Kya. She has great taste in men."

I didn't mind making small talk with Sadie, but I couldn't help but worry about Kya, especially after the phone call. "Did she change her mind about coming?"

"Ah, no. She had a little something come up, so it was going to take her a few extra minutes to get ready. I told her I'd keep you company, but I figured she'd called you to explain." She raised her hand, and the waiter came over, and she ordered a drink.

As the waiter walked away, I eased back in my seat, glad to hear she'd be along soon enough. "Good."

"So, what do you think about this Whit White asshole?"

"I think you're right to call him an asshole, for one. I can't wait to nail his balls to the floor. He's not been very kind in the things he's said about you and Kya. I couldn't stand for it any longer."

"Wise choice."

"How is Susan? Any word on her condition?" I thought it only polite to ask about her since I'd heard it was Sadie who'd found the woman to be their lawyer.

"She's stable now. Her daughter is still with her, taking care of her, so I'm sure she's about ready to jump from a building."

"Oh? I figured you were a friend of Susan's."

Sadie smiled. "She's okay, and I didn't mind having her as a lawyer, but I talked to her a lot, and let's just say, it didn't take long to see she was a piece of work."

The two of us shared a laugh, and then the waiter brought our drinks. I had just brought mine to my lips when Sadie's head came up across the table, and she smiled. "There she is."

I turned, expecting to see Kya standing alone, but instead, she held the hand of a small, beautiful girl who looked surprisingly a lot like Kya when she was little. She gave me a half-hearted smile as she approached, leading the little one with her.

I rose to greet them. "Leo, this is my daughter, Addison. Addie, this is my friend, Leo."

I suddenly felt fuzzy in the brain as the little girl held onto Kya's leg and looked up at me with eyes that were somehow strangely familiar. She looked so much like her mother, it was eerie.

"Hi, Leo." Her voice was so little like she was, and I pulled her out a chair, and she sat next to Sadie. "Hi, Aunt Sadie."

Sadie leaned over and gave her a hug. "What are you doing playing hooky?"

Kya took the other seat next to me and across from her daughter, but I figured Sadie would help manage the little one. Kya offered an explanation, "She didn't feel good, so she says. I decided to keep her home anyway just in case, but I have a feeling it's the Sadie blues again."

It was odd seeing her in a whole new light, and even though I'd never like dating women with children, I felt like this had to be the one exception to the rule since I felt like I'd known the little girl my whole life.

I took a long pull from my glass and waved the waiter over to order another. Kya got the two of them settled and ordered something for her and her child. I turned and met her eyes, doing my best to give her a warm smile even though I wanted to ask her where the father was and about sixty other questions that would have to wait while we were alone. "I can't get over how much she looks like you," I said, knowing I needed to say something.

"I'm sorry, Leonard. I was going to tell you I had a daughter. It just never came up and didn't feel like the right time."

"The two of us, right, Mama?" the little girl said.

Kya smiled lovingly across the table. "That's right, sweet pea."

She was an adorable little girl, and it was clear she was the apple of Kya's eye. I felt kind of foolish for thinking she'd not been with anyone since me, foolish and a bit hypocritical. Maybe a little jealous that she had someone else in her life, someone she loved so much.

Sadie cleared her throat. "Maybe we should get down to business?"

"I think that's a good idea," said Kya.

The little girl sat up on her knees when the drinks came a moment later, and then she sipped the cherry cola her mother had ordered her while giving me glances. She looked like she might spill her drink at any moment, but neither woman was concerned. I wasn't used to being around children, at least not since I was one.

Finally, the waiter left after taking our orders, and I felt it okay to start. "I'm going to ask for a little over half, the contract to be dissolved, including any and all past rights. You'll be able to do whatever you want."

Sadie sighed, her shoulders relaxing as she eased back in her chair. "That will be a relief. I was starting to wonder if I was going to have to cough up part of our YouTube earnings. I mean, hey, he's taken half of everything else."

I shook my head and gave her a reassuring look. "Not anymore. I'm going to take that asshole down." I realized as soon as I said it that I shouldn't have cursed in front of the little one who began to giggle. I turned my attention to Kya. "I'm sorry."

Kya reached over and placed her hand on mine. "It's okay. Addie knows that sometimes those words slip out."

"Yeah, Mama says them all the time." Her little cheeks turned red, and I couldn't help but laugh as Kya's eyes widened.

I looked down at her hand on mine and turned my palm up to hold hers. "Is that a fact? I wonder what else Addie could tell me about her mother."

Kya pulled her hand away and pushed her hair behind her ear. "Let's not get sidetracked. As you were saying, I think that's a fair offer considering."

"I think so, too, but they won't take it. That's when we hold strong at half." I glance over to see the little one was digging a cherry from her drink by the stem. She was making me nervous and as the glass turned sideways, the drink nearly spilling over, but not, I reached over and took it from her hands. "Careful there."

That earned a hard glare and then a look of confusion from Addie. Sadie and Kya exchanged a look, and I had to recover or else I'd look like a real asshole. "Here, let's get a spoon. Then you can dip as many of those cherries as you want." I unwrapped my silverware and handed her the spoon.

"Thanks," she said. She went back to spooning cherries, and Kya smiled.

Sadie spoke up. "So, we take half?"

I nodded. "Assuming he's spent half, it's your best bet. Some of that money will have been spent. And if he doesn't bite, then we take it to court, and I will tell you this, with the media attention, the case will be moved up on the docket."

"Whatever you think," said Kya.

Our food came, and while we were getting settled, I heard Addie clear her throat, and then there was a tugging on my cuff. I looked up and leaned in as she handed me her knife. "Oh, you want me to help?"

"Yes, please."

Kya made a move to reach for the plate, "Here, let me help you, Addie."

Addie shook her head at her mother. "Leo is going to help."

"Yeah, I got this." I shrugged like it was the most normal thing in the world for me to tend to the needs of a child, and in fact, I guess it wasn't that big of a deal.

I got that task out of the way and appeared to win the girl over, which was fine by me. She seemed like a good kid, and I knew if Kya had anything to do with it, she was. Still, I couldn't help feeling betrayed, and after we finished, when Sadie offered to take Addison to the bathroom, I took the chance to learn more.

"So, you have a kid."

"I'm so sorry, Leo. I mean, I know it shouldn't be a big deal, but I just wasn't sure how you'd react."

"That's why there were finger paintings on the fridge. I saw them across the counter." I let loose a deep breath and tried to shake off being upset. "Well, she's amazing and really beautiful like her mother."

"She intimidates you, doesn't she?" She gave me an apologetic look.

"It shows? I haven't even been around kids a lot, but I could get used to it. Especially a nice kid like her."

Kya laughed. "Oh, she has her moments."

"Well, she must get that from her father." I'd hoped to segue into the subject and took the chance while I could.

Kya turned pale. "He's not in the picture."

"At all? That's too bad. He's really missing out on a nice little family."

Kya tucked a loose strand of hair behind her ear and tucked her chin like she wasn't sure what to think. "So, does it turn you off of me?"

"No, not at all. I mean, it decreases my chances of sleeping over, but it makes me want to fight for you even harder knowing that asshole took not only from you but from Addie too. I'm going to make this better for you, Kya. For both of you."

"I know you will. And as for sleeping over, Sadie loves to babysit." She gave me a warm smile, and I leaned over and gave her a quick kiss on the lips before Sadie or Addie returned.

22

KYA

Addie was so full of energy after lunch with Leo and enjoying her day with Aunt Sadie so much that she had apparently forgotten she was supposed to be sick. As we arrived at our house, with Sadie a minute behind, she climbed out of her booster before I could even kill the car.

"I like Leo, Mama. Is he coming over too?"

"No, but I'm glad you like him. I've known him since I was your age almost." I opened the car door and climbed out, but instead of letting me open her door, she climbed over my seat, and I helped her to the ground safely.

"Were you little kids?"

"Of course, we were, no bigger than you once, and we lived next door to one another." I remembered those times and smiled. It seemed so odd to me that even though we went through high school together, those younger years were the ones I cherished. But then, Leo had become such an introvert, locking himself in his room and playing Zombie games until most everyone in our class forgot about him. Except for me. I never did. I just wondered what I did for him to not want to hang out with me anymore.

Even though I could have told her about him all day and never tire, she forgot all about me and Leonard as soon as Sadie got out of her car. She ran over and attacked Sadie's legs. "Aunt Sadie! Will you paint my fingernails again?"

Sadie looked up at me for approval, and when I nodded, she turned back to her. "Sure, sweetie. What color this time?"

"Blue! I want to be a mermaid again!" She took off to the door and waited while I got my bag from the car and locked the doors.

A car passed slowly by, and a man stuck a camera lens out the window and started to snap photos.

"Shit, keep your head down, Addie. Sadie, let's get in the house." After a tense moment, we hurried inside.

I dropped my bag on the kitchen counter while Sadie plopped down on the sofa and raised her chin to peek out the window across the room. "I can't believe those vultures are already starting."

"Yeah, it's a bit early for that." The man's camera was as scary as a gun being pointed at us. I preferred to keep my life private off stage, especially where my daughter was concerned.

She shook her head. "He's still out there."

"Yeah. I think he followed us from the restaurant. He'll go away." He wasn't the first asshole to try and take our pictures without permission, and the sad thing was being used to it.

She turned her attention back to me. "That meal was amazing, Kya, and Leo was nice to treat us, but we need to talk."

I walked around to join her as Addie went to her room. "What do you mean?"

"I thought we were meeting with him to discuss hiring him, but it seems he's already hired."

"No. I told you he was taking the case."

"You said we were meeting with him about him taking the case. He's one of the best in the city, and I'm not sure we can afford him, especially since he's going to try and get half of what we're asking for."

I suddenly realized we didn't see eye to eye on the case. "Do you want this to go to trial? To be long and drawn out? I know we've talked, and you said otherwise."

She turned and glanced down the hall. "Have you told him?"

"Told him what?" I shrugged not sure which of the hundred things the case involved that I might have failed to mention. "He knows everything we told Susan. He's prepared for this better than anyone, and he even has a look at the other side. We can't lose."

Sadie looked at me like I was daft. "You know damned good and well that's not what I mean, Kya. Did you tell him about Addie?" She lowered her voice and glanced over her shoulder again. "You know, that she's his daughter? Cause it sure seems like you didn't."

I knew she was right, but I still felt like baby steps were the way to go. He'd been out of sorts just finding out I had a child. He'd flip out knowing he had one too. "I'll tell him. It's just never the right time."

"And what happens when he finds out you lied? It could backfire big time, Kya. Especially if you want to pursue something with him. He needs to know now."

"Okay. I'll tell him. I thought you wanted to come over and discuss the case and the next YouTube video, not what I should do about Leo."

Sadie shrugged and moved to the edge of her seat. "Fine, I think he should go for more than half. I want Whit to pay, and Leo's idea just feels like a slap. Besides, the asshole needs to do time."

"I agree, but I don't want my daughter or our careers, for that matter, to suffer a drawn-out court case in the public eye. You know how the press can be brutal. And look," I gestured to the window where out in the street, the man was parked waiting for us to go out again. "That is only going to get worse."

"You could have asked me about hiring him, and how are we paying?"

I got up and went to the kitchen to fix a drink. "He's doing it for free, so stop worrying about that. Do you want something to drink?"

Sadie ignored my offer as she got up and followed me. "Free, huh? Let's just hope he doesn't take it out of your heart this time."

"It's different this time. We both realize our past mistakes and what a waste of time they were." I poured her a glass of lemonade anyway, and she took it leaning against the counter with me where we stood to finish our conversation.

"Which is all the more reason to tell him about Addison before it's too late. You're lying to him, Kya. Every single day you don't tell him is only going to add to the pain when he learns the truth."

The truth hurt, and I took a long pull from my glass and closed my eyes. "I know you're right, okay. I'll look for the right time next time I see him, and I'll tell him." The thought of doing so scared me to death. I didn't want to lose him again.

Sadie let out a long sigh. "I thought we'd covered the dos and don'ts of contour and highlighting. Someone's got to tell these girls that putting a big glowing dot on the tips of their noses is only going to make them cross-eyed in a few years."

"I'm with you, and thanks for keeping me straight too. I've just been so nervous with him back in my life. I mean, what if it's just for a little while? I guess a part of me is afraid that if things don't work out, it might not just be me with the broken heart."

Addie walked through the door with three colors of blue nail polish she'd gotten from our bathroom. "Mama, will you let me paint each finger a different color?"

"Yes. But take that to the table before you drop it. I don't want to clean up busted bottles from this tile."

She headed to the table, and Sadie followed, picking a bottle from the collection. "Hey, I remember this one." She held up a bottle of blue metallic that I'd bought on the road in Columbus, Ohio.

"That was a great show. I'd bought a metallic blue dress that matched, remember?"

"Yes, how could I forget spending an hour cutting slits in it to show off the fishnet body stocking you had on beneath it." She laughed so hard, she snorted.

"It looked great. That's before I had my baby body." I slapped my hips and then rubbed Addie's head.

She turned her head, glancing up at me with a smile.

Addie separated the bottles into groups. "I want to do these three."

"I'll do mine too," said Sadie, "and if we're lucky, we'll get your mom to do hers. Then we'll all match."

"Can we go and show Leo our nails?" asked Addie bouncing in her seat.

"He's probably working, sweet pea. We'll have to wait and see if we see him again. Besides, you should probably take it easy since you're not feeling well, remember?" Sadie and I exchanged a smile.

Sadie brushed the polish onto Addie's tiny nail. "Do you like Leo?"

"He's nice. He cut my chicken faster and smaller than Mama, and he's handsome." A little giggle chimed from her throat. "Do you think he likes me too?"

"I'm sure he loved you, kiddo."

"Can I make him some cookies?"

Sadie frowned and looked up from her hand. "Hey, as long as you remember your Aunt Sadie's sweet tooth, I'm good with that."

"Maybe tomorrow. It's Saturday."

Addie's eyes widened. "No school tomorrow too?"

"That's right, you little faker, no school tomorrow too." I gave her a wink, and the three of us laughed as Sadie finished painting her nails.

As I watched, I wondered if Addison had made as big an impression on Leo as he had on her.

23

LEO

I hadn't heard a peep from my father or Jon since I'd left, and I was more than curious if my father had given Jon the case. I had a feeling since he was already involved that it would fall in his lap, and I not only wanted to go down and talk to them about my latest move but find out if I was right and apologize to my friend for bailing on him.

As I walked into the office, heads turned, and you would have thought I'd stormed in cursing, rather than offering the kind smiles I gave them as I passed. I rounded the corner and went to my father's end of the hall, and when I walked into Edith's office, she stood from her desk.

"Leonard! It's good to see you, honey. Your father is with Jon."

"Then, I'll just go on in." I shrugged, and as I headed over to the door, she came around the desk after me.

"Wait, I'll let him know you're here."

I reached the door before she did, so I opened it and went on in. "Hello, gentlemen."

My father rose from his desk. "You don't work here anymore, and you're not welcome to come barging into my office."

"It's good to see you, too, Dad." I walked over to where Jon sat and shook his hand. Then, I took the seat next to him. "Jon, how's it going?"

"Hey, Leo. You look like you're in a good mood. I'm not sure I want to know why."

"I just wanted to announce that I'm officially representing Sabbath Sundae in the lawsuit and let you know that, as of this morning, I've filed for a hearing. I thought I'd give you a head's up."

"We don't need your head's up, Leonard," said my father. "I've got Jon on the case now. He's willing to do what it takes to get the job done, so you better watch your back. We're going to clean the courtroom with you and that Kya Campbell."

"Kya is doing great, by the way. She had a daughter, lives across town in a fine home. You know, in case you were wondering about our old friend." I still couldn't believe he was going against her. I turned my attention to Jon. "No hard feelings, man. I know what it is like for the old man to have you by the nuts. I wish you luck."

Jon didn't look pleased. He gave me a nod but otherwise didn't have a lot to say. Which was fine with me.

My Dad, however, wasn't finished. "I hope you know what you're doing, son. Not only have you gone against your father, but the best lawyer, and people are going to see you as a traitor. Your entire reputation is on the line, and you'll end up looking like a fool when we win this."

"It's a chance I'll have to take. I have to worry about my integrity, a little something you know nothing about if you think it's okay to try and spin this against Kya. And Jon, I know my father is probably suggested you do the same, but I warn you, friend, make sure you don't."

Jon's expression turned grim, and he looked away from me, which told me all I needed to know. My father had already put the ball in motion to try and pin something on Kya or make her look bad.

"I'm prepared to offer a settlement, so when it comes down, I'd be prepared to take it. Deep down, you know you're going to lose. Jon knows it, too, but your ego won't let you admit I'm right." I got up and straightened my cuffs and tie and walked over to the door.

"Have a good day down at the new office, son."

I turned back with a grin so wide it might convince someone I was happy with the situation. "Son? I've never been a son. To you, I was nothing more than a mistake. You've made that painfully obvious through the years, and even clearer now with this case. If you cared anything about me, I'd still be down the hall."

"Well, as it turns out, that's Jon's office now." It didn't surprise me that Jon had taken the opportunities as they came, and I couldn't blame him. His record wasn't as good as mine, and he couldn't just walk away from my father as easily.

I walked over and offered him a hand. "Congratulations, man. You deserve it." After he reluctantly took my hand, I squeezed his firmly and met his eyes. "Seriously, no hard feelings."

I turned and left, unable to get out of there fast enough. My jaw was set so tight, my smile permanently locked on my face, at least until I got to the parking garage where I let out a growl like a feral dog. I couldn't believe the audacity of my father or the way he was willing to try and pit my friends against me. By the looks on the faces of my former coworkers, he'd told them all about the way I'd left, but probably not the reason why. No, he'd never tell them anything to make himself look bad.

I shrugged it off as I got in my car. It didn't matter. None of them did. The only people I had to be concerned about was Kya and her band and that sweet little girl of hers. If my father dragged Kya into this as a knowing accomplice, which they'd first have to prove, it could be horrible for not only her but her daughter. If her career was tainted with scandal, it could threaten her livelihood.

I sped out of the parking garage the very same way I had the last time I'd been to my father's office, and while I didn't regret the visit, I knew it would be a long time before I ever came back.

I checked the time and wondered if I should head back to the office or if I should take a detour and see if Kya was home. I took the next exit without much thought and hoped I'd find her alone.

I pulled up to her house, and when I opened the door to get out of the car, I saw a man in a car across the street who appeared to be pointing a camera in my direction. About the time I started to call out to him, Kya opened the door, and he put up his window.

"I see you met my new friend. I call him Snoop."

I walked up to the house and looked back over my shoulder to see the man was looking straight ahead as if he hadn't just been trying to take my picture seconds before. "How long has he been out there?"

She stepped aside and waved me in. "He was here Friday when we got home from the restaurant, and he came around for a few hours on Saturday and Sunday. I had to put a scarf over Addie's face this morning to get her to school, and thank goodness the asshole didn't follow us, but he's been here ever since."

"I'll go out and talk to him."

"Are you sure that's a good idea? The press knows about the case, and they just want a glimpse at how I'm doing with everything going on. I've already explained things to Addie, and it's not the first time we've had to hide from paparazzi. I have sold millions of songs, remember?"

It was hard to remember sometimes that she had a following. "I don't want him stalking you. Besides, don't you want to know who he is? It might not be case-related." I turned and reached for the knob, and before she could stop me, I was halfway down the front walk.

The asshole was looking down at something, and when I tapped on the glass, he looked up, his brows raising over the sunglasses he wore, even though it was cloudy out. And then I saw it, the tattoo on his arm that told me exactly who he was. "Hey, Milton. I see the old man is already working his angle."

"You know it's the way the game is played. I was told to keep an eye on her."

"And find dirt?"

"You being here in the middle of the day is very interesting, to say the least."

"Yeah, well she called me up and told me there was some horrible asshole out front taking pictures of her and her minor daughter. So, unless you want me to call and report you for child stalking, I suggest you roll."

"Fine, I will roll out today, but I'll be back. I do have a job to do, whether you like it or not. And hey, I hear you've got your own place, so I don't mind giving you the same deal as your old man if you ever need my services."

"Leave her alone, and I'll keep it in mind."

He threw his head back and laughed. "Now, Leo, you know I can't do that. A deal is a deal, and I'm going to dig something up on that little lady friend of yours. Something really juicy."

"Beat it, or I'm calling the police." I stepped away as he started his car, and by the time I got to the door, he was gone.

My adrenaline was pumping even harder than before, and as I walked into the house, Kya met me at the door. She placed her hand on my arm. "What did he say?"

I hated to admit why the asshole had been stalking her, and it was just like my father to try and dig up dirt on Kya with no regard for me or my feelings on the matter. "I'm afraid it's my fault he's here."

"What?" She narrowed her eyes.

"My father. I should have told you, Kya, but I'd really hoped that by my leaving, he wouldn't go through with it."

"Go through with what? What are you talking about?"

"My father wanted me to try and make it look like you were an accomplice in the embezzlement. He wanted me to try and build the case to look like even though Whit had done those things, you were the orchestrator."

"What? How? It doesn't even make any sense. I'm the one who filed the lawsuit against him."

"Yes, and Dad wanted to make it look like you were jilted in some way, that you filed the suit to get back at Whit and falsely accuse him."

She met my eyes and folded her arms in front of her. "How could your dad do that to me? I mean, I've known him all my life."

I knew how she felt. "I've known him all my life, too, and it hasn't stopped him from being a complete asshole to me. Or from trying to push me into shit I didn't want to do. So that's the main reason I quit the case, aside from not being able to go against you and the fact that you're my oldest friend."

She stepped closer as I took her in my arms. "Damn, I always knew your dad was a piece of work, but shit. What does he think he's going to find?"

I kissed her forehead. "It wouldn't matter if he finds something or not. Even if he invents something, it could cause enough doubt, and you'd lose the case."

"That's crazy."

"I agree. Look, don't worry, okay? I'm not going to let anything happen to you." I pressed my lips to hers and kissed her deeply.

24

KYA

Knowing Leonard's father was coming after me had hurt more than anything, but with Leonard on my side and offering to help me through it meant everything. I hated that I'd come between them, and as he broke the kiss, his eyes meeting mine, I had to tell him so. "I feel like this is all my fault, you leaving your father's firm. I mean, I know the case is my fault, but you two shouldn't be fighting because of me. He's your father."

"He's wrong. What he's doing is wrong. I care about you, Kya, more than I've ever cared about anyone else, and I meant what I said. I'm going to fight for you and protect you." His lips crushed back down to mine, and I melted against him.

I'd never realized how much I did need and want him in my life, not only to protect me or take care of me but to just have someone by my side. I had to tell him what happened five years ago, and I wondered if he'd done any of the math.

I'd found out I was pregnant two weeks after we'd hooked up, and while I was certain it was his, I was still broken and bitter about him jilting me. He'd returned to his life, and since he had just come off another graduation, another milestone in his life, I didn't want to ruin his path. It had been part of the reason I'd turned him down the first time. I knew we were heading in different directions, and who was I to impose myself in his life? He had a great big future ahead without me.

His hand brushed up my back and down again, and then he cupped my ass and brought me closer as his lips caressed mine. I never wanted the kiss to end, but when it did, his mouth found my breasts, and as he slid his hand up my shirt, cupping them from below, the thoughts about the past slipped farther and farther away.

"Can we go to the bedroom?" he asked.

I took his hand and brought it away from me. "Yes."

He followed me down the hall and leaned close to my ear. "Do you have to pick Addie up from school?"

"Yes, but not until three, so we have a little time." The warmth of his breath gave me tingles, and as I opened the bedroom door, he lifted up his shirt and pulled it over his head.

I followed his lead and pulled off my T-shirt, and then I slipped my yoga pants off as he kicked off his shoes. When all of our clothes were on the floor, he pulled me close, and his hand fell on my face, softly caressing me, his lips devouring mine as we lay back on the bed.

He rose up and met my eyes. "You took such good care of me last time that I want to return the favor." His hand rubbed against my mound, brushing the short crop of hair as he parted my folds and rubbed my clit.

As the pleasure coursed through me, I giggled. "I was a good girl, huh?" I smiled as he leaned forward and kissed my nipples, tugging the tender flesh gently with his teeth.

"You were amazing." He waggled his brow and dipped down to kiss my tummy. Then, his tongue trailed all the way down to my center where he stroked and licked until I came.

As the pleasure curled my toes, he continued relentlessly worshiping my sex until I begged, "Please, I want you inside of me. I need it."

He looked up and chuckled. "I'll tell you what you need, baby. You need more of this, and besides, I like to hear you beg for it." He dipped his head and returned to his task and this time, he pushed two fingers deep into my channel and stroked my slick, tender walls, spreading his fingers to stretch and prep me for his thick cock.

I imagined it there, filling me up, curing the ache that was coiled deep. "Please," I begged, but he didn't stop.

I felt a rush of ecstasy come over me, and soon, my walls clenched tightly around his fingers. He kissed my inner thigh as he worked me with his hand, and then he kissed my clit, licking and flicking as the pleasure continued to quake.

Only when I was soaked, my honey coating his fingers, did he pull them free and push them into my mouth. "Taste it. Taste your pleasure."

I sucked his fingers clean as he rose up and centered his cock at my entrance. "Yes," I whispered, happy to get what I wanted.

He teased me with his head, rubbing it up and down my slit. "You are so eager for it, aren't you?"

I moaned, knowing how amazing it was going to feel when it penetrated me. "Yes, I need it." I moved my hips, rubbing against him, coaxing him to give me what I wanted.

He reached down and hitched me up, bringing my ass off the bed against him as my legs went over his shoulders. Then, he sank deep, giving me more of his cock in one thrust than ever before. I cried out and moved against him, grinding my hips, riding his cock as he stood still.

All of a sudden, the world went topsy-turvy, and he rolled us over. I settled on top of him as he held me close. "Ride it. It's all yours." He settled back against the pillows and bucked his hips to bounce me. My breasts jiggled, slapping together in a steady beat.

I moaned, and when the feeling of pleasure came over me, I looked into his eyes, leaned over, and kissed him. I had never had anyone give me so much and take me to limits I'd never felt like he did. He made sex exciting, almost like a new experience, and I knew at that moment, I would never want to be with anyone else. I'd never need more than the experience I shared with him.

Before I knew it, he was rolling us back over, and he picked up the pace, slamming his hips into me, but when he came, he pulled out and shot his load across my tits.

When I looked down at my chest, he reached over to the bedside table for a handful of tissues, which he promptly used to clean me up. I wasn't sure why he'd suddenly decided to pull out, but I had a feeling it had to do with the fact that I already had one child, and he probably didn't want to get caught up fathering a baby.

"I'm on shots. I can't get pregnant."

"I know, but I just thought I'd take extra precaution. You never know, and I heard that once you've already had a kid, you're easier to get pregnant."

"Right. Which is why I take the shots. But don't worry, it's no big deal." For some reason, as silly as it was, I felt rejected. I turned my head and was about to get up when he took my hand.

"It's obviously a big deal."

"No, it's not." I wanted to say he could have taken extra precautions five years ago, but even though Addison had come as a surprise, I had never regretted her. She was the one shining light in my life, and I wouldn't trade her for anything in the world, not even Leonard.

" I didn't mean to upset you. I just think that you've got a kid, so maybe we shouldn't take any chances. Besides, I don't want any."

The comment cut me deeply. "I see." I got up from the bed and found my robe.

"No, hey, don't be upset. That came out all wrong."

"Look, it's no big deal. It's your choice where you put your load, okay? I'm not making an issue of it, and I get it. You don't want kids."

" I didn't say I don't want any. I do someday, but can you honestly say you want another one right now?"

"No, I don't, especially not with you."

"Ouch." He walked around and grabbed my shoulders. "What's this all about?"

"Nothing, okay?" I sure as hell wasn't going to tell him Addison was his, not seconds after he'd said all of that. To make sure he knew I was okay, I leaned in and kissed him.

He pulled away, staring deep into my eyes. "I thought we might take a shower. You still have time."

"Okay. I'll get the water going."

He slapped me on the behind and then followed me into the bathroom. He reached and turned on the water and then pulled me against him. Our mouths met, and that was fine with me because I had nothing more to say. I didn't want to fight with him and needed to enjoy his company in a way that would take my mind off everything that had happened with the case and his father and even what had happened five years ago.

He stepped behind me, moving my hair over my shoulder so he could kiss my neck. His hands moved up my front, stroking my breasts, and while it felt amazing, it also seemed distant, and I didn't want things to be that way with him again.

I spun around and gripped his cock and stroked it, taking charge, and as he lifted me up, putting my back to the tiled wall. "For a minute there, I thought I really messed things up." He moved against me, holding me tight as he moved me up and down on his cock.

"It's going to take a lot more to get rid of me this time, Leonard."

"Good, because I don't plan on going anywhere. And nothing is going to make me want to mess up as I did before." He rocked against me and met my eyes, and I knew I could still trust him.

After giving me another orgasm, he put me down to give our legs a break, and as soon as my feet hit the floor, I dropped to my knees and stroked his cock. And when I closed my lips around his head, I licked the tiny slit with the tip of my tongue gathering a taste of him. The spray hit my back, and he shivered as I grabbed his balls and gave them a tug. "Fuck that feels amazing. I'm so close, Kya."

I looked up and met his eyes, relaxing my throat to take him deeper still. When he hit the back of my throat, I fought my reflexes and pushed, settling his head at the very back of my throat, and when I pulled away, he cried out, his primal growl announcing his release.

When I got to my feet, he took me into his arms and pulled me close. He buried his head in the crook of my neck, and we stood there, letting the hot water run for what seemed like forever. The two of us without a word between us, until he pulled back and met my eyes. "I've needed that, just to hold you, for a long time now."

I looked up at him and realized that he really did miss me as much as I'd missed him. It was time I told him about Addison, but as I went to speak, I couldn't.

As if he saw the pain in my eyes, he drew me close. "What is it?"

"I just don't want the moment to end, is all. And, well, I better go get Addie." I had chickened out, but considering we'd already had one awkward moment between us, I wanted to think of a better time and place.

25

LEO

I checked my phone for the time as I got out of my car, and before I went inside, I turned and checked over my shoulder for Milton's car. It had been two weeks since I ran him off, but he'd only been scarce for the past few days. I guess he realized he wasn't going to find anything on Kya. And if anything was said about me being over so often, I'd tell him my hanging around was only because he'd been hanging around.

The case had hit a lull, and now that we were waiting on the hearing, which had been pushed back a week because of another high-profile lawsuit we still hadn't been able to make the offer to settle. Other than another press conference, which was why I was on my way to pick up Kya, things were moving slowly.

I had been around an awful lot, and not only was Kya and I stronger than ever, but Addison and I had hit it off. How could I not fall in love with a tiny version of Kya who baked me cookies?

I walked up to the door, and Addie opened it as Kya ran up behind her. "I told you not to open that door until he knocked." I'd told them to be very careful about opening the door for just anyone, and I'd told them I'd use a secret knock.

"But I saw him through the window."

"Still, we don't want that man taking your picture again."

I knew better than to undermine her authority, so I kept my lips sealed until after my hug. "How are my favorite girls?" I leaned in toward Kya to get a kiss as Addie tugged my suit coat. I leaned down to get a big kiss, and then she ran off to the kitchen.

"You'll never guess what I made you!" she screamed all the way to the kitchen.

I glanced at Kya. "More cookies?"

"She's in a creative rut, but she did make these with extra chocolate chips."

"My favorite."

Kya giggled, and as she stepped away, I got a better look at her. She had put on a pretty purple dress, and even though she played down her makeup and hair, she still looked like a rock goddess. "You look amazing."

"Thank you. As do you." She let her eyes wander, and I relished in the attention. "So, are we ready for this conference? You know the press is going to rail you for switching sides."

"I'll have to tell it like it is, that there was too much corruption on the other side." I would have to keep my answers short and sweet, and hopefully, we'd make it through the thing without any surprises.

Addie walked around the corner with a plate of cookies. "Look, double chips." She took one from the plate, which she was dangerously close to spilling, and yet, once again managed not to. "Here, taste it."

I hadn't planned on eating anything before the conference, but I couldn't say no to her. I took the small cookie and bit it. "Mm. Absolute perfection. You are quite the little baker."

"Really?" She smiled.

"Yes. You're so talented, just like your mother."

"I'm going to sing too," Addie said. "I'm going to have a concert in the park under a rainbow."

"That would be amazing."

"She calls the stage lights rainbows because they're blue and pink," Kya explained.

"Yeah, and I want smoke, too, but not the stinky kind. Mama has a smoke machine that makes the place smell like cotton candy."

"That's Papa Blitz's vape, sweetie, not the stage smoke."

"Oh, right."

"Papa Blitz?" I hadn't ever heard her talk about another man in their lives, but I knew Blitz Hunter was a friend of hers.

Kya nodded and offered an explanation, "Blitz Hunter from The Deathgrips. She calls him Papa Blitz. He's like a grandfather to her."

Addie put the plate on the floor and sat down beside it. "Papa Blitz is the best. Uncle Stones said he loves me more than him, and he's his own son." She picked up a cookie and bit it.

My eyes widened. "Stones?" What kind of name was Stones?

"He's Blitz's son and Sadie's boyfriend. He's going to watch Addie while we go down to the conference."

I figured she must have known him well to ask him to watch Addie for her, but that was her business, not mine. "That's quite a name."

"He's named after the Rolling Stones. He's got a brother named Zep and one named Angus, but those two aren't musicians."

"Well, maybe he'll like me if I tell him my last name's Skynyrd," I teased.

"Is it?" asked Addie, who munched the cookie while stacking the others one atop another.

The doorbell rang, turning our attention, and Kya went to answer it. Sadie came in dressed like a million bucks, followed by a long-haired guy who had so much ink, if he got another tattoo, he'd have to hold it in his hand.

"Uncle Stones!" Addison got to her feet and ran across the room to jump up in the man's arms. I felt a pang of jealousy I knew I had no right to. He kissed her cheek, and she wrapped her arms around his neck like he was her most favorite person in the world.

"Stones, this is Leonard. He's my friend and our attorney."

"What's up? Cool name," said Stones as he held out his hand.

I shook his hand. "Thanks." I turned and glanced at Kya who smiled. "I guess we can leave whenever you ladies are ready?"

"Yeah, give me a minute, would you?" asked Sadie, who was holding up a hair clip. "I'll meet you in the car." She headed to the bathroom, and after telling Stones and Addie goodbye, Kya and I walked out to the car.

"Seems like Addie loves him a lot." I tried not to sound bitter and convince myself it was good for her to have role models in her life, father figures.

"Yeah, he's been around her whole life. She grew up on the road with us for the most part. I've only recently settled us down so she could start school in an actual classroom, but her on-the-road tutor, who's about to marry my bassist Liam, worked wonders with her."

"And what about her father? I know you said he's not in the picture, but who was he? Someone from a band?"

Her eyes widened, and then she looked over my shoulder to Sadie coming. "I'll tell you all about it later, but now's not the time."

I wondered if Sadie was as in the dark about Addison's father as me. Maybe she didn't like him or something, and maybe that's why Kya didn't want it brought up with the woman about to get in the car.

I dropped the subject and hoped it was going to be okay to ask again. I felt like if I would be in her life, I should know those kinds of things. And I did plan on being around. For a long time.

When we got to the courthouse media room, the crowd was already forming, and I held hands with both ladies to make a united front.

It didn't surprise me to see Milton there, and he was talking to a woman in the back of the room. Jon and Whit stood together feet away to observe, and even though I wasn't happy Jon had remained on the case, I couldn't blame him. I had left him in a tight spot with very little options.

After a moment, we were introduced, and I stepped up, bringing the two women up with me. "Hello, it's good to see you all again, and unlike last time, when I didn't have all the facts in the case, I'm here to say it is now my belief that Mr. White owes these women and their band what's rightfully theirs and what he stole from them. Justice will prevail in this case."

The media went nuts, a million questions coming at me at once. "One at a time, please. I'd like to try and answer your questions."

"I have a question," said a gray-haired man from channel four. "Why did the band agree to hire you after you were already against them on the defense team?"

"As I said, when I first agreed to represent Mr. White, I wasn't aware that he had been deceptive. But I'm also a man of integrity, and when the opportunity to help on the case arose, I knew it was my duty to take the right path in finding justice for the real victims in this, the members of Sabbath Sundae."

Another voice came out of the crowd, "Is it true that you and Ms. Campbell are having an affair?" A woman stepped up, the same woman that Milton had spoken to before the conference started. "Is it also true that you're the estranged father of Ms. Campbell's daughter?"

"That's completely false." I turned, and at the look on Kya's face of such pure shock, I froze.

"You two have a long past, don't you?" said the woman. "In fact, you grew up just next door from one another? Is that completely false as well?"

The conference was falling apart, but I had to regain control. "While it's true Kya Campbell and I do indeed have a friendly relationship, we're here today to focus on the case. According to the evidence, not only did he steal from Ms. Campbell, but he also falsified payroll to afford himself luxury vacations. We're prepared to offer Mr. White a plea agreement." I glanced across the room where I saw Jon. My eyes widened at him, and he gave me a shrug in return. This was his and my father's doing. They had Milton wait outside that house, and they'd put two and two together and come up with the whole thing based on Kya having a child. I couldn't believe I'd told them that. I'd given them the bullet.

It didn't matter, though. All I had to do was take a paternity test and prove that none of their silly allegations were true. I just hated it for Kya, having to go through something like this and being dragged into it. She had suffered enough.

I couldn't believe Jon had gone along with my father and betrayed me that way. He knew how much Kya meant to me. This time, blaming my father alone wouldn't do. I blamed him too.

I answered and avoided a few more questions about the case while Kya stood next to me like she'd been slapped across the face, and Sadie stood with her, equally shocked.

As soon as we got away from the press and into a private room, I spun around and was about to tell Kya how silly it was and apologize for what they'd said, but she broke down in tears.

She fell against me. "I was going to tell you. I'm so sorry you had to find out that way."

I stiffened. "What?"

"I wanted to tell you, but I guess they saw your name on her birth certificate."

Sadie excused herself and went out a side door to give us some privacy.

"Addison is mine?" I still wasn't processing her words when Jon opened the door and stormed into the room.

"I swear I didn't know that was about to happen, man."

Kya took the distraction to run out of the room crying, and even though I spun around to stop her, she left. I turned back to Jon and held my hands out.

Jon tried to close the distance, but I stepped back for every step he took forward. "I promise you, Leo. This was all Whit White."

"Well, turns out, it's true. It's all true."

26

KYA

I ran after Sadie when Leo's friend came into the room, and even though I wanted to stay and fight to explain, all I could think to do was flee. I'd wanted to tell him so many times, and I knew I was getting closer to being able to tell him the truth, but it had always seemed like something was getting in the way. Whether it be Addie and him getting along so good that I didn't want to spoil it, or if it was us in an intimate moment where it seemed like dropping a baby bomb was going to ruin his mood, I just hadn't found the right time.

The biggest reason for keeping up with my secret, though, was wondering if he would bail on me or worse, if he'd try to take our daughter from me.

Sadie called us a car, and we headed straight home. When we walked in, Stones and Addie were watching princesses on the TV. Stone was sitting on the floor, slouched down so Addie could reach his head, and Addie was brushing out his long hair.

"Hey, Mama!"

Stones looked up, his eyes filled with concern. "Back so soon? That didn't take long." He got a peek at my tears, and his nostrils flared. "What happened?"

Sadie cleared her throat. "Addison, why don't you go pick out some polish, and I'll do your nails."

Addie cheered and then disappeared into the bedroom. When she was out of sight, Sadie walked over and took my hand. "Do you want to talk about it?"

"I should have known it would backfire."

Stones cleared his throat. "Hey, someone want to tell me who I need to kill?"

"Easy, killer," whispered Sadie. "Leonard found out Addie is his."

"Holy Shit. That guy?"

I hadn't exactly told anyone else, and apparently, Sadie hadn't informed Stones either.

She swatted his arm. "Yeah, our attorney Leonard. They hooked up the night before we signed Whit."

"And you are just now telling the man?" Stones' judgmental look sent a fresh wave of tears rolling from my eyes.

"I wanted to, but it was so hard. He just looked so shocked. I know he's going to hate me."

Stones walked over and brought his arms around me. "It's okay, Kya. He probably just needs to let it sink in. He'll come around. You're a great little family, and he's got to see that. Hell, a blind man could."

"That's right. He's probably in shock. He was caught totally off-guard."

They were trying, but it wasn't making me feel any better. There was only one person who could do that, and I'd left him back at the courthouse.

Stones walked me to the couch, and I sat down, grabbing the stuffed bunny Addie had left there. Sadie went to the kitchen to get me something to drink. When she came back in the room, there was a knock at the door. My head turned, and Stones went to the door.

"You want me to let him in," he called over his shoulder.

"Yes." I needed to get through this. I'd let it go on this long and had no one to blame but myself. Whatever he needed to do, curse me, yell at me, say goodbye and leave me, I owed him the right to do it.

Sadie handed me the glass of water. "Wait. We'll get Addie and take her for a walk. You two need time alone to talk." I agreed, and she went to get Addie as Stones opened the door.

Leonard stood toe to toe and eye to eye with Stones and looked like he'd come prepared for a fight. "Is Kya here?"

"She's all yours. We're going to take Addison for a walk." Sadie came out of the room, and Leonard watched her as she walked by.

"Hi, Leo! Sadie's taking me to the park!"

Leo stiffened, his eyes turning red as he looked down at her. "That's great. I love the park. Have a good time." He didn't take his eyes off of her until the door was shut and then he slowly turned and looked at me. "I thought her eyes looked familiar. She looks like you so I didn't really bother trying to figure out if she looked like anyone else, especially me. I mean, why would I? It's not like I had any reason to think you'd keep something like this from me."

"I'm sorry, Leonard." I didn't know what else to say.

"It's Leo. I haven't been your Leonard for a long time. But you'd have known that if you'd bothered to call and tell me you were pregnant. I'd have shown you what kind of man I wanted to be for you and our daughter."

"I thought you wouldn't want to give up your life to us. You'd just finished law school, and I was on tour."

"And you never gave me that choice. Did you?" He glared at me as my eyes welled with tears. "I just really came by to make sure you and Sadie made it home. I came out of the courthouse and found you gone.

"Leo, don't go."

"You haven't needed me around for the past five years. You'll be okay while I figure this shit out." He turned and walked to the door, and even though I stood up and called his name, he shut the door behind him.

I could have run to him, but I knew he needed time. I went to my bedroom and lay on the bed crying. Twenty minutes later, Sadie came in. "Stones has Addie and suggested we take her with us. She doesn't need to see you upset."

"He didn't want to talk. He was just being polite and seeing that we made it back. He probably hates me. I can't blame him. I hate myself."

"Hush, you do not. You're Kya fucking Campbell. You're going to pick yourself and dust off and be strong for your daughter. And if that sorry SOB doesn't want to be with you, then who needs him It's his loss."

"What if he wants to take her? He's a lawyer, Sadie."

"Which reminds me. When you get this all out of your system, we need to figure out what this means for the lawsuit. I'm not even sure we can move forward. If he decides to quit us, too, then we may as well give up."

"I'm sorry I made a mess of things. I know you hoped to get your money back."

"Hey, you and Addie are much more important to me than any amount of money, so you remember that, okay? I wanted this to nail that prick to the wall, so Addie would have better. You guys are family. You're what matters to me. Nothing else." She threw her arms around me, and we held each other tight.

"I'll just take a few hours." I pulled away from her and reached beside my bed for a tissue.

Sadie got up and walked to the door. "We'll take her to my house and then bring her back later tonight. I'm sure she just thinks Stones and I want to spend time with her, which we do."

"Thanks," I said as she turned to walk out.

She stopped and looked over her shoulder. "That's what family's for." She closed the door behind her, and I heard the three of them leave a few minutes later. I rolled over and cried against my pillow. And that's when the past five years came flooding back to me.

I'd started getting sick during the show and having to leave the stage about two weeks after Leonard and I had hooked up. At first, I thought I was just having a hard time eating shitty road food and getting motion sickness on the tour bus, but then I noticed it was especially horrible in the mornings, and Sadie had encouraged me to get a test.

We stopped off at a drug store in Austin, and with Liam and Rob both waiting with Sadie out front, I peed on the stick and watched the indicator as it revealed a pink plus sign.

When I came out of the bathroom crying, the three of them had huddled around me consoling me and telling me it was all going to be okay. We kept it under wraps until I saw Blitz about two days later, and I'd never forget him walking up to me that day at the Dallas venue. "You have a glow about you, love."

At first, I'd thought Sadie had told Stones, and they'd spilled the beans to Blitz, but then he leaned in closer and brought his arms around me. "No, I just know these things. I've been through it three times with two different women, and I'm telling you, it's always the glow."

I remembered putting my hand to my face and the way he chuckled and asked me if I was going to keep it.

"Of course," I'd said, trying hard not to be offended. I had imagined he was about to kick me off the tour, but instead, he squeezed me tighter and then made me get off my feet.

"That's wonderful news. I never believed in killing off my own, and babies are fucking awesome. You're going to have to take it easy between shows, you know. And I'll make sure you get a room at every venue. You shouldn't be sleeping on that bus so much."

"Thanks. I'm a little scared."

"How does the father feel about all of this?" He gave me a bit of side-eye, and I knew he had to be curious if I even knew who the father was. It wasn't like I had a bad reputation, but I was on the road in a rock band, and anything was possible.

"I don't know if he can't handle it. I told my parents. That went over horribly, so I just don't know if I can face rejection from anyone else."

"Well, my opinion is, he has the right to know. But I'll also respect your wishes, and I won't judge. But if you plan to go into it this way, I'll be here for you, and I'd advise you never try to find him or ask for anything. Shared custody is a bitch on the road. Take my Melinda. She tried to take Angus from me once. Said my lifestyle was unbecoming of a father. Careful what paths you choose because once your feet get the feel beneath you, it's hard to change your course."

As I stared at the ceiling wondering if Leo was ever going to come back, I realized I'd taken Blitz's advice to heart. I had let myself get so used to my lifestyle, I hadn't allowed myself to stray from my path, even though I knew not telling Leo about our child was wrong.

I let my mind drift back to the day Addie was born when Stones and Sadie rushed me down to the ER, and Blitz, Liam, and Rob all made their way down from the venue to see the new member of our tribe. My heart was so full of joy, and though I knew it was wrong not to call Leonard, I never wanted that feeling to end.

27

LEO

The sun peeked through my window announcing it was morning, which was fine with me. I hadn't slept a wink. No matter how hard I'd tried, I couldn't get Kya and Addie out of my mind. I hadn't talked to her since the day of the conference and really didn't know if I could look at her ever again.

As much as I loved her, I couldn't help but be pissed off. I needed a little more time before I went to her and wasn't totally sure what course of action I wanted to take.

Addison was my daughter, and I'd been cheated out of her life since the day she was born. I'd missed out on all the firsts, the walking, the talking, the first day of school, her learning to say daddy, and every single day she could have known who I was, and I could have known her.

I wanted to punch a wall. I got up, knowing I couldn't be alone, but I couldn't really talk to Jon, and even though Dad was the last fucking man I wanted to get a lecture from, I needed to speak to him.

As I brushed my teeth and trimmed my beard, I knew I had to find out why he'd done this. Not only that, but he had a granddaughter he didn't know. Did he even want to see her? Even though

I'd been a total disappointment, maybe she'd make up for it somehow.

I walked to the closet and pulled out some comfortable jeans and a casual, button-down shirt and slipped them on. I found my shoes by the dresser and stepped into them while I grabbed my wallet and shoved it into my pocket. On my way out, I grabbed my keys and headed out to my car.

Being Wednesday morning and so early, the sun had barely begun to shine, I knew my dad had to be home. He never went to the office too early, and on Wednesdays, he liked to have a nice breakfast at home and practice his golf swing for an hour before heading in to work.

I drove up to his new house and wondered if he ever thought about getting remarried after Mom had died. He'd been alone since, and while I knew he'd dated a few women, nothing had lasted.

I walked up to the house and knocked on the door, and a moment later, he answered wearing his long red robe with the black trim. He'd always worn the same kind, and I knew it was because my mother had bought him one every other Christmas for years before she died.

He held his hand up to me and gave me a hard look. "Before you start with me, Leonard, I didn't know Milton would spill what he knew to the press."

"Why even put him on the case in the first place? I told you Kya didn't deserve that, that this case was a joke, and you hired some asshole to stalk Kya and Addison, looking for dirt."

He walked away from the door, leaving me to walk in and close it behind me. Then he waved his hand dismissively when I turned around to go after him. "I didn't know anything about the baby rumor, but it isn't anything a paternity test can't fix."

It was scary that I had also come to that conclusion when I thought it was a mistake. "Oh no, it's not just a rumor. Turns out, it's true. Congratulations, you're a grandfather."

His face paled, and suddenly, he was at a loss for words. We stood in silence, and I gave him a minute to collect himself. I knew how rough that shock could be. He finally looked up from the floor and met my eyes. "You mean to tell me it's true. You really have a child with that woman?"

"I saw Kya five years ago, and yes, I got her pregnant. And I only just found out about it at the conference." I felt like a loser admitting that. I had this amazing little human being in the world, and I didn't even know it. "You should see our little girl. She looks just like Kya but with my eyes."

Dad put his hand to his lips and then held his hand over his heart. "Your mother's eyes?"

"Yeah, Dad. Mom's eyes."

My father turned and began to pace the room, and after a few times back and forth, he stopped and turned his attention back to me. "I regret what happened at the conference, but we're not encouraging the client to take a deal."

I knew he would be stubborn about the case. He had never been one to back down. No matter how much he needed to. "He's going to lose, Dad. There's no way you can win."

"So? I get paid anyway, son. Jon is prepared for trial, and we'll let the cards fall where they may, but I need you to be ready for it."

I had only one more warning for him. "Don't go after Kya. She's the mother of your granddaughter, and the little girl needs a stable home and a stable family. If you do anything for any of us, make sure you don't disrupt that."

He waved his hand as if to calm me down. "Jon already took care of that. He threatened to quit if I insisted he bring Kya up in court. And believe it or not, in light of the child being involved, I agree."

"Her name is Addison, Addie for short." I took out my phone and pulled up a picture I'd taken of Kya and Addie together. "See? Your granddaughter."

Dad's eyes narrowed as a smile played over his face. "She does look like your mom."

"I don't know if I can do this. I've thought about it all night. I want to be with Kya, but this is hard. I'm not sure if I can forgive her. I'm not even sure I can defend her."

"You know, son. I've thought about what you said. How you think I'm disappointed in you. The truth is, I've always been tough on you because I want you to reach your fullest potential. I know there's greatness in you, much more than there is in me. You're a much better man, and I promised your mama I wouldn't let you waste your life not giving it your best. I need you to know you've never let me down, son. Not once. I've never been disappointed in you, not even when you walked out at work. And now, that woman needs you, and so does that little girl. The only thing that could disappoint me is if you let another five years of that girl's life go by without you in it."

"Thanks, Dad."

"I love you, son. I know I don't say it enough, and hell, I barely show it, but I love you, and I'm proud of you." He glanced back down at the phone. "You two sure did make a beautiful kid."

I looked down at the picture too. "She's got good genes."

"I'll see you in court?" His brows rose as he waited for my response.

"Yeah, Dad. I'll see you in court. But I think I should call Jon. I want to make sure things are set and let him know I'm not angry at him."

"He's a good egg, that one. Too bad this case won't improve his record any." We shared a chuckle, and I let myself out.

I walked away from my father for once feeling like things were okay with us instead of like everything was falling apart.

I got in my car and took a deep breath knowing that as badly as I wanted to run to Kya, it was still a tad early and she would be taking Addie to school, so I decided to find Jon, who I figured would be sipping coffee at the office.

I drove down, and this time when I walked in, there weren't as many glares or people looking at me like I was out of place. And sure enough, I found Jon sipping coffee and chatting it up with some of the office staff. They cleared out when I walked over to Jon and extended my hand. "Hey, man. I wanted to talk."

He took my hand and pulled me in for a hug. "How are you?"

I raked my hand through my hair. "A father. Can you believe that shit?"

Jon shook his head and blew out a long breath. "As many women as you were banging, it was bound to happen. Hell, who knows? She might even have a sibling out there somewhere in the world."

"Shit, you're right," I said. "One secret baby at a time." We shared a chuckle, but mine was half-hearted. I had really been a man-whore, and now I had a little girl to be worthy of.

Jon crossed his arms and leaned back on the counter of the office coffee bar. "So, when do I get to meet her?"

"I'll bring her around sometime after I go talk to her mother. I haven't since the press conference, not really talked, you know. I didn't know what to say to her, and I was so angry that I thought if I stayed around, I'd only make it all worse."

He turned and picked up his coffee and took a sip. "You'll figure it out, man. You'll be a great dad."

"Thanks, but speaking of dads, mine told me you stood up for me and Kya, and I appreciate it." He'd finally taken his own stand against my father, and I respected the hell out of him for it.

He turned a soft pink. "Hey, man. That's what best friends do, right? Besides, that's the mother of my best friend's kid. And I have a feeling if I did anything to hurt either one of them, you'd hunt me down and castrate me."

"With rusty scissors." I held my hand up to vow. "Yeah, I had a good talk with the old man earlier. I dropped in on him and was prepared for things to go south, but instead, it was actually the best conversation we've had since I was a kid."

"That's great, man," he said. "Maybe you should have been on your own all along, you know? Paving your own path without all of his pressure."

"I don't know. I have a feeling all of his pressure shaped me, you know. It's hard to believe I'm saying it, but I really feel that's true. I also have a feeling Addison could bring us together and make us closer like Mom used to."

"Addison? That's your daughter?" he asked. Those words were

strange, and claiming a daughter was even stranger, but it also felt kind of nice.

I swelled with pride. "Yeah, we call her Addie." I turned on my phone and showed him a picture.

He leaned over to look and gave me a nudge. "Wow, a beautiful woman and child. You're a lucky man."

I felt a sinking feeling in my chest. "Only if I make things right." I had to get to Kya and tell her how much I loved her and wanted her in my life. I checked the time and saw I had a little while yet. The anticipation and not knowing what would happen had me wound as tight as a coil.

Jon took his last sip of coffee and tossed the cup into the trash. "Well, I know you're probably going to win, but I want you to know I'm going to refuse the settlement. I think my record can handle a loss. Besides, once this shit is over, I'll get all of the cases you would have gotten, so I'm pretty sure I'll get my fair share of winners."

"I think so, too, man. You're a damned fine attorney. This Whit White prick doesn't deserve you."

Jon elbowed me. "Fuck that; *I* don't deserve his sorry ass."

"Too true, brother. I guess I should let you get to work. I think I'll head over and be waiting on Kya when she gets back home."

Jon offered me a fist bump, and I took it. "Good luck, man."

"Thanks," I said. "I need it." I wasn't entirely sure Kya was going to want to keep me in her life.

28

KYA

I woke up on Wednesday morning with the ache still in my heart. I hadn't heard from Leonard since he walked out the day of the conference, and I didn't expect I'd ever hear from him again. Surely, if he was going to remain professional and do all the things he'd promised us on the case, then he'd show up for the court date.

As I dragged myself out of bed and headed down the hall to wake up Addie, I decided that if I hadn't heard from him by lunch, I was going to call him. I didn't want to walk into that courtroom not knowing what I was facing from Whit and his new lawyer, much less be blindsided by my own. If he owed me anything, it was finishing the job he started.

I opened the door to Addie's room and walked over to turn off her nightlight and switch on her lamp. I took a deep breath and slapped on a happy grin, which was so forced, it was nearly painful. All of my feelings aside, I wasn't about to let my daughter see me down.

As I flipped the switch and the room brightened, I gave her my usual morning greeting, "Good morning, sunshine. It's time to get up for school, Addie."

Addie rolled over and groaned. She opened one eye and then brought her fist to her mouth and coughed.

"No, you don't. You didn't have a cough all day yesterday, and you are not laying out of school again."

"But, Mama. I'm feeling really bad. I think my toes are going to fall off."

"Your toes are not going to fall off, but if you aren't up and dressed and at the breakfast table in ten minutes, I'm taking away your TV privileges for a month."

"No more princesses?"

"Nope, I'm not playing around with you. I have too much to do today," Tears welled in my eyes, and my voice cracked. "You're going."

Addie's eyes widened, and she got up from her bed. "I'm sorry, Mama. I'm going." She ran to the bathroom, and even though I hadn't wanted her to think she'd done anything wrong, I'd wait until she was at the table eating before I explained.

I dried my eyes on the way to the kitchen and then washed my hands and had everything ready to pour us both a bowl of cereal.

She rounded the corner and sagged, dragging her little backpack with her. "I don't want cereal again, Mama. Could we go to the diner today?"

I hadn't been to the bank in a week and with me not working to bring in any jobs and taking half of our savings to pay Susan Costanzo her retainer fee, things were tight. Sure, I could dip into the vacation fund, the bill money, or Addie's college fund, but it didn't seem smart to do that for pancakes I could make myself. And if we lost that case, things would be even tighter until I figured it all out. "Not today, sweetie."

"What's wrong, Mama?"

"Life's hard sometimes, sweet pea. It gets hard and makes me sad. And it doesn't help when you fight me on school or where we eat breakfast and other things. You have to learn that I know what's best for you and let me take care of you." I wiped another tear from my eye.

"I'll help. I'll take care of you, too, Mama." She climbed up to the table and pulled the bowls in front of her. Then, she carefully poured us both some cereal.

"Thanks, sweet pea. I'll do the milk, okay?" I took the milk and poured, and as she took her first bite, she looked up and winked. "The two of us." She held out her spoon, and I tapped mine with hers.

"The two of us." I felt another fresh tear escape and quickly wiped it from my cheek. It had been the two of us for so long now, and even though I wished Leo would be a part of our lives, too, I guessed it always would be. It wasn't that I needed a man in my life, but it would have been nice to have someone else around to share in the responsibilities and take care of us both for a change.

Without another fuss, Addie ate her cereal and then grabbed her bag up from the floor when it was time for school. And when we walked out to the car, she even held my hand.

"Mama? Are you going to see Leo today?"

"I'm not sure," I said as I unlocked the car and boosted her into the back. "Why?"

"Just wondering. Maybe he could cheer you up since I'm going to school."

"I bet he could." I gave a half-hearted smile thinking of all the ways he'd made me feel good before. But those times were most likely long gone, another part of my life that used to be.

I took her to school, and after I was done driving her, I went to Sadie's house. She'd asked me to stop over and plan another tutorial, this time on natural looking brows and the sins of over-tweezing. I'd told her I would, but now that the time had come, I really didn't feel up to it.

She opened the front door before I could knock. "Hey, girl, how are you feeling?"

"I'm okay."

"You've got tear streaks, Kya, so I don't buy it. Come on in, and I'll make us some coffee." I followed her in and to the kitchen where she offered me a seat at her bar while she made quick work with the Keurig. "So, have you heard from Leo?"

"No, not since the other day."

"Well, as much as I would love to be mad at him, I guess I can't blame the guy for being in shock, but he needs to grow a pair and come around." She passed me my cup of vanilla cappuccino and then started making her own.

I glanced up from my steaming cup. "I don't know what we're going to do, Sadie. What if he doesn't show up for the trial?" I hated to even think about walking into that courtroom alone only for the judge to see our attorney hadn't even bothered to show up. We'd not only look ridiculous, but we'd lose the case we were a shoe-in to win. "I'm not going to let this go on another day. I plan to call him. I just hope he answers."

Sadie took a stool at the end of the bar to join me. "Well, Leo or not, we're going into that courtroom with our heads high and fight." Sadie raised her fist and bumped mine. "Atta girl. And if he doesn't come around, it's his loss. You've never needed a man in your life to accomplish anything—well, other than becoming a mom, but let's face it, if you wanted that to happen, you could have gone down to a clinic and paid for that."

I knew she was just trying to cheer me up, but it didn't do too much to raise my spirits. All I kept thinking of were all the times I'd missed out on having Leo in my life. It was my own dumb choices that had gotten me in this situation. "I feel like it's all my fault."

She shook her head and reached across the bar to hold my arm. "No, he made the choice to leave this time."

"I mean going back all of those years. If I hadn't broken his heart the first time or let him go even the second time, then maybe he'd have been around that next morning when Whit showed up."

"Life is full of maybes, Kya." She pulled her hand back and raked it through her long, blond hair. "We do the best in making choices when we make them. We can't go back and wish it was all better and live a life of regret. You did the best with what life you had. Would you give up the songs, the tours, the experience you had by living your dream to be a stay-at-home mom and the wife of a lawyer?" I shook my head. "Or do you think poor Leo would have lasted one minute on the road to help you pursue yours? Maybe it's meant to be this way. You have a great life and a family, the best, even if I'm a little biased."

That seemed like it made sense to me, but I couldn't help feeling like there was more to it. "Why can't it be wonderful with Leo in it then, and why did he ever come into my life at all?"

She lifted her shoulders and smiled. "To give you Addison. Maybe she's the only reason."

I put my hand on my heart and rubbed the tender spot. "No, I don't think it would hurt this much if that were true."

"I'm sorry, Kya. I wish it wasn't so bad. I mean, what the hell is up with this guy? Can't he call? He obviously cares, or he wouldn't have come to your house to make sure we made it back. I think he needed to see you. He just didn't know what to say or do."

"It can't be easy. You know the kid never had so much as a puppy growing up. That day at the restaurant, when Addie was drinking her cherry cola, I thought he was going to lose it watching her try to manage the glass. He was like that when he was a kid. Kind of awkward, you know. Now he's back in my life, insisting I call him Leo and so confident that he's not the same guy, but I see him. I see the changes, and I like them, but there are other times when that lanky, geeky four-eyed braces-wearing kid rears his head, and for me, that's okay too. I always loved that kid."

"That's because you're in love with him. I'm jealous of that, you know."

"Come on. You have that with Stones."

"No, I don't. Stones and I probably won't work out. He's never home, and to be honest, when he's gone, the only thing I miss about him is the sex. Honestly, you and Leo have more going on. I'd put my money on the two of you."

"You really don't think you'll make it?" I couldn't believe she thought that, and suddenly, another dream seemed helpless. I had always seen them as the perfect couple when they were together, and even though I knew they kept an open relationship, I'd never seen her with anyone else. Was love an illusion?

She shook her head. "Nah, but don't worry about me. I'm good. One day I'll meet Mr. Wonderful, and he'll sweep me off my feet. Besides, Stones already has a true love, and her name is Wanda." She rolled her eyes, and we both shared a laugh. Wanda was Stones' pride and joy Les Paul. The two had bonded over their instruments, and Sadie's own precious Sally was her mistress as well.

"I think I'm going to pass on YouTubing today. I've got some things to do around the house since I've been in zombie mode."

"No problem. We can wait until Saturday if you want. We'll either use it as a celebration, or we'll both be crying through the whole thing."

"At least we're doing eyebrows and not lashes. We're good." I got to my feet and gave her a hug. "I'll show myself out. You sit and enjoy your coffee. I'll let you know if I hear anything."

"Good, and hey, keep your chin up, Kya. It's all going to work out. We're going to go down there tomorrow and hope for the best."

As I gave her one more hug, I knew she was right. It was going to hurt for a while, but everything was going to be all right.

29

LEO

I had left the office and stopped for coffees and pastries on my way to Kya's. I thought we might have a lot to discuss, and since I hadn't had anything to eat, I didn't want to show up empty-handed.

But when I got to her house, she wasn't there, even though I figured she'd had enough time to go to the school and back. I had a feeling she'd gone to do errands or stopped off to see Sadie. I wondered if she'd brushed herself off and went about life without me as she'd done for the past five years, and before bitterness could set in or anger me, I took a deep breath and then got out of the car. The feel of the warm sun on my face helped a bit, and instead of getting back in the car, I grabbed the pastries and coffee and sat down on her stoop to wait. With my stomach making awful sounds, I decided to nibble the pastry, and before I knew it, I'd gulped down my coffee and finished off two of the pastries.

I'd been stupid to leave without settling things the other day, but I'd felt like I needed time, but now, sitting on the front steps of her house, I felt like time couldn't pass quickly enough to bring her back home.

Just when I thought about giving up, a car approached, and I got to my feet as it slowed and she pulled into the driveway beside my car.

She killed the engine and got out of the car. "Hey," she said. Her voice was rough, and her eyes were puffy from where she'd been crying. I felt a pinch in my chest, and even though she seemed miserable, she was still the most beautiful woman I'd ever laid eyes on.

I held up the box of pastries. "I brought breakfast, but it's cold. I guess I should have called."

She walked past me and unlocked her door. "Yeah, I was at Sadie's."

I turned and wondered if she was going to invite me in or leave me on the front steps. "I figured. I wanted to see you. I thought if I called, you'd tell me to stay away until the trial."

She shook her head as she pushed the door open and went inside. "I wanted to see you too."

I waited for her invitation, knowing I wasn't about to take anything for granted.

She dropped her bag to the little bench by the door. "Are you going to come in or what?"

I hurried in, and she walked away as I shut the door.

"I had to take Addie to school. She didn't fight me today."

I followed her to the kitchen. "She usually fights you?" I placed the pastries and coffee holder down on her kitchen counter.

"Lately. It's a phase. She likes to spend time with Sadie, and since she knows I work with her, she wants to tag along. She usually loves school. She's quite smart for her age, and well, I guess she gets that from you."

It wasn't exactly how I thought the conversation would begin, but as long as we were talking, and I could get to know Addie better, I wouldn't complain. Especially since she'd actually invited me inside instead of leaving me out on the front steps begging. And I would have begged.

"What else is she like?" I wanted to know everything I could and keep her talking as long as possible.

Kya took a deep breath and seemed to think a moment. "She's

creative like me. Likes to perform, but she's cautious around new people like you. I'm not sure if she'll choose to be a brain surgeon or a painter, but I know one thing for sure. Whatever she does, she'll shine at it."

"She already shines, in my opinion." To me, she was completely amazing.

She leaned against the counter, rapping her hands on the top. "That's because she's your daughter. You're biased."

"I guess you're right. I do see her in a new light. She has my mother's eyes, you know, and while I thought she was so familiar and so much like you, I never noticed the resemblance. Now, it's all I can see."

"Strange, isn't it?" She kept her eyes on the counter.

"Yeah." The conversation lulled.

Kya took a deep breath and squared her shoulders. "So, are we all set for tomorrow?"

"Yeah, of course. I think I have everything in order. I know we'll present a good case, and I don't anticipate any surprises."

"But what about what happened at the courthouse? The conference was pretty brutal."

"Yes, it was, and I'm sorry about that. I guess I should explain. I did go to my father and Jon and talk to them about it. The investigator was hired by my father to find something, and in that process, he must have figured out Addison was mine."

Kya nodded. "It probably wasn't hard to do since your name is on the birth certificate."

"Really?" It came as a surprise that she'd done that, but I was glad she had.

"Yeah, I never intended to keep it from you, Leonard. I knew I wanted her to know you. I just—Hell, I don't know how to say I'm sorry. It doesn't seem like enough or like you'd even believe how sorry I am."

"I know, believe me. And look, it was Milton who told the press. My father didn't think it was true, and once he and Jon found out, they don't want to do anything that's going to jeopardize your or

Addison's safety or lives. They promised their plans to drag you into it are not going to happen."

"What if they're backed into a corner? They could still bring up the fact that you're the father of my child."

"That won't matter, and if they do, I'll proudly claim Addison. She's mine, and I'm not ashamed of that. Who would be?"

She nodded and looked back down to the counter. "Thank you. And look, I understand if you don't want to see me. I won't try to keep you from her. I know I owe you a lot of time, and I'm prepared to give it. All I ask is that you ease her into it. I don't want to shock her little system. But we'll tell her as soon as possible."

I reached over and rested my hand on her wrist. "I have a lot of time to make up with you both, and if you think I'm letting either of you go, you're sorely mistaken."

Her face turned up to meet mine, and a tear slid down her cheek. I quickly brushed it away. "Hey, no more of that, okay? We're here, we're together, and it's going to be okay."

She nodded and sniffled, wiping her eyes with her free hand.

I walked around the counter and brought her into my arms. "We both probably made some mistakes between us," I said. "But what's in the past is in the past. I want to look to the future, starting by winning this case together. Then I want to come back here and celebrate our victory with *our* daughter."

A weak smile turned up the corners of her lips. "Its nice hearing you say that. I've always wanted to hear it. I've dreamed of you saying it."

I brought her closer, and she laid her head on my shoulder. "You have no idea how nice it is for me to say it. I keep thinking I'm dreaming and it's not real. But then it is real, and honestly, while it's a lot to get used to, I'm ready for it."

"I shouldn't have cheated you out of the last five years." She trembled as she took a deep breath, and I felt as if she might cry again.

"Sh. No, let's not sit and think about that anymore. The truth is, I've done well, I've matured, and I'm probably a better man for her now than I would have been back then. Maybe this is how it's supposed to have been, and who are we to say otherwise?"

"You're just too good to me. Trying to cheer me up."

"I don't like to see you cry. Never have. Remember that time you fell off your bike? It scared me so badly that I picked you up and carried you home?"

She smiled a lot brighter for me. "I do. You doctored my knee and shared your Easter candy with me. I remember everything we did together."

"Yeah, that was the first time I saw you cry, and I knew you were hurting. I wanted to make it all better so you'd stop. I remember feeling a pain in my chest, and wondering if that pain was sympathy or love."

"Did you ever figure it out?"

"Yeah. It was both." I brought my mouth down to hers as she hitched a breath, and soon her body was pressed up against mine, melting against me like there was nothing but the two of us in the world.

When the kiss broke, she caught her breath and then brushed my hair back from my face. "Do you mean it? I mean, we're a lot to take on, both set in our ways and stubborn, and we can be a handful."

"That sounds like heaven to me." I closed my eyes as if savoring the moment, but then opened them to meet hers. "And yes, I mean it, Kya. I've always known I love you. Now, I'm finally going to have a chance to show it. I only regret I didn't sooner."

"Now, now," she said, shaking her finger at me. "If I can't speak of regrets, neither can you."

"Fair enough." I kissed her again and turned her back on the counter.

"Do you have to go to work?" She looked up at me with her gorgeous green eyes. They were the color of sea glass and glistening with tears I hoped were from happiness.

"No. I took the day off. I had a very important meeting with a very special woman, and I hoped it would take all day." I pressed my hips against hers.

Her hands slid down to my ass, and she ground her hips into me. "Well, I think you're in luck because I happen to have all day too."

"I like being lucky. Maybe we should have this special meeting in the other room."

Her hand slipped around to the front of my pants, and she undid the top button and made quick work of my zipper. "Or, we can start here, and work our way across the house."

"Have I ever told you that I like the way you think? Nice and dirty, just the way I love it." I hissed in a breath as she reached into my pants and gripped my heavy sac. They were tender and full, and I was ready to go.

30

KYA

As my back pressed into the kitchen counter, all I wanted to do was hop up on it and spread for him. Instead, I rubbed his big sac and then stroked his cock from base to tip.

He pressed his hips forward. "Are you sure you want to do it right here?"

I nodded. "Yes," I whispered in his ear before biting his lobe. "I want it right here and now."

"Mm. I like it when you get creative." He lifted me up, my ass landing on the countertop that I usually used to prepare and serve dinner, which made it even naughtier. I would never so much as spread butter on bread without thinking of what we were about to do.

I wrapped my arms around him and drew him close for a kiss, but then he flattened his palm on my chest, just above my breasts and urged me back as he kissed down my front.

He reached for the hem of my concert T-shirt and lifted the thing up over my head. Then, he lifted my breasts up out of their cups and kissed each tight nipple, sucking and licking as he let one go to undo the clasp in back. He stepped back and reached for my waistband and let his own pants fall to the floor as he pulled mine down to my knees, kissing my thighs once they were exposed, all the way to my knees and to my feet, where he stopped and dropped the clothes to the floor. He brought his mouth up to my thighs and parted my legs, nudging his way between them before he pushed two fingers between my lips.

I sucked his fingers as he smiled at me, and then he pulled them away, sliding them so deep inside of me that I moaned out, my voice breaking as my walls tightened.

"Relax for me, Kya. I want to make you feel good." He nudged me back and dipped down between my thighs, his tongue finding my clit, the flicking movement driving me insane. It felt so amazing, and it was like all the stress and pain of the past two days had been stripped away with my clothes. His tongue soothed me. Slowing his pace, he lapped softly as his fingers slow fucked me, his fingers curving upward to rub my most tender spot.

The pleasure built there as he continued, and soon, I felt the coil unwind with my first release. I chirped out a sound that not only expressed my pleasure but sped things up. His hands moved even faster, and soon I was coming again, the first seeming pale in comparison.

He took my hand, and when he helped me off the counter, I reached for his cock and stroked it as he led me around to the living room, stopping at the sofa. "Here?"

I nodded, but I had a few ideas of my own. I lay down on the couch where I hung my head off the edge and put my feet over the back.

As I curled my finger to call him forward, he grinned. "You're a dirty girl, aren't you?" He straddled me, and I gripped his cock, and he leaned over and licked my clit which was much easier to access.

I must have been crazy thinking that taking his cock in this position was going to be easy, especially considering how rough and gaggy it could get with him. But I trusted him to be gentle. He slowly entered my mouth and rocked his hips. Then, he put his hand on my throat gently and fucked my mouth.

I swallowed and sucked, licked and gagged. "Fuck, Kya, this is the best blow job of my life. You're amazing."

I backed up and he rolled me over, coming up from behind me. "I need you." He pressed a finger to my back door and teased, and then he bent down, and his tongue rimmed me, darting in and out of me as his fingers plunged deep into my pussy. His feverish strokes gave me a little bit of indication of what I was in for, and as I braced myself for whatever he wanted to do to me, he stepped forward and pressed into my slick channel and continued to finger my ass, never once dipping his finger, at least not until I begged.

We spent the next hour in the living room, changing positions and moving around from one couch to the other until we made it to the bed.

He laid me back, but I was too into it to lie still. I rose up on all fours and backed into him. And he gave a little growl of pleasure as he cupped my breasts while buried deep in me. "Fuck me hard, Leo." My voice was but a whisper, barely breaking audible, but he heard it, and as his hips began to pound, his balls slapping against my clit, I cried out in ecstasy.

I needed the hard pounding, and it made me feel so alive and so connected to Leonard, that I finally felt at peace with all that had happened. Even though I wasn't excusing my actions, I'd no longer be hard on myself for them. Like Leo had said, no more regrets because the future was what mattered.

He stepped back, and I rolled over prepared to take his load on my tits. Instead, he gripped my thighs and pushed himself back inside me and pumped me nice and slowly, looking me in the eyes, not saying a word, but not having to. There was so much understanding at that moment.

"I wanted to look at you," he said. "My beautiful Kya." He stiffened, and his cock erupted, spilling his seed deep and soaking me to my core. There was no pulling out this time, and I brought my legs up around his ass to hold him inside me.

We were hardly finished, and as he readied for round two, I knew I never wanted the day to end.

After he came again and had given me too many to count, we curled up against one another beneath the blanket.

"I should shower," I said with a lazy voice. "I have to get Addison in half an hour."

He stroked his hand through my hair and kissed my shoulder. "I'll help, and then we'll both go down and see her if it's okay."

"Of course, it is. We have a lot to figure out, I guess. How are we going to do this?"

"What do you mean?"

"Well, will she stay with you on weekends or would we all live together?" We both had houses, and while I wanted us to live together, I couldn't possibly ask him if he wanted to get rid of it.

"I'd like us to be together all the time. But I know it's going to be an adjustment and take time. I don't want to impose on you guys or anything. But I do want that to be the goal." He met my eyes. "Is that what you want?" He didn't sound too sure it's what I'd want.

"Of course, I think we should figure out which house we're going to use."

"Maybe we should just keep Addie settled. She's close to her school, she's adjusted here, and besides, my office isn't too far now."

"Okay, so are you just going to move in?"

"Eventually, I mean, not today or anything. We haven't even told Addie." He shrugged and got a dour look on his face. "What do you think she's going to think about all of this? I mean, I know she's okay with me being around on weeknights, but I'll be moving in. We'll be together, and she might hate it. She might start to hate me."

I couldn't help but laugh. "Leonard, she's not going to hate you. You're her father, and even though we've never really discussed it, I'm sure she wondered who you are."

"Did she ever ask?"

"Not really asked as much as mentioned. She said there were other girls in her class with just a mommy. And another girl with two daddies. She didn't really understand what normal was, I don't think."

"I guess I'm just nervous. I want her to love me as much as I already love her." He put his head down, but I cupped his face and brought it up for another kiss.

"You're going to be a great father." I stroked his bottom lip with my thumb. "Let's get cleaned up and then go get our daughter."

He raced me to the bathroom, and we had fun showering, even though we had to make quick work of it. We quickly dressed, and he grabbed his wallet and his keys, and we headed out hand in hand.

As we rounded the circle drive, Addie recognized Leo's car and jumped to her feet, snatching up her bag. She tugged her teacher's arm and then pointed as I stepped out of the car.

"Hi, Mommy! Hi, Leo!" said Addie as she ran up to the car. I pulled my seat up and let her into the back where I buckled her in.

"How was school today?" Leo asked as I got into my seat and buckled up.

"The best! The teacher said we get to remember a poem. I get to pick any I choose."

I gave Leo a grin. "That's wonderful news." I glanced back as I heard her backpack open. "Don't take too much out in the car, Addie."

"But I want to show you the picture I made." She gave me a pouty look.

"You made a picture? Let's see it." He gave me a wink. Addie held the paper up between our seats, and I took it.

There was a large square house with a triangle roof, and inside were three stick figures and outside were two.

"That's you and me and Leo in the house, and Aunt Sadie and Uncle Stones outside. They're coming over to visit, but I didn't have time to draw all of the cars."

Leo glanced over. "I think it's perfect, Addie. Just perfect. You're a very talented little girl."

"Do you think so?" she asked from the back seat.

Leo turned out of the school road and headed back to our house. "Yeah, I really do."

"Then you're not mad?" she asked in a small voice.

I turned around in my seat. "Why would he be mad, sweet pea?"

"We were drawing pictures of our family, and I told Anna he was going to be my new daddy. Like I drew in the picture." I could tell by her tone that she thought she might be in trouble. And as we neared the park, Leo turned in and stopped the car.

"Would you like it if I were your dad?" He shifted in his seat to face her.

Addie looked up at us with big brown eyes. Her little shoulders were drawn in. She glanced at me and then nodded. "Yes, I'd like that very much."

He smiled and lifted his chin. "Well, it just so happens I am your daddy."

"Really?" Addison looked like she wasn't sure he was telling the truth.

"Yes, it's true. We were actually going to wait and tell you, but I think now is as good a time as any." I raised my hands, and she let out a little squeak and cheered.

"Does this mean you'll live with us too?"

We exchanged another glance, and I could tell he was very careful with his promises. I nodded, letting him know it was okay. "Yes, when you're ready."

"Good." She smiled, folding her arms in front of her. "I'm ready now."

Leo and I both chuckled, and he pulled the car into a parking space, turned off the ignition, and then opened his door. I gave him a puzzled look, "What are you doing? Aren't we going home?"

He grinned. "Yeah, but first, I'm taking my family to the park."

Addie cheered. "I like my daddy."

We got out of the car, and Leo took her hand, and the two headed for the swings. I knew all of our problems weren't solved. I'd still have to explain where her father had been and why, but we were okay for now. We still had to get through the court case, but no matter what the turnout, I already felt like a winner.

31

LEO

Even though I'd tucked my daughter in the night before and then went down the hall to make love to Kya, I left around midnight so we'd get enough rest for court. Besides, until we figured out what we wanted to do about our living arrangements and I moved all of my things, I'd still have to get dressed and trim my beard in my own place.

I'd gotten up at the crack of dawn to be ready and couldn't wait to see Kya and ask how her morning went.

I arrived at the courthouse and went to the café where I'd asked Kya and the band to meet me. Jon must have had the same idea because he was there sipping coffee and looking at his phone at a table alone.

"Great minds do think alike," I said as I walked up and shook his hand.

"Yeah, I can't say I'm in any hurry for this to start. I know I'm going to get my ass handed to me."

"I'll try to make it quick and painless, but no promises."

He chuckled and kicked out a chair. "Have a seat. We've still got time, and I want to know what's going on in the land of new fathers."

"We just told Addie yesterday. She's very excited about it, which is good, but I'm not sure what we're going to do about our houses and where we should live. She's got her place, and I've got mine. It would be best if Addie stays in hers. She's close to everything, but if we take mine, it's not much more of a commute to take her to school and pick her up. But, I don't know. Decisions are much harder having to make them for three and not only me."

"Well, you look happy," he said. "Fatherhood looks good on you."

"I can't believe it still. Seems like a dream." About that time, a short, petite blonde who I'd spent the night spinning on my cock walked by and gave me a wink.

Jon stared at her ass as she walked away. "You might want to send out a memo. I don't mind taking on all of your old girlfriends, by the way."

"The old clients weren't enough, huh? I'll tell you what. You send out the memo, and they're all yours." I only had eyes for one woman, and it was Kya Campbell.

"Looks like Kya's radar is on." He gestured to the door, and she walked in with Sadie and two men behind her. "And it looks like you better behave or that tattooed posse of Kya's is going to smash you with a guitar."

"That's Rob and Liam. They're in the band. Looks like my gang is all here." I got up, and he held out his fist.

"Good luck in there."

I bumped his fist with mine. "Thanks, and right back at you."

I walked across the room and joined them where they were already drawing a crowd. Kya waved me over. "It's a bit stuffy in here."

I should have anticipated the press would be all over them after that last conference. "Let's go down the hall, and I'll see if I can find us a private room."

"That would be great," said Sadie. "Rob hates reporters."

Once we were good and settled into the private room, Kya introduced me to Rob and Liam.

Liam was tall and stood as straight as a soldier, which made him look even taller. His thin build wasn't lanky like I used to be, and he had that lean and laid-back rocker vibe going on. "It's nice to meet you. Kya tells me you're Addie's father."

"Yes, I am."

"Congratulations. She's a good kid."

Rob cleared his throat. He was more of the big and scary type, the kind of guy who couldn't help looking like a criminal even though he had a face the ladies loved. "I guess we don't have to tell you she's like a niece to us. We've been her family a long time, and we look out for her and her mother."

"I appreciate that."

"Do you? Because I really hope you do." His hard look was a warning, and while I'd never backed down from a fight, not even in my geeky high school days, the man was practically like a brother to Kya, and I'd give him all the respect due one.

Sadie laughed. "Knock it off, Rob. He's on our side."

Rob smiled big and then nudged Liam. "I think I had him going there." Suddenly, he didn't seem so intimidating.

Kya sat next to me and took my hand. "They're big jokers, those two. Always misbehaving and a handful on the road. But they make it fun, and they have my back."

The bailiff came to the door and waved us out. "We have to go. It's show time."

They all filed out, and we took our seats. I looked to the other side but didn't see Jon or his client.

Kya whispered to Sadie, and the two glanced over their shoulders at a woman sitting behind where Jon should have been. I looked around, wondering what was keeping him as the courtroom continued to fill.

"Is everything okay?" asked Kya. "You look worried."

"No, I'm just wondering where Jon and Whit are."

"Well, he can't be too far behind, not with Mona Star already here."

"She might be a witness. Who knows what they've got up their sleeve? I only hope they keep their promises."

It was a tense moment waiting for Jon to walk in, and when he did, he was alone. He got to his table and turned and shrugged at me.

We all rose for the judge, Sarah Carter, to enter the room and as she sat down, she announced for us to be seated. She was an old friend of my father's and of mine as well, and she'd always liked us both. Being on opposite sides of this case, I wasn't sure whose favor that could work in, but I gave her my warmest smile and hoped for the best.

It didn't take Judge Carter long to notice that Whit White was missing. "Mr. Hanson, where is your client?"

"I wish I knew, Your Honor. He hasn't shown up."

"Normally, I'd give you another five minutes to find your client, but I'm not in a giving mood. The allegations against Mr. White are too serious of a nature to warrant any leniency, and it is in my opinion that he doesn't see the severity of the charges against him enough to respect them. With that, I think it's only fair to the plaintiffs that I—"

"Sorry I'm late," came a voice in the back of the room.

All of our heads turned, and Jon's face reddened with embarrassment. I should have known the son of a bitch would be late to his own trial.

"Mr. White, I presume."

Whit grinned. "The one and only."

"What an asshole," whispered Sadie.

Whit wasn't done digging his hole. "Sorry, I'm late. I got caught up with life. I'm a very busy man as many here know. I hope I didn't miss anything."

Sarah's frown lines were deeply creased by the time he shut up. "What you missed was your opportunity to plead your case. I've gone over the preliminary evidence for the allegations brought against you, and I feel you've wasted enough of my time."

"With all due respect, Your Honor—"

She banged her gavel. "Not another word, Mr. White. I'm about to wrap this up for you since you're so busy. There is not only evidence that you falsified documents and embezzled funds, but you've wasted five years of these people's time by hindering their creativity for your own ego-fed purposes. I'm ruling in favor of the plaintiff and releasing Sabbath Sundae from any legally binding contracts between you. All of their rights and creative freedoms will be returned to the group effective immediately, and your assets will be frozen upon evaluation to determine what kind of restitution you owe the band, during which time, you will be placed on a two-year probation. My judgment is for the plaintiff." She smacked her gavel on the bench, and as I turned to Kya, Sarah continued. "The next time you have an appointment in my courtroom, Mr. White, you'll be on time."

Whit jumped to his feet. "You can't do this! You didn't even hear my case!" He stomped his feet and tossed Jon's case file to the floor.

Sarah banged her gavel again. "Bailiff, please take Mr. White down and show him our lovely accommodations. He'll be spending the next two nights in lockup for contempt of court." She banged her gavel one last time, and while we stood to celebrate, Whit was cuffed, and not even Mona Star wanted to have anything to do with him. She wasn't happy as she grabbed her big handbag and stormed out.

Jon came over to shake my hand. "Well, I have to say, even though we lost, I don't feel so bad."

"My father is going to be in a shitty mood, but at least you didn't lose the case as much as White gave it up."

"I wouldn't be too sure of your father's mood." He pointed behind me where my father was hugging Kya and greeting the band.

He slapped me on the back. "Congratulations, son."

"I hate to win a case I didn't even get to argue."

"A win's a win, and the best man came out on top. Now, when am I going to get to see my granddaughter? I'm not getting any younger, you know."

Kya and I exchanged a look. "I suppose we could come by later if you want?" I said.

"How about we all meet up for ice cream? My treat." My father's smile beamed so brightly, I should have worn shades. "She likes ice cream, right?"

"Of course, and we'd love that. Thank you, Mr. Pace."

"Thanks, Dad." It was nice to see him excited for a change, and I hoped that maybe Addie would bring a little light to his life again. He'd been so hardened by all the time without Mom, and Addie was the perfect cure.

We cleared the courtroom, and as we filed out into the parking lot, the reporters gathered around us wanting a statement. "Justice prevailed," I said. "And now, I'm going home to see my daughter."

After some quick goodbyes to Sadie, Liam, and Rob, we hurried to my car. Once we were inside, I leaned over and kissed her full on the lips. I didn't care who knew, who photographed us, or about anything else.

Kya slumped in her seat. "That was the craziest thing ever. I can't believe the judge tossed his ass in jail."

"And don't forget she's going to make sure you get paid," I said, holding up a finger. "That's the best part. By the time she's done with him, he'll never want to screw anyone over again."

"Good. That's what I really wanted, for no one else to have to suffer what he's put us through. He'll be lucky to show his face in public." Kya reached over and took my hand.

I squeezed it tightly as she leaned over and gave me a quick kiss on the lips. "Thank you for not only helping me through this but for being here for me and Addie now."

"I'd do anything for my girls, and I hope you know how much I love you, Kya. I've always loved you."

"I love you, too, Leonard. Sorry, Leo."

I leaned over and gave her a quick peck on the lips. "You know, baby? You can call me anything you want."

32

KYA

"Kya?" Leonard called from the hall.

"In here, red door." Venues were always a maze when it came to backstage accommodations, and Leonard wasn't used to navigating his way around.

He stuck his head in the door, and then he and Addie walked into my dressing room. "Jesus, that crowd is insane out there."

I didn't want to think about the crowd or how packed it was or that it had been a year and a half since I'd been onstage performing anything, much less being one of the main acts.

Now that we were out of our contracts and free to tour on our own terms, I'd signed us up for a seven-show deal playing just ahead of The Deathgrips, who were the headlining acts. A new band, Seventh Wave, was our opening act, and they were currently in the wings waiting to be introduced.

Addie climbed up into Sadie's chair beside me. "You look pretty, Mama."

"Thank you, baby. Did you happen to see Aunt Sadie out in the hallway?"

"No, but I did see Uncle Stones and Papa Blitz. Papa Blitz said he was going to come and see me soon."

"Yeah, and speaking of grandfathers," said Leo, "my father sent his love and told me to tell you to break a leg."

The door opened, and Sadie rushed in. "Have you seen Stones?"

Addie handed me my lip gloss and turned to her aunt. "He was out in the hall, Aunt Sadie."

She paced the room back and forth. "I don't know what I'm going to do. I don't know if I can do this!"

"It's just a sold-out crowd. You'll be fine. We've done this a million times now." She always panicked when it was a larger crowd than before, but this overreaction was stranger than usual.

"It's not the crowd."

"Is Stones screwing around?" It wasn't unusual for him to have groupies hanging all over him before a show, not that he would have instigated it, but they were imposing that way.

"He better not!" she said, her voice breaking.

She was beginning to worry me, and Leo's eyes were already wide as he stared at her hand. "Sadie? What's wrong?"

She walked over and slapped something down on the table in front of me. I looked down, and my mouth hung open, my eyes widened as big as Leo's. It was a pregnancy test, and the indicator showed a pink plus sign, the same as I'd gotten when I was pregnant with Addison.

"Oh, Sadie." I covered my mouth, and she covered hers. I knew she hadn't expected her and Stones to last, but so far, they'd been holding strong, and over the past year, they'd become even closer, with him taking more time off to be with her when he could.

Sadie's eyes filled with tears. "I don't know how this happened."

Leo cleared his throat. "I'm pretty sure you do."

She gave him a glare and then began to pace again.

Addie was confused. "Is Aunt Sadie having a meltdown?"

Leo got up and moved across the room to a sofa where there were a TV and a platter of fruit and cheese. "Yeah, sweet pea, I'm afraid so." He popped a grape into his mouth, and Addie got down and joined him.

Stones walked into the room, and Sadie stopped walking. "There you are, babe. I wanted to see you before you went onstage. Did you see my newest strap for Wanda?"

"Sally has it. I borrowed it, remember?"

"No problem. Just give it to me after the show." He kissed her lips and then glanced over at the table where I was getting ready. "Holy shit, Kya, you and Leo expecting? That is a pregnancy test, right?"

Sadie's eyes widened. "Actually, babe. That's mine."

Stones looked like he was going to faint. "No fooling?" His eyes grew wild with happiness, and he stepped closer, pulling her into his arms. He held her stare until she nodded.

"No fooling."

"Whoohoo!" he screamed. He lifted her up off her feet and spun her around.

The door flew open, and Blitz hurried into the room. "What's going on in here?"

"Sadie's pregnant!"

"You're having a baby?" Addie asked, her little eyes wide with wonder. "When do we get to see it?"

Leo looked up at me. "You're the one explaining where the baby comes from."

I walked over to join Leo as Blitz hugged Sadie and Stones. "Well done, my son. You're going to be great parents." He turned and picked Addie up in his arms. "And I'm going to be a Papa again!" He spun her around and kissed her cheek until she giggled.

"I'm so happy that you're happy." Sadie held him tightly, and the rest of us decided to slip out and give them a moment.

As we walked down the hall, Papa Blitz was strutting as proud as a peacock holding Addie's hand while Leo and I followed.

We hung around and waited for the call. And finally, we took the stage. Sadie was full of energy, and I knew she better enjoy it while she could. She had a lot to go through for the next nine months, and I was excited that I would finally be an aunt too. The two of us were rock and roll soul sisters, and I couldn't have asked for a better friend.

Leonard and I had both owed her a lot, especially when it came to babysitting, so we'd soon be returning the favor.

After five songs, I needed a break, so Sadie took the mic and performed a solo. In the end, she took my hand and addressed the crowd as the band played low. "Hey, Chicago, I've got a little surprise for you tonight."

I thought she was about to announce her pregnancy and thought she'd done lost her mind. It was way too early for spilling that kind of information, and the press was going to eat it up. Instead, she turned around and out walked Leo.

He walked out, and I could see Blitz holding Addie just off the stage where she could see, and suddenly, my heartbeat was so strong, it nearly beat out of my chest.

"Hey, Chicago, I hope you don't mind indulging me, but I think you'll all agree, this is one hell of a woman."

The crowd went wild, and my cheeks reddened. I held his hand tightly, and Sadie stepped back, nodding her head as she played a riff.

"She's so amazing, I just can't let her go. So, I wanted to ask her tonight, here in front of all of you fine people, in the presence of our beautiful daughter, a very important question."

The crowd was going nuts, and things got crazier in the audience as he got down on one knee. "Kya Campbell, I've loved you my whole life and always will. Will you do me the honor of becoming my wife?"

I held the mic to lips. "Yes." I barely choked out the words, and we embraced as the band continued to play.

"You're crazy!" I said. I couldn't believe he'd planned this.

"Yeah, well, when I asked Blitz for his blessing, he said I better make the proposal a good one."

I glanced off stage where Blitz was holding Addie's hand, and he let it go, telling her it was okay to join us. She ran out onstage, and the crowd cheered even more. I readied my mic and signaled Sadie, and while I geared up for the next song, Leo picked up Addie, and I sang them my latest ballad titled *The Three of Us*.

I ended the song with a kiss and then put my arms around my family. It was the best night on stage ever and one I'd remember for the rest of my life.

After the show, Liam and his wife took Addie for us since Sadie and Stones needed a little time to themselves as well, and Leo and I drove home.

I kicked back in the seat, and it felt good to have on comfortable shoes instead of my thigh-high boots and to have my hair brushed out instead of spiked. And now, all I needed was to get home, take a shower, and make love to my man. "That's what I love about playing a hometown crowd. I get to go home to my bed when it's over."

"That was some show. Your voice was strong, more powerful than I remember it."

I thought of him on his roof back when we were kids and how I'd found out he used to sneak and listen to me. "And at least this time, you weren't stuck out on a roof spitting sunflower shells." I wondered if he realized I remembered that. It was so long ago. We were so young. It was hard to believe how far we'd come over the years.

His cheeks turned red. "I was your biggest fan back then too. When you crawled through that window, wow, you were my perfect fantasy. For a minute, I thought I was dreaming. Always and forever." He gave me a sideward glance as he slowed down to turn down our street.

"I still think you should have come to see me back then. I'd have rocked your world. We'd have had a lot of fun, you and me." I moved closer to the seat and held his hand.

"But I couldn't because it was too soon to knock you up or ask you to marry me." He gave a chuckle and pulled into our driveway.

"Yeah, you do have a way of taking my shows to the extreme. They bring out the wild man in you, don't they?" I reached over and squeezed his knee.

He shut off the car and took my hand, kissing my ring. "Are you happy?"

"I'm over the moon. I don't think life could get any better."

"The night could get better," he said as he put his hand on my knee and moved it up my thigh.

He brought his lips to mine, and I pulled away. "I think you're right about that, so why don't we go inside?"

"I can't wait to get inside." He wagged his brows, and then we got out of the car and hurried inside where we immediately fell together in a passionate kiss, our hands working to undress one another. We left a trail of our clothes on the way to the bedroom, and when we finally reached the bed, he picked me up against him and laid me back.

"I know it's a weird time to ask, but you do want other babies, right?"

"After we're married and enjoy a little time as newlyweds, of course." I searched his eyes as he braced himself against me and smiled.

"Good, because I want another one. I love Addie so much, but I can't help wishing I'd gotten to see her grow from a little tiny baby into the little girl she is now. I want to see our baby grow, get the whole experience. And I want to try for a boy. I'd like a son, someone to carry on my name and maybe pass my car down to."

I felt horrible knowing I'd cheated him out of the opportunity with Addison, but I was thankful I could give him that gift again. And this time, we'd share in it together.

"I'd like a little boy too. One exactly like you." I brought my lips down to his, and as we made love, I couldn't think of anything I'd want more than a little boy as special and sweet as his father.

"Good. I love you, Kye."

I smiled. "Only me?"

"You're my one and only." He pulled me down for another kiss. I had no doubt he was speaking truth. I felt like the only girl in the world. His girl. Forever.

EPILOGUE
LEO

"Daaaaddy!" Addie's bloodcurdling scream sent chills down my spine and brought me to my feet. When only seconds before, the hum of the vacuum cleaner had been normal, now it growled like a beast with something caught in its snout.

I got up from where I was sitting in the laundry room and rushed down the hall to her bedroom on the other side of the house. When I rounded the corner into her room, she stood away from the vacuum, tugging on her silky purple curtain that it had grabbed.

"Back up!" I ran over and switched the thing off, and she covered her mouth as her eyes filled with tears.

"I'm sorry, Daddy. I tried to make it stop." I knew I shouldn't have let her run the vacuum alone, but she'd been so confident she could do it by herself, and I'd checked to make sure everything was off the floor, except for her curtains apparently, which draped low enough to get snagged.

"No, sweet pea, I should have made you wait." With Kya due home from her two-month tour, we wanted to surprise her by cleaning up the eight weeks of roughing it without Mom before she got home. The last time she'd stopped in for a quick visit, which was over a week ago, she'd compared our home to a pigsty.

I reached down and tugged the curtain, but the gauzy fabric had been sucked in so deep, it wasn't coming out without damage. As I gave it a hard yank, the fabric tore before pulling free. Dark marks and a whole lot of dirt stained the fabric too.

"Did I ruin the big surprise?"

"No, just the curtains. But I've got an idea." I pulled the bent rod down and removed the two long panels. Then with Addie following behind, I went to the laundry room where I'd left my mound of laundry to find Kya's emergency sewing kit.

Addie's eyes widened. "Are you going to sew it up?" She didn't seem to have a whole lot of faith in me.

I shook my head. "Nope. I'm not much of a seamstress, but I do have an idea. I lay the two pieces of purple fabric down one atop the other and carefully cut the length down. "Now, you'll just have shorter curtains. This should work." I handed her one of the panels which she examined closely and gave me her thumbs-up approval. "Now, we'll go hang them back up."

She followed me out of my laundry nightmare where piles of clothes were still stacked all over the washing machine, the dryer, the folding counter, and even the floor, and we went back to her room. "Then can we do the banner?"

"Yes. We'll hang the banner and bake the cookies, and if my calculations are correct, everything will be perfect when your mother comes home."

"Good. I want this place in tip-top shape." Addie ran ahead of me, and before we could make it across the living room, a slamming car door brought our attention to the front window.

"Looks like your mom is early."

Addie dropped her curtain panel to the floor and ran to the dining table to get the banner we'd worked the entire night before painting so it would be dry. "Help!"

I grabbed an end of the paper, and we stood there waiting with the big banner rolled out for her to see along with our smiling faces.

She opened the door and smiled as we cheered. "Welcome home!"

Kya tilted her head and dropped her bags. "Thank you both so much. I've missed you, and this is perfect." As she walked over and gave us hugs, I realized the banner was upside down, but I knew better than to say a word to Addie who had worked so hard to make everything perfect.

Kya looked down to the curtain panel in my hand, and then reached down and picked up the one Addie had dropped on the floor. "What is this?" Her eyes widened as she must have figured it out.

Addie hugged Kya's legs. "I'm so sorry, Mama."

I patted Addie on the head. "It was my fault. I let her vacuum while I tackled the mountain of laundry. Bad call."

Kya laughed. "It's nice to see things are falling apart without me, and I have to say, this place looks great. You guys have really outdone yourself."

Addie grabbed my wrist and pulled me down to whisper in my ear. "We didn't do the cookies."

"We can make them together later," said Kya, who had overheard as she looked at the curtain's new raw edge. "Your doing?" She held out the drape and looked down at its length. "Not a bad idea."

I dusted off my shoulder and blew on my knuckles. "Well, I've always fancied myself a problem solver."

We made our way to the couch where Kya plopped down and put her feet up on my lap when I joined her.

Addie climbed up beside her. "I've missed you, Mama. Are you really home for good?"

Kya snuggled her close. "Until the next tour, but don't worry, that's not for a long time." I smiled, knowing that if the opportunity came her way and the money was right, she'd take it. It was the nature of her business as a singer, and I was okay with that.

For the moment, I was just so glad she was home; my little world, my family, back together where we belonged.

"How was the show last night?"

"It was good but poor Sadie was miserable. Stones filled in for her on three songs. Being seven months pregnant on the road, now she knows how I felt when I was pregnant with Addie. It was brutal. I had to wear a lot of scarves to hide my baby bump." She rubbed Addie's belly, and the two giggled.

"At least it works out, and by the next show, she won't have to worry about it."

"Right." She closed her eyes and let out a deep breath.

"Mama, will you be home for my birthday?"

Kya smiled at Addie. "Yes, I'll be home for your birthday, but that's not for another few months." She closed her eyes and groaned. "I have so much to catch up on."

With her looking so tired, I wasn't sure if it was the right time to tell her about my surprise, but I hoped it would not only make her happy but take a lot of pressure off her. *Here goes nothing.* "About the list of to-dos, I have a surprise for you."

"Another surprise? Better than the banner and the curtain makeover?" She gave me a lazy smile.

"I hope you think so." I searched her eyes.

Kya nudged me with her foot. "Tell me."

I took a deep breath, hoping she'd be pleased and not overwhelmed. "I booked The Regency for next Saturday."

"The Regency? As in the most beautiful, luxury indoor garden in the world? The very same place I wanted for our wedding, but it was too booked up?"

I chuckled. "Yes. That one."

Kya let out a squeal of delight that was quickly replaced with panic. "Wait, next weekend? As in a week from right now?"

"Yeah, they had a last-minute cancellation. They knew I'd shown interest, so they gave me a call. I couldn't turn it down, and besides, I want to marry you as soon as possible."

Addie got to her feet and jumped up and down. "We're having a wedding?" She looked back and forth at us. "I have to find something to wear." She ran to her room, and I looked over at Kya to judge her mood.

She looked at me with uncertainty in her eyes. "But what about invites and food? I have my dress, but I'd hoped there would be cake, champagne, a wedding party."

"We'll make phone calls, be creative, and do a lot of crazy, quick shopping. We've got a week and the money. How hard can it be? As long as we're all together, our family and friends can make it, which I happen to know your entire side won't be working since the tour is over, and all I have is my father and friends at the firm. And Tabby, of course."

"Of course," said Kya with a half-hearted smile. "You make it sound easy."

"You're upset. It's a horrible idea, right?" I should have thought this out more, but I'd just wanted to give her the very best.

"Hell, no. I want to get married too. It's just a lot to take in. I thought I would come home and get to rest, and instead, I'm going to plan my wedding in a week." She sat up and turned to lie in my arms.

I brought my lips down to hers for a quick kiss and then met her eyes. "You'll have all the time in the world after to rest."

"You're right, and don't get me wrong, Leo. It's a wonderful surprise. I've always dreamed of having my wedding at The Regency. I guess my mom was always right. Good things happen in a hurry." She smiled and seemed content with the idea, which made me relax a bit.

"Speaking of parents, do you think yours will come?" I hadn't even thought about them before she'd mentioned her mother, and surely, they'd want to be there for her on the big day. How long could they hold their grudge? Sure, she'd left home right out of high school to be in a rock band, but she'd been very successful and was a wonderful person and mother.

"I'll invite them, but they haven't been any less distant since you've been around trying to make an honest woman out of me. If they don't, it's not the end of the world for me." She seemed convincing enough, but I had a feeling that deep down, she wanted them to be there if only to see how happy she was.

"I don't understand them. They have this great daughter, an amazing granddaughter, and they'd rather ignore that because of your career choice?" I couldn't think of anything that would make me ever stop loving or talking to my daughter.

Kya reached up and touched my face, her warm fingertips brushing through my stubble. "I stopped trying to make sense of them a long time ago. You should too."

I hated to see the disappointment in her eyes over them. If I could get them there, I would, but then a part of me wondered if that was the best idea with her music family present. Looked like I had a lot to think about as well.

"I can ask Sadie to stand up with me. And Addie can be our flower girl. I think she'd like that." She held up her hand and counted off on her fingers as she went down the list of ideas.

"I'll ask Jon if he'll be my best man. Maybe we can do our own cakes?"

"Whoa there, baby. Let's figure out how many people are coming, and then we'll decide. I'm sure we could find someone to do a cupcake tower or something simple, so it's one less thing to worry about." She snuggled closer, and I could already see her wheels turning.

I'd known it would be a challenge, and knowing she was up for the task made me feel so much better.

She turned her head and kissed my lips. "Thank you for my surprise, by the way. I do love it, and I love you too."

A moment later our heads were turned as a clanking noise sounded across the hardwood. "Can I wear this to the wedding?"

Addie had dug out one of her yellow princess dresses and a pair of pink plastic heels that had little fuzzy feathers on the toes.

Kya laughed as we exchanged a quick look. "Daddy is going to buy you a new dress, sweet pea. One that will match Aunt Sadie's. That way you can be my flower girl."

Her eyes widened as she ran over to join us. "I get to be a flower girl?"

"Yes," said Kya. It was nice to see that special moment between them, especially when Addie fell into her mama's arms.

Then she turned to me. "Did you hear that, Daddy? I'm going to be a flower." She turned back to Kya. "Can I be a daisy?"

Kya

AFTER EXPLAINING the role of a flower girl and spending the rest of the evening making plans and lists over dinner, we tucked Addie into bed together and then retired to our room.

We both readied for bed, undressing to our undies and crawling beneath the covers.

It was nice to spend time in my own bed, especially with Leonard, who wasted no time pulling me against him to snuggle. "I've missed my beautiful soon-to-be wife," he whispered in my ear.

"I've missed you too. More than you know."

He lifted my chin and turned my face to meet his. "Are you happy?"

"Yes, I'm very happy. I know it's a bit of a rush, but I love my surprise, and I'm glad we're jumping in headfirst to make it happen. And Addie was excited." I'd never seen her smile so much. She had grown a foot while I was away and carried a little less baby fat, her round cheeks slimming as her features sharpened.

Leo chuckled. "I think she was happier when she thought she was going to dress in a flower costume, but I like the compromise you gave her."

"A few white daisies in her basket and my bouquet will be pretty, and they're her favorite flower. I want it to be special for her too. How has she been?" I hadn't been too sure about leaving him at home alone with her, but here we were at the other end of things, and they were both alive, and the house was nearly the same as I'd left it.

"Good. It wasn't as hard as I thought it would be. She's a good kid. Her mama raised her right."

"Her daddy is doing a hell of a job too. Did she do okay at school?"

"She was good. She got in trouble for talking in class, but that sort of thing is bound to happen. It was nothing I couldn't handle. I signed the slip and returned it to her teacher."

"That's not too bad. Was she behaving at home? Didn't give you too much trouble?" I had been afraid she'd con him into eating a lot of junk food, and I had found two empty ice cream tubs in the garbage.

He shrugged. "Nah, it's easy when I let her have her way and anything else she wants."

"Oh no, you didn't," I said, laughter filling my voice. "Please tell me you didn't spoil that child and completely ruin her."

"Not completely, but we did take out stock in McDonald's and made such an impact at Dunkin' that the cops are still pissed about the doughnut shortage."

"No wonder she grew so much. I thought the two of you were going to try and cook at home while I was gone."

"No, two nights of that, and she told me the cold, hard truth. My spaghetti, the one thing I thought I was good at, turns out, it stinks. Her exact words were, 'Daddy, I love you, but this stinks.'"

I could almost hear Addie telling him that. "She can be brutal for a five-year-old."

"You're not kidding. And she wouldn't even let me try to make it again. She said I should call my father and ask him how to make it. Apparently, he makes the best."

"How is Richard?" His father had really come around since Addie had come into his life.

"He's Dad. You know, grumpy until he sees Addison. He cleared out the spare room for her. Turned it into a toy room that is complete with a frilly white daybed and even put in cable TV, a computer, and bought copies of all of her favorite movies."

"He's going to spoil her." It was hard to believe sometimes how his father had actually been against me at the trial. He'd tried to force Leo against me, but Leo had quit, leaving his best friend Jon to take over. In the end, it had all worked out for the best, and they'd decided not to go that route but only because of Addie.

As soon as the old man had learned he'd had a granddaughter and seen her eyes were the same as his late wife's, he had called off the dogs and had a change of heart. We'd been okay since, and he'd apologized, telling me he wanted to make things right.

He'd even met my family over the holidays, and he and my friend Blitz, who had taken me under his wing, had surprisingly hit it off.

Leo looked at me like I should know better. "Too late. He already has her rotten."

"Those two are quite the pair." I giggled thinking of them and the way they acted when they were together, more like having two children instead of one.

"Yeah, he was angry I hadn't brought her over sooner."

"We'll have to make sure we go. I guess we have a big announcement to make. I hope he's not upset we're rushing."

"He's always asking me when I'm going to marry you, so the next time he asks, I'll know what to tell him."

"Yeah, I just don't want him upset that we're not having a bigger occasion or Sadie for having to walk down the aisle looking like she'd smuggled a beach ball under her dress. Are you sure we shouldn't wait?" Waiting would mean I couldn't have my venue, but at least everything else would be right, and if it kept everyone in the family happy, I was all for it. I didn't need to be greedy with the whole standard "my big day" bride ego. No, I had to consider Leo and Addie, and they were much more important to me.

His smile faded a bit as he got a serious look on his face. "What's that all about? We're doing this."

"Are you really sure you want to marry me? And the crazy ass family that comes with me?" I had a lifestyle that might be a little hard to keep up with at times and being out on the road got harder and harder each time I had to leave. There was a lot of trust involved on both sides, and so far, we'd managed to hold it together.

Leonard gave me a sideward glance. "Are you kidding? Addie is my daughter, and I'd like her to have parents who are married to each other. As for the rest of the crazies, I think they like me, and I like them, they did help me propose. Besides, I've wanted to marry you since I was a gawky teen with thick glasses and braces."

I nudged him. "Well, what took you so long?"

We both laughed, and I couldn't help thinking about the first time we'd been together at a party when we were just eighteen. It had ended badly, with me telling him I didn't want to be with him because it would ruin our perfect friendship. Little did I know, that statement would lead to a series of events including us hooking up five years later to conceive our daughter, only for him to do me the same way.

But thankfully, that didn't last, and when I'd taken my manager to court, our friendship had rekindled.

"Better late than never, right?" He shrugged and drew me closer.

I laced my fingers with his. "You know how you mentioned a long rest after the wedding?"

"Yeah?" His voice was so close to my ear it sent chills down my spine.

"Well, I was thinking, if we're planning a small wedding, then maybe we could do a nice honeymoon. Maybe go to a nice secluded island somewhere for a couple of weeks and lie out in the sun and stare at the ocean."

"That sure sounds romantic, but what about Addie? You just got back. You can't expect her to stay behind."

"I don't. She could come along with us. We'll go away another time for romance, but I want to be lazy with my family and enjoy some time where I don't have to hem curtains and finish the monster pile of laundry in the washroom."

"That's all clean. I just haven't finished folding it. In all fairness, you did come home earlier than expected." He chuckled softly in my ear.

I turned and faced him, brushing his hair back and planting a kiss on his mouth. "I'm teasing, Leonard. I'm not worried about that. I just want to enjoy some downtime with my two favorite people in the world."

"I agree, but let's get the wedding plans behind us first, okay? I know the quick walk to the altar is saving us some money, but we'll have time to book something special, and we'll have to see about Addie's schooling."

"She can take it on the road. She's used to that kind of life, but I agree, first things first. I've got to take the gown in to make the final adjustments. Then, there's Addie's dress, and we should buy Sadie's. With the baby coming, I think it would be a nice gesture, and I'm letting her choose something she likes with that baby bump. Now is not the time for a bridesmaid dress from hell."

"You're so thoughtful." He kissed my shoulder, and his hand cupped my ass. "What do you want me to wear?"

I smoothed my hands down his bare chest. "A tux. Also, I'd like to discuss the rings."

He met my eyes. "Bought, and I can pick them up whenever." He kissed my neck and slowly made his way up to my ear.

"Another surprise?" I wasn't worried that he'd managed that task alone because the two of us had already picked out the ones we liked. We'd actually done a lot of talking about how we wanted the wedding to be, so I wasn't surprised he'd felt confident enough to take the initiative.

"Well, you keep talking, and you'll find I'm full of them." He gave me a wink. "Or don't and see what else I'm good at." He rolled his hips, and I could feel his large erection pressing into my center.

The heat blossomed between my legs, and I was overtaken with need. Exhaustion aside, I ground my hips against him, and he moved over me, nudging himself between my legs.

"I thought about you every night, even after our calls." I had called him every night whether I was on the bus on the road or in a hotel room across the country, and I had even called him late nights after my shows. We'd mostly said our good nights, but some nights, we'd had long, naughty talks to keep the passion between us burning.

"You did?" I couldn't wait to hear about that. "Tell me." I could already picture him in the shower, his hand between his legs as he worked himself.

He chuckled and gave me a sly smile. "I'm sure you already know how that story ends."

"Then show me," I said, as I bit his shoulder. "Show me all of the things you said you wanted to do to me during those long calls."

He reached down between the covers and rubbed my mound, his fingers slipping the lace of my panties aside to gain entrance. "I thought you'd never ask."

∼

Leo

I HADN'T BEEN to my father's office in a while, and now that I had big news, I couldn't think of a better excuse to do a pop in. I stepped off the elevator and into the hall that used to lead to my office before I'd walked out, and as I went around the corner to my father's end of the building, I hoped I'd caught him and Jon before they'd left for lunch.

Having worked with them for so long, I knew their routines, and neither had been in the habit of heading out early. Sure enough, when I approached his door, I could hear the two men talking.

Their heads turned as I rounded the corner and stepped into Edith's office. My father's secretary had announced her retirement and was going to be moving to California with her daughter's family once she finished out her month.

"Hey, son. What brings you around?"

"Just thought I'd take the two of you to lunch and tell you the good news." I looked around for Edith, but she must have been on an errand.

"Well, you caught us about to leave if you want to join us. I owed your buddy here steak and lobster for his recent win." My father headed to the door, and Jon and I followed.

"Oh? Did you finally win a case?" I teased.

Jon rolled his eyes and huffed. "I've done quite well since your sorry ass left the firm and stopped hogging all the good cases."

We approached the elevator, and my father pushed the button as he turned to us. "He's done quite well filling your shoes, but I do wish you'd reconsider my offer to return."

My father had offered me three different times to come back to work for him, but I'd refused. It was time I made my own way. Tabby and I had settled into the office, and she'd even hired a few others to come in and help us because business had picked up so well.

And even though things had been crazy playing the part of a single parent in Kya's absence, I'd still managed to keep a high rating that I could be pleased with.

We filed into the elevator and made small talk as we headed down to the lot where I offered to drive.

Once we made it across town to the steak house, I handed over my keys to the valet, and we went inside and waited to be seated.

The hostess smiled and looked Jon up and down as she took us to our table. When she walked away, I leaned over and elbowed him. "She's hot, and she couldn't take her eyes off you."

She still had his attention as she walked away, and before she slipped into the back, she turned and gave him a smile.

Jon cleared his throat. "She's in here every time I come."

"You should ask her out."

"No, thanks. I've dated her type before. She's probably working her way through school with a butt load of student debt and either she'd clean me out or be working so hard, I'd never see her."

"You're too picky," said my father, and I had to agree.

Jon raked his hand through his hair. "I'm not ready."

He'd had a four-month romance with a woman who'd not only broken his heart but smashed it into a million pieces. Things had seemed good for a little while with them, but two months in, she started taking off in his car, spending his money, and apparently, it was all to impress another man. He'd walked in on them one day when he went home early from lunch. She'd been using his house while he was at work. He took the key back and kicked her ass to the curb, but he'd been miserable ever since.

"You have to get back on the horse," Dad said.

"And you're one to talk. You haven't dated anyone since Mom passed away."

Dad squared his shoulders. "I see women. Just because I don't flaunt it in your face, doesn't mean I've spent all of my time alone."

The admission surprised me. "How come you don't bring them around? I'd like to see you happy with someone else. It's way past time you moved on."

"Maybe I will." Dad smiled and turned his eyes to the menus.

Our waitress showed up to take our order, and as she sauntered away, she had my father's attention. The woman was attractive, but a little too old for Jon's liking, although she was a little too young for my father.

"Seems like this place has a little something for the both of us," Dad said.

I knew it was time to tell them the news. "Well, maybe you should both leave here with a date. I have the perfect place you both can bring a plus one. Kya and I are getting married this weekend at The Regency."

My father's head snapped up in surprise. "This weekend?"

"Yeah, I surprised her with the venue when she got home. It all happened pretty fast when they had a cancellation, and since it's the place she was hoping to be married, I wanted to make it happen for her."

Jon looked at me as if I were crazy. "Yeah, I can't believe you got that place. But a week to do a wedding?"

"Well, the good thing about marrying in the garden is you don't need a lot of decorations, which they frown upon anyway, and since we've talked about the big day on more than one occasion and bought the rings and the dress, there's not a lot to do but gather and do the ceremony. The restaurant at The Regency will cater, all I have to do is pay for the food and choose the menu, which is being done later today."

My father offered me a warm smile. "That's wonderful. I'm proud of you, son. Kya is an easy woman to please."

I couldn't agree more. "That she is. The very best."

"Wow, I can't believe Leonard the Legend is officially off the market."

I gave him a sour look. "I've been officially off the market for over a year."

"Yeah, but now it's different. You'll be married. Like, no going back."

"I don't want to ever go back. Kya's the one for me." I had been with enough women to know when I'd found the right one. Kya was everything to me, and my only regret was that I hadn't found her sooner. With our lives getting adjusted and the tour, we hadn't been able to marry right away, and that was part of the reason I wanted to hurry up and get it done. The ceremony was just a formality, but I already felt in my heart that we were husband and wife, two souls connected forever.

When the waitress came to the table, Jon nudged me as my father stared at the woman's ass. I cleared my throat and tried not to laugh as she placed our food in front of us. "Someone's getting a big tip," I said with a chuckle as she strolled away.

We dug into our food and continued to make small talk.

My father took a sip of his drink and then cleared his throat. "What does my granddaughter think of this rushed wedding?"

"She's happy that we're getting married. I don't think she understands much else. She's excited about being the flower girl, and Kya's asking Sadie to stand up with her. There's actually another thing I need to take care of. Jon, I was hoping you'd stand up with me for the service. You're my closest friend, and I can't see anyone else doing it."

"Of course, man. I'd be honored."

"Perfect. We're going to get tuxes for the service, and if you're not busy this week, we'll go in for a fitting."

Jon cut into his steak and readied the piece to his mouth. "Sounds like a plan." He popped the piece into his mouth.

My father pointed his fork at me. "Is Kya's parents coming?"

"If they do, it will be because I invited them, and I'm not sure it's a good idea. They loathe the lifestyle she lives and that she had a career in an industry that's plagued with so much scandal."

"I remember Donald and Elise. The two of them used to be a lot of fun until Donald got caught with his pants down. Then Elise gave him an ultimatum, and they started going to church. They probably weren't happy when Kya started playing that *devil's music*." My father got a big kick out of calling it that, and he laughed when Jon held up the horns sign.

"Yeah? I never knew that." Kya and I had talked an awful lot about our lives at home, but nothing of the sort ever came up about her father. I'd known her parents from living next door, but it was the same way that I'd known anyone's parents. We weren't close or anything.

"Kya might not know it either. They eventually stopped attending, but maybe her mother just doesn't want her to have it as rough as she's had."

I'd never considered why her parents were so dead against her career choice, but I guess it kind of made sense. "I just don't want to do anything to upset Kya on her big day."

"Then stay out of it," Dad said. "Don't try and fix it for her."

Jon leaned up to the table. "Did you know her parents growing up?"

"Of course. They were our neighbors. They seemed like nice people. The mother was a little quiet and kind, and the dad worked an awful lot of hours, but that wasn't anything too out of the norm." Even my father had worked long hours.

I let the conversation die down, and when my father spoke again, he changed the subject. "Did you tell him what happened to Whit White?"

Jon shook his head and finished his mouthful of food. "No, I hadn't had a chance."

"Having trouble on house arrest?"

"He was arrested for a probation violation. He and his girl, Mona Star, they were headed out of the country. Seems he tried to cut out early on his two years and got caught. He told Jon he didn't think anyone would notice."

"That man has an insane ego," I said. "I'm glad I'm not the one stuck with his bullshit."

Dad waved the waitress over to the table and then turned to look at me. "Oh no, I told him to get a new lawyer. I'm done with his bullshit too."

"It's about time." I finished the last bite of my steak and threw my napkin on my plate. "You've already done more for the man that I ever would. His kind is what gives us a bad name as lawyers."

As my father asked for the check, I turned to Jon. "I'll get with you this week over the details, and I'm sure we'll do a quick rehearsal on Friday."

"As the best man, do you think I'll be able to squeeze in a quick bachelor party?"

I thought a moment about our plans, and even though I wasn't about to get sucked into some long night out of drinking and lap dances, I knew with some traditions, Kya might not want to spend the night before together. But since this wasn't a traditional ceremony, she might have already thrown that out the window.

"Let me ask Kya. I think she and Sadie might get together." I turned to look at my father, who was slipping the waitress his card along with a healthy tip. "Dad, do you think you could watch Addie for us on Friday night?"

"Of course, I can. She likes to stay with me." He smiled proudly, and it felt good that he could help with my daughter. Their relationship had already grown stronger than mine and his, and Addie had him wrapped around her little finger.

"That's because you spoil her and let her walk all over you. You can't let her get away with that because then she comes home, and we get to spend a week getting her in line." We shared a smile.

Dad shrugged. "When she's at Grandpa's house, she can do and have whatever she wants."

He had never let me get away with half the stuff he let her. "How come you didn't ever spoil me that way?"

"Because, your mother ruined you long before I had a chance, and because you weren't as cute."

"Ouch," said Jon with a laugh. "The man is brutal."

As we chuckled, I couldn't help but think about how much my own father had changed when it came to his granddaughter. Addison had a way of making things all better, and it was my hope that she would do the same for Kya's parents.

Kya

AFTER DROPPING Addie off at school, I ran a few errands, and by lunch, I'd already made arrangements for the cake and made an appointment to choose the menu for the big day.

I still needed to ask Sadie about standing up with me, and even though we'd talked about it since our early days on the road, I knew that her big baby bump was going to make her hesitate.

At least I'd chosen her favorite place, and if I could get a delicious diner burger into her, I could convince her of anything.

As the doorbells announced my entrance, Sadie looked up from her glass of soda and waved me over. "I hope you don't mind this table. I know you prefer the other side, but I needed to sit down."

I eased into the booth. "No, this is perfect. You look beautiful today."

She rubbed her round belly. "I'm a bloated cow, and these maternity pants are cutting off the circulation to my legs."

"That's because its time to go up a size." She hadn't bought any new clothes since her second trimester started, and now that she was in her third, her pants looked like she was ready for a flood with her growing belly pulling the length up.

She shook her head. "No way. I have already gone up enough, and with just a couple more months to go, I don't want to spend any more money on clothes."

"Come on, Sadie, it's not like you can't afford it, and you're going to need your legs when the baby comes, trust me. And besides, I think we should do a little shopping this week."

She narrowed her eyes. "Why do I get the feeling you have something up your sleeve?"

"Because I do?" I gave her a sly smile.

The waitress took that moment to walk over with her pen poised at her pad. "What can I get for you?"

"I'll take a BLT on wheat."

Sadie leaned forward, her belly hitting the table. "I want the biggest, juiciest, bacon double cheeseburger with grilled onions. Oh, and add a fried egg, well done with mayonnaise, mustard, and ketchup on the side." She glanced at me from the corner of her eye. "What? I'm starving, and I've gone two months without one of these delicious burgers. I wanted one last night, but Stones said I could wait until today. He didn't want me up all night." She turned back to the waitress. "Oh, and could you put some extra pickles on the side. And fries. The waffle cut, not the shoestring."

"I got it," said the waitress. "Want another soda?"

"Yes, with cherries this time, please." Sadie looked across the table, and even though I didn't drink much soda, I decided what the hell.

"I'll take a cherry cola too." Sadie gave me a pointed look. "Okay, fine, scratch the sandwich and bring me the same, but no extras, just a bacon cheeseburger all the way."

The waitress took a deep breath and scratched out the first order, changing it to the second. Without another word, she walked away.

When she was good and gone, Sadie shrugged. "What?"

"No wonder your pants are cutting off your circulation. If you keep eating like that, you're going to have no choice but to go shopping."

"Do you think that just because I ordered food, I would forget you have something you need to tell me."

"Oh, I do. I'm just not sure you're going to be as excited as you might normally be."

"Why wouldn't I?" Sadie asked as the waitress quickly brought our drinks. She hurried away as if to avoid us before Sadie could add to her order, or I could change mine.

"Because I know you. And when I tell you that Leo and I are getting married this weekend, and I want you to stand up with me, you're going to—"

"This weekend!" She grabbed my hand across the table. "You want me to go to your wedding swelled up like a beached whale?"

"No, I want you to stand up with me."

She made a sound that had heads turning. "You know I want that more than anything. I just can't believe you didn't give me any warning."

"You're beautiful and glowing, and you're not that big. And this is just the reaction I expected." I gave her hand a squeeze. "Leo sprung it on me when we got back. He reserved The Regency for me and everything."

"The Regency. Oh wow, that's been your dream forever."

"Right, and they had an open spot because of a cancellation. He grabbed it, and so since I have my dress, and we have our rings, we wanted to do a quick service there."

"I think it's a perfect idea. And I'll stop my fussing about it. I don't mean to spoil anything."

"Don't be silly. My day will be perfect, and you're going to look beautiful in your dress, and Leo, and I want to buy it, anything you choose."

"Any color?"

I looked up and saw the waitress coming through the swinging doors. "Well, that's something we maybe could talk about over these monster cheeseburgers coming our way."

"I can't eat that thing! I'll gain a ton before Saturday."

"No way. I changed my order so you wouldn't have to eat so much alone, you're not backing out on me now." The dishes were placed in front of us; two of the biggest burgers I'd ever seen sat on each plate.

She gave a sigh. "It does look yummy." She wasted no time digging in; then she wiped her mouth. "I can't believe we've only been home for a couple of days and you're getting married. You're going to be exhausted by next week. I hope he's taking you someplace nice."

"We've talked about going on a trip to an island, but we'll bring Addie along. More of a relaxing family getaway than a honeymoon, but we have our whole lives for romantic getaways."

"I could always watch Addie another time, and a beach sounds nice. I hope I get my bikini body back." She rubbed her tummy again.

"I'm sure you will." I gave her a reassuring look as she picked at the burger's bun.

"Let's talk colors." Sadie bounced in her seat. "How about red? Plum? Royal blue?"

"I like those. I was thinking a deep red and blush. Not pink. But maybe we should go and see what the shops have to offer. I'm wide open, really." I had no idea was more like it. I liked so many colors and had never really pictured anything too colorful. Since I was the only one who was supposed to wear white, I had thought a pale blush or green would be nice in the garden.

Sadie nodded. "I know it's a touchy subject, but are you going to invite your parents?"

My heart stung every time I thought of my parents not being at my wedding, but I wasn't the one being difficult. My mother had always been hell-bent against my lifestyle, and my father, with his addictions, was the reason. I'd known about their rocky marriage, my father's many affairs, and the way he'd abused drugs and alcohol to the point of near overdose when I was a junior in high school. "No, I don't think that's a good idea."

"It's your big day, though. And I don't understand why they don't want to see their granddaughter or at least be happy you're no longer going to be a single mother living in sin."

"It's more about their issues than mine. Always has been. I'm not going to let them push their issues off on me. I've been in this business for a long time, managed to keep my nose clean, stayed away from all of the temptations, and worked hard for a good reputation, but they won't ever see that, no matter how bad I want them to."

"Well, not if you don't ever ask to see them," she said softly.

"I keep in touch just enough to find out if they're both alive, and I figure the papers will tell them if something happens to me. It's not like they ever try to reach out." That had been the way of it since I'd left home, and the only time I tried to reach out was when I was pregnant with Addison. They hadn't bothered to come down to see me or her in the hospital. I didn't think they'd come to my wedding.

"I guess it would be kind of strange."

I laughed. "You have no idea." She gave me a pressing look and knew I had to explain. "I didn't tell Leo about my dad. In fact, you're the only person I've told."

"Wow, Kya. Don't you think he should know before you two get hitched? I mean, that's kind of something I'd think he should know about."

"It's not that big of a deal, is it?.Besides, he's never really asked for details, and I just kept it simple. They don't like my lifestyle. It's the truth, so why complicate things? Besides, he'll want to know why I waited so long. But he wasn't around in high school, our friendship had taken a hiatus, and it all just sort of came to a head. I was good at hiding it. Didn't want my friends to know my parents were so screwed up."

"I can understand that. I just hope it doesn't come back to bite you in the ass. How would you feel if there was something Leo was keeping from you?"

"If it was about his parents, it wouldn't matter. That's not the kind of thing that he can hold against me."

"I'd want to know if it were Stones."

"You know everything about Blitz, probably too much. We've seen his naked ass, for fuck's sake." To be fair, he liked to moon the audience, and it was one of his usual stage stunts. All of America had seen it.

"You don't have to remind me. But look, take my word for it. Let Leo know. You'll feel better not having any secrets."

I shrugged it off, not really thinking it was a big deal. The fine details of the situation weren't that important. "I have a meeting with the venue coordinator. I have to choose my menu, and I'll be able to see what kind of flowers they have. I'd like to coordinate if I can, and I thought maybe you'd like to come along."

"That sounds like fun. I'm not doing anything. Some of us kept a clean schedule so we could rest."

"I could tell Stones to plan you an impromptu wedding for next weekend if you want."

"No way! I think we'll do the baby thing first. It's all I can handle. And besides, my dream dress doesn't allow for a baby bump."

We shared a laugh and finished our burgers over small talk, but I couldn't get my parents out of my mind. I wanted to dismiss the thought of them attending my wedding, but deep inside, I'd always wanted them at the ceremony. Knowing they wouldn't come, I couldn't handle asking them if they were just going to say no.

Leo

THE WEEK HAD FLOWN by fast, with lots of planning and spending, but by Friday, we'd come to a few conclusions. For one, we weren't having bachelor and bachelorette parties. Neither of us really wanted to do that, and with Sadie pregnant and needing her rest and Jon undecided about what we should do, Kya and I agreed we wanted to throw tradition out the window and spend the night together. Since my father had already planned to get Addie, it would be the perfect night at home alone. Just the two of us.

As we loaded into the car to take Addison to my father's, Kya looked at her phone, going down our to-do list to make sure we hadn't forgotten anything. "Food is done, dresses and shoes are bought, suits are rented, flowers, cake, and the judge."

I reached over and patted her knee. "I took care of the rings, and we called everyone we know and loved to spread the word."

"Is there anything we've forgotten?" She put her hand on her temples and closed her eyes.

"Yes, there is," I said, starting the car.

"What?" She looked down at the phone.

"You forget to breathe. Just relax, okay. Everything is going to be fine. We practiced, and everyone knows their places. We're all set. Now, all we have to do is let the clock run out."

"I don't know how you can be so calm."

Deep inside, I was nervous, but I wasn't going to make it worse for her by letting her know that. I had also taken it upon myself to invite her parents, a big surprise I hoped wouldn't backfire.

"I have been practicing throwing my petals too," said Addie from the back seat.

"And you're going to do a great job."

"My dress makes me look like a real princess too. Even though Mama wouldn't let me buy real high heels."

"They don't make tall heels in your size for a reason. Little girls don't wear heels."

Addie sighed loudly. "It's not fair."

"You'll have your whole life to wear tall heels, sweet pea, and your mother is right. I want you to be my little girl forever." She was so ready to grow up, already wanting to wear makeup and heels. I wanted to lock her in a closet until she was eighteen. No, thirty.

I looked in the mirror at her wide eyes and realized that if Kya's parents did show up, the only one of our parents missing would be my mother. I liked to think that part of her spirit was always with me and maybe she would see the thing through my daughter's eyes that were exactly like hers.

After fighting a little traffic, we made it to my father's house, and as soon as I stopped the car, Addie undid her booster and jumped out of her seat. By the time I made it around to get her out, she had already done so and was halfway to the door where my father waited with open arms.

She ran to hug him, and I grabbed her suitcase and walked around to join Kya.

"There's my sweet pea!" He tucked a piece of chocolate into her small hand and lifted her up in his arms.

"Dad, it's a bit soon for chocolate. She hasn't even had dinner." I knew Kya had gotten onto me for the crappy diet we'd had in her absence, and she wanted us all to do better.

Dad squared his jaw. "I've said it before, and I'll say it again. When she's at my house, it's Grandpa's rules. Besides, it's one piece of chocolate. It's hardly going to spoil the pizza I ordered for dinner."

Kya and I exchanged a look, and Addie cheered as she unwrapped her chocolate. "Is it the same kind as before?" She popped the candy in her mouth.

"Yes, ma'am, I know how much you love pineapple and ham."

I remembered as a child begging my father to order pizza, only to have him tell me no, but Addie didn't even have to ask. Suddenly, the tin man had a heart. He carried her into the house, and we followed.

When we were inside, I saw a blanket fort set up in front of the TV next to his recliner. "I've got us all set up to watch movies, and we'll have popcorn too."

Kya spoke up, "Grandpa, remember there's a wedding tomorrow. I don't want her to be sick with a tummy ache." It was her polite way of telling my father he better slow down on the junk food, and I had to agree.

"Yeah, no eating past seven-thirty, and no more candy." I kissed Addie on the cheek, and Kya did the same.

We left the two to their fun, and then Kya and I made our way out to the car.

As we drove away, she eased back in her seat. "We're really doing this. Tomorrow."

I reached over and took her hand. "Yes, we are. And I can't wait to see you walk down that aisle, for the moment you take my hand and we say those I dos." I brought her hand to my lips.

"Me too." She eased over in her seat. "I just hope everything goes off without a hitch and people show up. You never know with last-minute planning."

"The people at the office are coming, Tabby's bringing the new man, and Edith is excited she's going to make it before her big move. Then the rest of my father's people will be there, and I'm sure they'll come, or he'll have their asses. All of my cousins, and mom's sister." I turned onto the freeway and hit the fast lane.

"And my family. Everyone should be there except my parents, of course. The best thing I did was not invite them."

My back stiffened, and when I didn't make a sound, she turned and looked at me.

"What's wrong?"

I glanced her way but couldn't hold her stare.

"Oh, no." Kya turned in her seat to face me. "What did you do, Leo?"

"They may not come. I mean, when have they ever, right?"

"You invited my parents without telling me?" She folded her arms and turned away from me. "I can't believe you did that without discussing it with me first. You don't even know the situation."

"I just thought they'd be glad to know you're getting married and that things are good in your life. I don't see what the big deal is, Kya. I didn't think it would hurt to make an effort, and I hoped that if they did show, it would be a nice surprise."

She feigned laughter. "A nice surprise? Sorry, but the last thing I need tomorrow is my addict father showing up with my bitch of a mother so they can either cause a scene or blame me for their troubles."

"What?" I hadn't ever heard of her refer to her father as an addict before.

"Yeah, as I said, Leonard, you don't even know what the issues are."

"Why don't you tell me?"

"I really didn't want to go into it right now or anything before this wedding. Shit. What did they say?"

I let loose a long breath, wishing I'd listened to my father and not tried to fix things. I should have talked to her first and respected her to handle it herself.

"I called them Tuesday. I talked to your mother who sounded good, and she remembered me. I told her we were getting married, that her granddaughter and you would love to see her for the big day. She said okay, seemed like it was not the worst thing she could think of doing on a Saturday, and then asked where it was. She asked about my father and, you know, made a little small talk."

"My mother made small talk with you?"

"Yeah." I shrugged like it wasn't a big deal, but Kya shook her head.

"You're kidding me. Do you know that when I get her on the phone, she never makes small talk? Hell, it's hard enough to get her on the phone, much less get any kind of human response from her. When she does talk, all she does is ask me if I'm still hanging out in bars and wasting my life."

"I had no idea. I'm so sorry." I felt like I was shrinking with each and every word. "I wish you'd told me. When did your dad become an addict?"

"Well, he's always messed around on my mother, but it got worse when I was a junior. I pretended things were okay and didn't ask for a whole lot of support, you know. I just hid in my music, put all my focus and energy into it. I guess that's part of the reason my mother hates it so much. I disappeared into my music and left her to deal with it alone. It wasn't like she could be supportive and come to my shows. That would put her and Dad in the bars. That would put Dad in the path of a relapse."

"And then, when I had my friends come over to do practices, we had to do them one a month. My mom was sweet to my friends, hid it well, you know. But when there was no one around, she was a mess over my father. She finally gave him an ultimatum and told him he needed to reform his life, to start attending church and being a member of society. So, my hanging out in bars was only a temptation. I didn't want to stick around and watch my family fall apart, so I bailed just as soon as I could."

I couldn't believe what I was hearing. I'd been right next door and not known, and even my father didn't know the whole truth. "You could have told me. You could have talked to me, Kya. I'd have taken care of you."

"Don't you see, Leonard? I knew that. I didn't turn you down because I didn't want to ruin our friendship with a relationship. I just didn't want you to find out the truth."

I took the next exit and then turned down our street. "I'll call them and ask them not to come if you want, but, and while I know this is out of line, I think you should really consider letting them see what a great person you are. You don't have to let them into your life every day, but once in a while, it's good for the soul, and I think it's time you healed." I held my breath and waited for her to yell at me. Not twenty-four hours from the ceremony and here we were in disagreement.

But she took a deep breath and nodded, which was not what I expected. "You're probably right. Deep down, I know I want them to come, but I really didn't want to have to face the disappointment if they didn't."

I pulled into our driveway and stopped. "Let's just have a little faith, and if they don't, we'll agree that it's their loss, but then, at least you can know you were the bigger person."

"You were the bigger person, Leo. And thank you. It was a sweet gesture; I just hope they come. I'd like them to meet Addie before she grows up. She won't be young forever." A tear formed in the corner of her eye, and she quickly wiped it away.

"It's going to be okay, Kya." I leaned over and pulled her into my arms. "Let's go inside, and I'll draw us a nice, hot bath, and then I'll give you a long rubdown."

"That sounds good." She brought her mouth down on mine, and after a long, deep kiss, we went inside.

❦

Kya

Leonard unlocked the door, and before I could shut it behind me, he had me off my feet. As he turned with me in his arms, he caught the door and shut it with his foot.

"I'm sorry if I upset you."

"I'm not upset. It's okay, really. I think it's all the stress getting to me. The tour, the wedding, all of it. I want to just relax and hold you and forget all about it until tomorrow."

He brought me to the bedroom and placed me on the bed where I lay unbuttoning my blouse as he undid his pants and kicked off his shoes.

My shoes fell to the floor in two light thuds, and then I leaned up to pull my top from my shoulders as Leonard removed his shirt. Before I could make it to my pants, he reached forward, hooking fingers into my waistband to pull them down.

He straddled my knees and then rubbed my hip. "I should go and draw that bath, hm?"

I reached up and held his arm, pulling him down closer to me. "I think it can wait another few minutes." Our lips crushed together, moving and mingling against one another's as our hands roamed each other's bodies. Mine went to his ass, pulling him closer, and he cupped my breast, moving down to pull my tight nipple into his teeth.

I gave a soft moan as he bit gently, sending a tingle of pleasure through me. "That's right. I love that sound. I've missed it so much. I don't think I ever want you to be away as long as you were this last time. I'm going to have to learn how to manage my time, so I can be there with you."

I brought my hand up his back and to his shoulder. "Or, I could not take as many shows. I've talked to Sadie about it. We both agree it might be best to wait a little while after she has the baby, like at least a year. Without me touring, it will give me some more studio time."

"How would you like a studio here?"

"Here?" The sound of that turned me on more than he knew, and I rubbed my hips upward as he pressed his thick erection into my middle.

"Yeah, I thought we might do one in the basement. We have that entire space down there going to waste. You don't even use it for laundry."

"That would be nice. I've thought about it before but just never wanted to hire anyone."

"I'll take care of it. It can be a wedding gift from me." He moved his hips, his rock-hard cock sliding between my lips and teasing at my channel.

I loved him so much, and he always thought of the sweetest gifts and wanted to do things to make me happy. I wished I had something I could do for him. "I don't have a gift for you, Leo."

He moved his hips, rolling them so hard, his hipbone ground into mine. "Yes, you do, and I'm about to take it." His voice was barely a whisper, and it sent chills down my spine, the aching in my core intensifying with need.

He reached down and centered himself at my entrance, moving slowly into me, inching himself until he was buried deep.

He filled me up, my lips stretched tight around him, and then he moved, his hips working slowly, grazing each and every tender spot on his way in and out. He had me over the edge in no time, and as I writhed beneath him, he stifled my moans with his mouth, kissing me hard.

All of a sudden, he rolled us over, his hands resting on my hips as he moved me up and down on his cock. "Fuck, baby, you feel so good." His pace quickened, and soon, he was filling me up, his seed warm as wax as it shot into me. I pressed my hands on his shoulders and rode him in a quick, steady pace, my tits bouncing up and down, slapping together, until he reached up and cupped them both. I moaned as he squeezed, and then my release soaked him too.

He rose up and brought his mouth to my breasts, his tongue licking, flicking my tight, little buds. "Let me go run that bath. We'll get good and relaxed for round two."

"That sounds good." I wanted the intimate time with him, and it was strange knowing the next time we were together like this, we'd be married.

I moved off of him, and he took my hand as he led me to the bathroom. "Let's get the water set. Then, I'll turn on the jets." He turned on the water as I sat on the edge of the large tub and watched. He was so handsome, so tall, and even though I would always see my special Leonard from school, I could see him now for the man he was, a man who cared deeply for his family, loved me and his daughter fiercely, and would do anything for us.

"That should do it. Won't be long now."

I got up and went to the bathroom closet. "I'll get us some towels." I chose the two largest, fluffiest towels we had because I knew he liked them best.

When the water was set, he turned on the jets and reached for my hand. Then, he helped me up the steps and into the water. Before I could sit, he stepped in behind me, and I settled between his legs. His stiff cock rested in my crack, digging into my back. I nudged against it, and he chuckled.

"Already so eager," he said.

"I'm always eager for you, Leonard." I always would be. There wasn't anyone in the world who made me feel as good as he did, and not just in a sexual way, but good about myself, about who I was and who I wanted to be for him and with him in my life. I couldn't have asked for a better father for my child and husband, and I felt truly blessed.

"Are you nervous?" he asked.

I took a deep breath. "Maybe a little anxious. Are you?"

"Same," he shrugged. "Isn't it strange? The two of us make a living working a crowd, and yet when it comes to standing up and taking our vows, we're anxious."

"I do feel like I do when I get ready for a show. Only this is a much smaller crowd, which is sometimes more intimidating only because it's a lot easier for me to be aware of who's focused on me."

He moved my hair to one side, exposing my neck. "That doesn't make much sense. I'd rather have to worry about sixty people focused on me than hundreds or even thousands."

"You only say that because you haven't worked a trial in front of thousands." I laughed, and he kissed my shoulders. He reached around and cupped my breasts and then dipped his hand down into the water to rub my mound.

"You're a goddess on stage. I get turned on thinking about how hot you look when you perform." He nudged himself closer, his thick cock pressed tight against me.

Our tub was so large, I could easily turn around and straddle him, so that's just what I did, only I didn't sit on his cock just yet. Instead, I straddled his legs and gripped it, stroking it nice and slow, feeling him harden even more, growing in my hands even more.

"It's a grower. And it's ready for you." He rocked his hips softly as I stroked him, kneading his balls in my palm as I worked it base to tip.

I moved back in the water and leaned down to take the head into my mouth, and he turned off the water and raised his hips up out of it to give me better access. I relaxed my throat, taking him to the back of my mouth, his thick head locking behind my tonsils.

He held me there, moving his hips up and down to fuck my mouth. He moaned and reached down to play with my nipples, and then he pulled me up and kissed my mouth. "I want inside of you, Kya. I need to feel your tight, little slit on my cock." His arm came around my waist, and I moved closer, straddling him, centering him at my entrance as I lowered myself down, grinding against his base.

"Fuck, yeah," he hissed.

I rode him hard, and he held on to me, and when I didn't think I could go on and the bathwater had turned cold, he moved me off him and got to his feet. "Let's go to the shower where it's warmer. I want to put you on the wall."

I loved it when he did that, and I smiled, taking his hand as he led me to it. He turned the hot on and then added a little cold before I stepped inside as the steam filled the room. He brought me closer, his mouth landing on my breast as his hands roamed and his fingers explored, plunging deep into my slit, stroking my walls and making me shudder as another release rushed through me.

My walls quaked, milking him, my back falling against the cool tile. I threw my legs around him as he lifted me up and stepped between them. He impaled me with his cock, and then bounced me up and down. When our legs were good and ready to give out again, he put me down, and I turned to face the wall. I looked over my shoulder, tilting my ass up to brush against the head of his cock, which jutted proudly from his hips still in need of attention. I rubbed my ass against it, and he leaned down, licking my tight star as he pressed his fingers into my channel.

Then he rose up, his fingers moving to tease my clit as he pushed his cock into me, tapping my G-spot with each and every thrust.

We worked ourselves into a frenzy, and I felt all of the stress and urgency melting away as we both came, him filling my channel as I spasmed through my orgasm, milking and clenching until we both stilled and moved to the floor where he held me as a steady stream of hot water flowed over us.

After a few minutes, I didn't want to move, not even when the water started to cool. He turned off the water and reached around to grab our towels. He pulled them around us, kissing my damp shoulder and rubbing my back in soothing strokes.

It was nice just sitting there together. "I don't think I can move."

"I know I don't want to," he said. "But we probably should. I'm sure if this feels amazing, then the bed is going to be fucking amazing."

We shared a laugh, and then he helped me up, and we dried off, walking to the bed where we climbed under the covers, both still supple from the water. We used our bodies to get warm, and soon I was comfortable, content to sleep knowing that I loved Leo with everything in me.

Leo

I PACED the groom's dressing room of The Regency and didn't think I could possibly be any more nervous.

"Relax," said Jon. "You're making me anxious. I don't think I've ever seen you like this before. You weren't this nervous during your first trial."

"It's Kya's parents. Dad's supposed to come in any minute and tell me if they made it. I hope his slow pace is a sign that the three of them are talking and reminiscing about old times."

"There's no telling with your father. He's probably out there talking to one of the ladies from the office." Jon looked in the mirror and straightened his tie. Then, he grabbed his shoes and went to sit on a satin-covered, padded bench.

"I hope not. I want them to be here. I don't want Kya walking out there to find they haven't shown up." I should have just minded my own fucking business when it came to them, but no, I had to put the only dent in the perfect day.

"I'm sure they'll be here, but if not, I could always go to their house and drag them here if you want."

"It sounds appealing, but I'm not sure that would solve anything. Apparently, the issues with her mom and dad were a lot deeper than I realized, and my surprise just might blow up in my face."

He straightened his sock and pulled on his shoe. "That's too bad, man. I hope it all works out."

"Well, at least you had a reason to ask that hostess out."

"Yeah, and we'll just see if she shows up too. She was supposed to meet me here since I had to be so early. Her name is Sabrina, and she's nice so far."

"Is she what you thought? You know, college student, buried in her work?" He had been so certain of how things would go with the woman before he had ever met her that I wasn't sure he was going to give her a chance.

Jon straightened out his laces. "No, she actually just graduated before Christmas. She's trying to get a job in her field of study, but there aren't any positions in the area."

"What did she study?" I asked.

"She's a radiation tech. We went out the other night. She wanted to have coffee and get better acquainted."

"Nice. Medical field."

"Yeah, she likes to take care of me." He waggled his brows, and we shared a laugh.

"Yeah, and you learned that on the first date?"

His response was a sly grin. It was nice to see him happy about someone, but I hoped the girl wouldn't stand him up. He needed someone good in his life. That reminded me of someone else who needed someone good to spend his time with. "Did you see who my father brought?"

"I think he's flying solo unless he has someone we don't know about, which is entirely possible."

I still couldn't believe he liked to keep his women a secret from me, and I wondered how many he'd seen since my mother died. "Yeah, today might remind him too much of my mother for him to bring anyone. He might be thinking of her today."

"Yeah, that can't be easy."

There was a soft knock on the door, and my father stuck his head in. "I have a bit of bad news, son. Kya's parents are not here yet, and you only have about ten minutes until you go out. I saw Sadie in the hall."

"They aren't going to come." I let out a long breath and sat down beside Jon to put on my shoes. "I should have minded my own business. I just wanted to make her happy. I hate that she doesn't have her parents in her life."

"She has a pretty good family from what I saw on that front row, and surprisingly, that bunch cleans up nicely."

Jon got to his feet. "I'm going to go on out and give you two a moment." He left the room and pulled the door shut behind him.

I looked around, and my father was holding a small box, and I suddenly realized why Jon made himself scarce.

"I wanted to give you something special on your big day. I hope you like it." He passed me the small, white gift-wrapped box. I could tell by how fancy it was that someone, most likely a lady, had wrapped it for him, probably Edith.

"Thank you, Dad." I pulled off the ribbon and then ripped into it, revealing a Rolex watch.

"I thought you might like that. Your mother gave me a watch on our wedding day. She said it was because I had a problem with being late." He let out a soft chuckle as his eyes grew red.

"I love it, Dad. I wish she was here."

"Me too, son. Me too. You know, when you and Kya were young, your mother used to watch you play. We had that old tree house in the backyard."

"I remember. It was really run-down."

"Well, it terrified your mother that one of you would get hurt, and then one day, she was at the kitchen window, and you two were headed up the ladder. She saw how careful you were with Kya. How you made sure you helped her up. Your mother said you were going to make someone a fine husband one day. She could see the way you doted over her. She sure loved Kya too. She'd always wanted a daughter so we'd have one of each, but that just wasn't in the cards for us. Having Kya around filled that void."

I could still remember how her smile could light up a room. It seemed so long since I'd seen it. "Mom was great. She used to send out cookies and lemonade. Always the best. I still haven't found lemonade that good."

My father laughed. "And you never will. She was something, your mother. And I know she'd be very proud of the man you've become." My father pulled me in for a hug and held me tightly as he patted my back. "I'm proud of you, too, son."

We pulled back, both wiping tears, though my father looked away so I couldn't see his. "I guess we should get out of here."

"We certainly should. You've got to get into position." He straightened my tie, and then we walked out together.

While I passed the door to Kya's dressing room, Sadie popped her head out. Dad went on ahead as I stopped. "Hey, do you know if Kya's parents showed?" Her voice was barely a whisper, and I could tell she didn't want Kya to hear. She stepped out into the hall.

"No. I wish I'd never asked them."

"Don't feel that way, Leo. You wanted to do the right thing, and I think you did. Whether they show or not will speak to their character, and it's nothing she didn't already expect. She'll be fine."

I had a feeling that since she'd shown concern, Kya must have mentioned it. "Did she ask about them?"

"She's mentioned them a few times. I think she's trying to prepare for the disappointment, but when she sees you at the end of that aisle, she'll forget all about her parents and their issues."

"I hope you're right." I took a deep breath. "Okay, tell her I'll be waiting."

"You look great. We'll be right out." As she returned to the room, I headed out for the ceremony.

When I walked in and saw everyone gathered, I waved and said a few hellos as I made my way up the front. I didn't see Mr. and Mrs. Campbell anywhere, and though it was a letdown, I wasn't going to let them ruin my big day.

Considering we'd done the last-minute ceremony with only a week to plan, there was quite a turnout, and though we'd only called about sixty of our closest family and friends, the room was packed, and it looked like everyone else we'd asked had arrived.

Judge Sarah Carter had arrived as well and stood at the front row with my father, both of them smiling and laughing together. They had been old friends since I was a kid, and Kya and I thought it was fitting that the judge who had found in her favor during the trial that brought us together would officiate our marriage.

Jon sat with the hostess from the restaurant, Sabrina, and they seemed to be getting along nicely as well. When he saw me, he gave her a kiss on the cheek and then got up and joined me. "Hey, is it time to get this show on the road?"

"Yeah, we better get in place."

Sarah Carter took her place, and I heard Jon mumble under his breath, "Latecomers. In under the wire."

I looked up to see Kya's mother and father, both looking great and dressed to the nines. I gestured to my father as I headed down.

As I approached, Kya's mother, who looked so much like her, hair, eyes, and even her teeth, which she showed with a wide smile as she saw me coming. "Leo?"

"In the flesh. I can't tell you how glad I am that you made it."

"We figured it was time to make things right." She put her arm around her husband, and he shook my hand.

"You've grown into a fine man, it seems, and a lucky one at that. Thanks for taking care of our girl when we didn't. I wish I'd done better by her. Then I could have been here to give her away."

As I shook his hand, I realized I hadn't even thought of that. Papa Blitz was prepared to give her away, but I had a hunch the man wouldn't mind sharing his duties. "I'm blessed indeed. If you don't mind giving me a moment, I'll see if I can arrange something." I held up and finger and walked over to where Blitz stood at the door about to go back for Kya.

"Hey, man. I know Kya is honored to have you giving her away, but I was wondering if you could help me in a bit of a surprise for her."

"Anything for Kya."

"Well, her parents showed up after so many years, and I know she really wanted them to come and didn't think they would. I thought maybe you could walk her down the aisle to her father, and do a sort of pass off?"

Blitz nodded. "That's a great idea. I'll make sure and let it be a surprise."

"Thanks, Blitz. You're an amazing friend to her, and I appreciate you always looking out for my girls."

"Glad you're in the picture, my man. Now, I better get my ass to the back or Kya's going to think I already had one too many." He gave me a wink and then headed off to meet Kya. I went back to find her parents still standing where I'd left them, talking to a few of our old friends, including my father.

"Mr. Campbell, if I could get you to stand in the third row, I've arranged for our friend to hand Kya off to you."

"That would be a dream come true, thank you. If it's not any trouble, of course."

"Kya will love it, trust me. She was so hoping you'd make it." I turned to my father as the music started, and I knew we had to get in our places quickly. "Dad, could you please show Mrs. Campbell to her place in the front row?"

Dad gave me a thumb's up and took Mrs. Campbell's hand as I hurried back up the aisle.

Jon leaned closer and whispered, "Is that her parents?"

"Yes," I said proudly. "And just in time to pull off an even better surprise."

Kya

As I stood in the hall with Addison and Sadie, waiting for the music to change, Blitz rounded the corner with a huge smile. "Oh, how mine breath hath been taken away," he said in his best dramatic voice. "You ladies are surely the picture of pure beauty."

"Thank you, Blitz." I moved my bouquet to one hand and then gave him a loose hug as not to muss myself.

"You're welcome, gorgeous."

"Do you like my dress, Papa Blitz?" asked Addie.

"Why you're the prettiest, my little flower. As sweet as the jasmine too."

The music changed, and it was time for Sadie and to send Addison out in front of her. "I'll see you soon, honey." I waved at Addie and gave Sadie a nervous smile.

She looked at me with reassurance in her eyes. "You've got this, Kya."

"Thank you for doing this, Blitz. I always wanted my father to do this, but I guess I should have made an effort myself to invite them. I suppose I haven't ever really done as much as I could have to make them see how much I need them in my life. It's just always been easier to let things be."

"It's an honor to do this for you. You know, having all sons, who I truly love, I've often wondered what it would be like to have a daughter and what she'd be like. I don't know what I would've ended up with in one, but I know if she could be anything like you, I couldn't be prouder or happier. You're a sensational woman, friend, and mother, and I'm honored you've allowed me to be in your and Addie's lives."

His words were everything I needed to hear, and I pulled him in for another hug, this time not minding if I got a little smooshed. "Thank you so much for that. I feel the same about you, Blitz. You've always been like a father to me, taken me under your wing and treated me with respect when no one else in the industry would. I owe you so much."

"If you want to pay me back, you can live a full life of happiness and bliss with the ones you love. That's all a man can ask from a daughter, or so I guess." He gave a little shrug, and we shared a giggle. Then, when the music started, he took my hand, and we slowly made our way out and around the corner.

Everyone rose, and I glanced up at the front to see my Leonard. He looked so good, my heart ached. His eyes were ringed with red, and his smile was so bright, it touched his ears. I knew I would love him forever and didn't think I could be any luckier. Not only did I have the best daughter in the world, and friends who loved me, but I had the hottest man in the world for my very own.

About halfway down the aisle, I glanced up at Blitz who leaned over and gave me a kiss on the cheek, and then he turned loose of my arm, and when he stepped aside, my father was there to take his place.

Tears stung my eyes as I fell against him, and he broke down too. "It's been too long, princess. You're so beautiful, and I couldn't be prouder." The words were choked out with tears, and my own throat was on fire with a lump that had me nearly suffocating.

"Thank you for being here, Daddy. I wanted you to come so badly." We continued down the aisle, and though I felt like I was ten feet off the floor, my father delivered me safely to Leonard's arms.

"We are here to join this woman, Kya Elizabeth Campbell, and this man, Leonard Michael Pace in matrimony. Who gives this bride to her groom?"

"Her mother and I do," said my father.

I turned to see my mother sitting next to Liam and his wife on the front row, and I totally lost it all over again as my father stepped away. By then, I was blubbering like a baby, and Leonard pulled me into his arms to hold me, taking my hand so we could get on with the union.

Sarah Carter read a moment and then gave us time to say our vows, which we'd written for one another, and then came the rings. We managed to get them on without a hitch, and I was bouncing on my feet when the judge proclaimed us husband and wife. "You may now kiss your bride."

Leonard gave me a sly smile as he pulled me into his arms. So many obstacles had come our way, but we'd managed to overcome them, and now we would have a happy life together. He leaned in and planted a big kiss on my lips as the crowd went wild. There were a lot of cheers and whistles and a "hell yeah" from Blitz who raised his fist in the air and whooped.

When it was done, I glanced over my shoulder to see my parents smiling, and then we turned to be presented to our friends and family as Mr. and Mrs. Pace.

"I'm so happy," I told Leo. Addie ran over and fell against Leonard's legs. He scooped her up, and everyone clapped for our little family.

We carried her out with us, and when we got to the back, he put her down, and I met Leonard's eyes. "They came! And my father gave me away! Can you believe it?" I searched his eyes and realized that he'd arranged it all. "You asked him to?"

"He said he regretted not being close to you and being able to, so I decided we had to make it happen, and Blitz agreed."

"That stinker, he knew the whole time!" It was perfect, every single moment of the ceremony. "I can't believe that all went by so fast."

Leo looked down at Addie. "Now, we party."

Addie cheered. "Do we get to eat the cake now?"

"Soon. We have to get a few photographs of it first, but yeah, we get to eat it." My cake looked beautiful, and everything about the ceremony had gone well too. I couldn't wait until the rest of the guests moved into the reception room, and while we waited, Leo's father rounded the corner with my parents in tow.

"Here they are."

My mother's jaw dropped when she looked at us and saw Addie, and I knew it was time for an introduction.

"Mom, Dad, this is your granddaughter Addison. Addie, this is your grandparents, my mom and dad."

"You mean I get a new last name *and* new grandparents?" We had discussed her name changing when mine did, and Judge Carter was going to help with that process.

My mother laughed. "You sure do, sweet pea."

Leonard and I exchanged a look. I had called her "sweet pea" long before anyone else, and the nickname sort of stuck. "How did you know what we call her?" I asked my mom.

"You mean you call her 'sweet pea'?" Mom and Dad exchanged a laugh.

"What's so funny?" I narrowed my eyes.

Dad explained, "I know you were too young to remember because she died when you were so young, but your grandmother Campbell used to call you that." My father's mother had died when I was still a baby.

"How strange. I guess it was meant to be, then. And thanks for being here. I'm sorry I didn't invite you myself. Leonard took the initiative, and I'm so glad he did."

"Indeed, it's been a long time, Kya. I hope we can move forward."

"I'm still who I am." I shrugged, hoping that the person I had become was enough for them both.

My mother put her arm around me. "So are we, but we've learned a bit of tolerance and acceptance goes a long way. We've started taking counseling, and it's been amazing for us." My mother held onto my father's hand. "This is a big step for us all, and I hope we can continue to get to know you even after today."

"Of course. It's all I've ever wanted, Mom." I wondered if she would still be against me having my musical career. As we filed into the other room, where our reception was, our friends clapped, giving us a warm welcome.

I felt a tug on my dress and looked down to see Addie on her tiptoes. I leaned down, and she spoke into my ear, "What do I call them?"

"I don't know. I suppose whatever makes you feel comfortable."

"Could I call them Grams and Gramps?"

My mother smiled, overhearing our conversation. "I think Grams and Gramps are quite appropriate." She giggled, and I hadn't realized until that moment how much she and Addie sounded alike.

"There you have it," said Leo. "And now, I want to have my dance with my bride."

He took my hand and led me out on the floor as the music got a little louder and the lights dimmed. Then he pulled me close, and I stared into his eyes, the rest of the room fading away as we made our way around it.

"Are you happy?"

"I'm in heaven. I can't believe we did it and pulled it off nicely if I do say so myself."

"It's this great venue. It made things easy. And, I have another surprise."

I couldn't help but laugh. "How many surprises are there tonight?"

"Maybe one or two more," he said with a wink.

"Tell me." I nudged.

"Well, you know how you wanted to go to a private island somewhere and forget all about the world for a while?" He wagged his brows.

"Yes! Don't tell me. You've already booked the flight?"

"Okay, I won't. But I can tell you we arrive tomorrow, and we're staying not just two weeks, but three."

"Three weeks! That's going to be amazing. Does Addie know?" I wondered if he'd shared the good news with our daughter. She'd always wanted to go to the beach, but I hadn't been able to take her.

"Not yet. I figured we'd tell her together. I've already talked to Sadie and Stones. They'll watch the house, get the mail, and make sure it looks like someone's at home."

"You've thought of everything, haven't you?" He was such an amazing man, and I didn't know how I ever made it without him.

He brought his head down, his lips kissing mine. A few of my rowdier friends whistled, reminding us we had an audience, and when I looked over across the room, my mother and father were talking to Blitz as Mr. Pace and Sadie watched on. My father had Addie by the hand, and the two of them were laughing. I wondered if he had told her one of his corny jokes and couldn't believe how many years it had been since I'd last heard him tell one. Never again would I let them stay out of my life. If I learned one thing from the rushed wedding, it was how special family and friends were and how each and every one of them played an important part in my life.

Leonard waved Addie over, and she turned loose from my dad and ran to join us. She looked like a little princess in her dress, her round cheeks flushed with excitement. "Mommy, Daddy, can I dance too?"

We each took one of her hands, and then Leonard picked her up in his arms, and we continued to move together in time with the music. "Are you happy, sweet pea?"

"Yes, I'm very happy, Daddy. I love my new family."

"And I love you both so much," said Leonard.

I lay my head on his shoulder. "I love you too."

Addie gave me a questioning glance. "The three of us, Mama?"

"That's right, Addie, the three of us."

The End

ABOUT THE AUTHOR

I'm a former firefighter/EMS guy who's picked up the proverbial pen and started writing bad boy romance stories. I co-write with my sister, Ali Parker as we travel the United States for the next two years.

You're going to find Billionaires, Bad Boys, Mafia and loads of sexiness. Something for everyone, hopefully. I'd love to connect with you.

www.westonparkerbooks.com

ALSO BY WESTON PARKER

Bad Boy Crime Novels

Toxic

Untapped

Bad Boy Billionaire Novels

Stealing First

Doctor Feelgood

Captain Hotness

Mister Big Stuff

With the Risk

Worth the Distraction

Worth the Effort

My First Love

Deepest Desire

Debt Collector

Hot Stuff

My Last First Kiss

Printed in Great Britain
by Amazon